MW01008190

rem. mark

The Prisoners of Cabrera

THE PRISONERS OF CABRERA

Napoleon's Forgotten Soldiers
1809–1814

Denis Smith

Four Walls Eight Windows
New York / London

Copyright © 2001 Denis Smith

Published in the United States by
Four Walls Eight Windows
39 West 14th Street
New York, NY 10011
http://www.4w8w.com

UK offices:
Four Walls Eight Windows/Turnaround
Unit 3 Olympia Trading Estate
Coburg Road, Wood Green
London N22 6TZ

First printing October 2001

All rights reserved. No part of this book may be reproduced, stored in a database or other retrieval system, or transmitted in any form, by any means, including mechanical, electronic, photocopying, recording, or otherwise, without the prior written permission of the publisher.

Library of Congress Cataloging-in-Publication Data:
Smith, Denis. The prisoners of Cabrera: Napoleon's forgotten soldiers, 1809–1814/Denis Smith.
p. cm.
ISBN 1-56858-212-9 (hardcover)
1. Peninsular War, 1807–1814—Prisoners and prisons, Spanish. 2. Prisoners of war—France—History—19th century. 3. Prisoners of war—Spain—Cabrera Island—History—19th century. 4. Cabrera Island (Spain)—History.
DC231.S53 2001   940.2'77—dc21   2001033899

Printed in the United States
Interior design by Ink, Inc.

10 9 8 7 6 5 4 3 2 1

Pages xii–xiii: *Carta Esferica de las Costas de España* (by courtesy of the map division, the New York Public Library, Astor, Lenox, and Tilden Foundations)

The brilliant campaigns of 1805 to 1807 stirred all our hearts. Austerlitz, Eylau, Jena were immortal victories that seemed to join our flags forever with Fortune, crowning our soldiers with a halo of glory. Young men went into the training camps with the sole concern that they would never win enough honors. Like so many others, I yielded to such insistent dreams, and, without waiting for a call-up, I became a soldier at the age of eighteen.

What illusions turned the head of that young man! Glory, pleasure, fortune, I saw them all in the career I had chosen; everything, except the thorns that actually filled it. But after all, what modern Cassandra could have predicted that my nation's star would so quickly lose its magnificence?

Bernard Masson, Sergeant
Sixty-seventh Regiment of the Line

TABLE OF CONTENTS

DRAMATIS PERSONAE

The French Memoirists, Prisoners on Cabrera

Henri Ducor, volunteered as a naval cadet at the age of twelve in 1801; naval rating aboard the French ship *Argonaute* under Royal Navy blockade in Cádiz Harbor after the battle of Trafalgar, 1805–1808; captured by the Spanish at Cádiz in June 1808.

Charles Frossard, conscripted at the age of nineteen in 1798; veteran of the battles of Marengo, Austerlitz, Eylau, and Friedland; sublieutenant in the Artillery Train of the Imperial Guard; member of the Legion of Honor; captured at Bailén in July 1808.

Louis-F. Gille, student, conscripted in Paris at the age of seventeen in 1807; trained in Lille; quartermaster in the Third Battalion, First Reserve Legion; entered Spain in December 1807; captured at Bailén in July 1808.

Robert Guillemard, conscripted to a regiment of the line at Perpignan at the age of nineteen in 1805; on board the French warship *Redoubtable* at the battle of Trafalgar; captured and repatriated to France; after service in Prussia and Austria, entered Spain as a quartermaster; taken prisoner by Spanish guerrillas and transferred to Majorca and Cabrera in March 1810.

Bernard Masson, sergeant, volunteered for service in July 1807, aged eighteen; attached to the Sixty-seventh Regiment of the Line; entered Spain in August 1808; taken prisoner in Catalonia and transferred to Cabrera in March 1811.

R. K. Amédée de Muralt, career soldier and captain in the First Battalion, Third Swiss Regiment; captured at Bailén in July 1808.

Louis-Joseph Wagré, apprenticed in his father's bakery near Compiègne; conscripted at the age of seventeen in 1807; corporal in the First Reserve Legion; followed his unit into Spain in the spring of 1808; captured at Bailén in July 1808.

The Prisoners' Council, Cabrera, 1809-1810
Sublieutenant De Maussac, Fourth Reserve Legion, chairman.
Lieutenants Avril, Carbonnel-d'Hierville, Degain de Montagnac, Deschamps, members.
Cruzel, Fouque, Joly, Lepeltier, Thillaye, Vallin, surgeons.

The French
Napoleon Bonaparte, emperor of France, 1804–1814.
Joseph Bonaparte, king of Spain, 1808–1813.
Joachim Murat, marshal of France, lieutenant general of the realm of Spain, 1807–1808.
Pierre Dupont de l'Etang, general, commander-in-chief, Second Army of Observation of the Gironde, 1808; defeated at Bailén in July 1808; repatriated, tried, and dismissed from the service; minister of war in the restoration government of Louis XVIII, 1814–1820.
Dominique Honoré Antoine Marie de Vedel, divisional general, Second Division, Second Army of Observation of the Gironde; captured at Bailén in July 1808.
Baron Privé, general, commander of the Privé Brigade of the Cavalry Division, Second Army of Observation of the Gironde; captured at Bailén in July 1808.
Louis XVIII, king of France, 1814–1824

The British

George Canning, British foreign secretary, 1808–1809.

Cuthbert Collingwood, baronet, vice admiral, commander-in-chief in the Mediterranean, 1805–1810.

Charles Cotton, admiral, commander-in-chief in the Mediterranean, 1810–1812.

William Cuming, captain, HMS *Bombay.*

John Hookham Frere, British minister to the Spanish Junta Central in Seville and Cádiz, 1808–1809.

Samuel Hood, viscount, admiral in the Mediterranean Fleet, 1808–1814.

Robert Mitford, captain, HMS *Espoir.*

John C. Purvis, rear admiral in the Mediterranean Fleet, 1810.

Arthur Wellesley, first duke of Wellington, general, then field marshal, commander of the British, Portuguese, and Spanish armies in the Iberian Peninsula, 1809–1814.

Henry Wellesley, British ambassador to the Spanish Council of Regency in Cádiz, 1810–1814.

Richard Wellesley, marquis, British ambassador to the Spanish Junta Central in Seville, 1809, and foreign secretary, 1809–1812.

The Spanish

Eusebio de Bardaxi y Azaña, minister of foreign affairs in the Spanish Council of Regency at Cádiz, 1810–1812.

Jerónimo Batle, commissioner for Cabrera under the Junta Superior of Majorca, 1809.

Nicolás Campaner, judge in the High Court of Majorca and member of the Junta Superior of Majorca.

Francisco Javier de Castaños, general, commander-in-chief of the Spanish armies in Andalusia, 1808; victor at the battle of Bailén, July 1808.

Charles IV, king of Spain, 1788–1808; deposed and exiled by Napoleon Bonaparte, 1808.

Antonio Desbrull y Boil de Arenós, marquis of Villafranca, chief of the urban police of Palma, commissioner for Cabrera under the Junta Superior of Majorca, 1809–1811; civil governor of Majorca, 1813.

Damián Estelrich, parish priest in the village of Porreras, Majorca; volunteered as chaplain to the prisoners of Cabrera, 1809–1814.

Ferdinand VII, king of Spain, 1808; deposed and interned in exile by Napoleon Bonaparte, 1808–1813; restored to the throne by Napoleon, 1813; king of Spain, 1813–33.

Manuel de Godoy Alvarez, prince of the peace, prime minister of Spain, 1792–1808; removed from office, 1808, and exiled with Charles IV.

Tomás de Morla, captain-general of Andalusia, 1809–1810.

Nicolás Palmer, provisioner to the prisoners on Cabrera, 1809–1810.

Joaquín Pons, commissioner for Cabrera under the Junta Superior of Majorca, 1809.

Teodoro Reding de Schwyz, Swiss officer in the service of Spain, general, commander-in-chief of the Spanish armies in Granada, 1808; victor with Castaños at Bailén, July 1808.

Nazaire Reding de Schwyz, Swiss officer in the service of Spain, general, military governor of Majorca, 1809–1810.

José Rodríguez de Arias, captain of the Spanish frigate *Cornelia.*

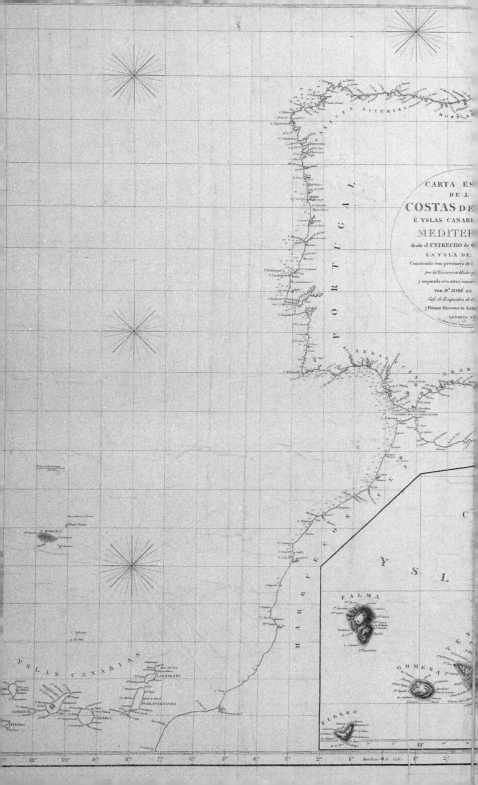

CARTA ES
DE L
COSTAS DE
É YSLAS CANARI
MEDITER
desde el ESTRECHO de G
LA YSLA DE
Construida con presencia de l
por la Dirección Hidrog
y mejorada con otros conoc
POR D⁰ JOSÉ DE
Gefe de Esquadra de la
y Primer Director de dich
LONDRES A

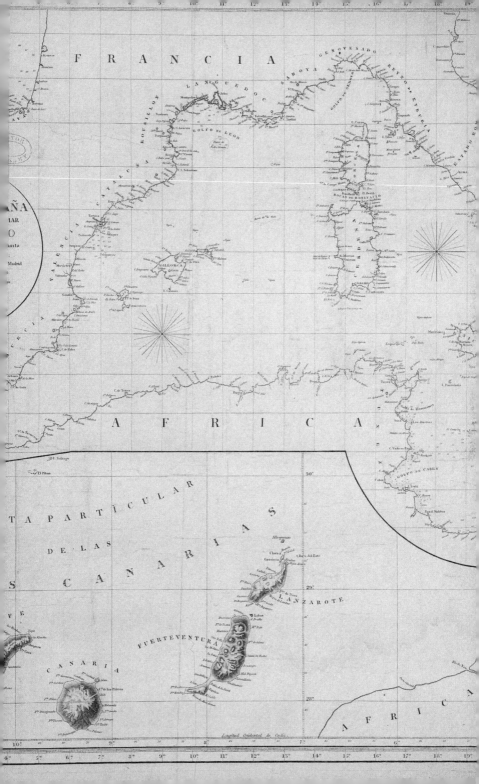

PROLOGUE

FIVE AND A HALF MILES OFF the Mediterranean island of Majorca and twenty-one miles from its port of Palma lies Cabrera, or Goat Island, the largest of a small archipelago jutting irregularly from the sea. On a clear day the outlines of the island, shimmering low on the horizon, can be seen from Palma's Bellver Castle. Approached by boat from the north, the island's rough scrublands and bare rocks rise abruptly from its shores. At the island's northwest point, two peninsular headlands give narrow entrance to the only safe harbor; and beyond this gateway lies a calm, roughly circular half-mile anchorage. From a high point on the headlands to the left, a rugged fourteenth-century castle surveys the port and the sea beyond.

Cabrera's medieval castle, rebuilt in the sixteenth century in defense against raids by Barbary pirates, is the only sign of human habitation visible on the seaward approach. Phoenicians and Romans left relics of their presence on the island, and early in the Christian era it was the site of a small monastery for wayward monks; but it was empty when King James I of Catalonia conquered Majorca in 1229 and awarded it to the prelate Don Ferrer de San Martí of Tarragona, from whom it passed through many hands in the centuries that followed. With the exception of the pirate watch, occasional goatherds, tenant farmers, and fishermen from neighboring villages in Majorca, the tiny island remained empty over the centuries—too dry, too barren and unforgiving to support continuing human settlement. In the harbor today, two small docks and a few whitewashed barracks recall Cabrera's recent history as a Spanish military training base. Rough gravel tracks wind up the valleys from the barracks into the scrub hills beyond; and near one of these tracks, "at a place on the island best seen from a distance" (now hidden in a pine forest), a stubby obelisque, dated 1847, honors "the memory of the Frenchmen who died on Cabrera."[1] The inscription recalls one of the least known but most dramatic events of the Napoleonic wars—and a dark anticipation of inhumanities to come.

For five years from May 1809 to May 1814 the island of Cabrera was an unwalled prison camp holding thousands of soldiers from Napoleon's conscript armies and elite guards. When they landed the prisoners were thrust alone into a virtual state of nature, guarded offshore by warships of the Royal Navy and the Spanish Navy, and supplied (when the weather was good) by sloops from nearby Majorca. They arrived on the island almost accidentally after their terms of surrender had been betrayed. Those who survived did so through tenacity, ingenuity, good fortune, and the occasional generosity of their guardians. Afterwards, a few of these Gallic Robinson Crusoes told their stories to fascinated audiences at home in France, where the tale of the prisoners of Cabrera became legendary. But in Britain and Spain, where the history of Napoleon's war in the Iberian Peninsula was written by the victors, there was slight interest in the prisoners' misadventure. The Frenchmen had been captured and their war had been lost. Their treatment remained an indistinct and disquieting memory, a peripheral incident in a long and vicious campaign, an embarrassment more conveniently ignored than recalled. Two hundred years on, when we recognize the Napoleonic Wars as a prelude to the indiscriminate brutalities of twentieth-century conflict, Cabrera's story could stand as an emblem of two callous centuries of war.

This is an account of that forgotten episode, as recalled in the memoirs of a number of young prisoners or recorded in the documents of their captors. The prisoners were all common soldiers or junior officers, relating what they had seen rather than reporting the officially embellished account of triumph and disaster. They knew nothing of their commanders' plans or the general course of the war. They had only their own stories to tell.

As the narrative reveals, the British were crucial participants in the Cabreran misadventure. Yet previous French, Spanish, and Swiss accounts of the affair, both memoirs and history, made no use of the materials in the British historical archives. These manuscript records of the Foreign Office and the Royal Navy offer essential evidence of Britain's determining part in the saga. The unusual absence of any British account of the Cabreran imprisonment has meant that this significant element of the story, involving military and political decisions at the highest levels, has remained untold for almost two centuries. Sir Charles Oman's monumental *History of the Peninsular War* (published early in the twentieth century) devotes one paragraph to the events on Cabrera, laying entire blame on the Spanish government for its "indefensible" treatment of the prisoners. But the Spaniards were not alone.

The soldiers who arrived on Cabrera were the losers in the battle of Bailén, in southern Spain, and ultimately found themselves—with their hero Napoleon—on the losing side of history. On Cabrera too there were winners and losers: on one side the fortunate, the strong, the ingenious, the opportunists; on the other the unlucky, the weak, the passive, the unimaginative, the dead. Those few who wrote accounts of their captivity were among the winners. So we have reports of, but no direct accounts by, those who were punished by their fellow prisoners, or those who became hermits and recluses in the island's caves, or those who died in captivity. The memoirs of Cabrera are tales told by the relatively fortunate. Beyond these stories the lives of the other outcasts on the prison island—like those of the defeated in every war—remain forever out of reach. In the words of Primo Levi: "We, the survivors, are not the true witnesses.... We are... an anomalous minority: we are those who by their prevarications, or their attributes or their good luck did not touch bottom. Those who did so, those who saw the Gorgon, have not returned to tell about it, or they have returned mute."[2]

I
ANDALUSIA

THE FRENCH REVOLUTION of 1789 and the execution of King Louis XVI and his Queen Marie Antoinette in 1793 set the monarchies of Europe against France in their determination to restore the old order and the European balance of power. Two decades of warfare (relieved by brief interludes of peace) were the result, ending only with France's defeat at Waterloo in 1815. The first decade of revolutionary tumult and indecisive continental war ended in 1799 with the accession of an extraordinary young Corsican general, Napoleon Bonaparte, as first consul of France under a new constitution. By 1802 he had arranged his own election as first consul for life; and in 1804, standing before Pope Pius VII in the cathedral of Notre Dame, he crowned himself defiantly as hereditary emperor.

Apart from a few months of peace with France in 1802–1803, Britain had for years maintained a punishing commercial blockade of Europe enforced by the Royal Navy, while Napoleon responded with his own continentwide boycott of British goods. To break the British blockade of Europe, the emperor gathered vast conscript armies at training camps near the channel in preparation for an invasion of the British Isles; but they were drawn away to Germany in 1805 to meet fresh threats from the attacking armies of Austria and Russia. At Ulm and Austerlitz, Napoleon shattered the forces of his continental enemies; and when Prussia joined them in the following year, he defeated it too at Jena and

Auerstädt. In 1807 his troops fought the Russian army to a blood-soaked draw at Eylau, and a few months later dispersed the Russians at Friedland. The Treaty of Tilsit offered relief to Napoleon's exhausted foes and brought temporary peace for France in the east.

The emperor was now at the peak of his power on the continent, and apparently invincible. Whole states were his playthings, their peoples and riches at his command, their institutions transfigured under his reforming will. But Napoleon remained annoyingly hemmed in by his last enemy Britain, which held decisive control of the seas after its defeat of the French and Spanish navies at Trafalgar in 1805. An invasion of Britain had become impossible. To confront that enemy by indirection, Bonaparte now turned his attentions southwards to the Iberian Peninsula. There, in 1808, he broke the regime of his ally Spain and the patience of its subjects.

In the early years of the nineteenth century the Spaniards, ruled by the inept Bourbon king, Charles IV, and his chief minister, Manuel de Godoy, were divided by factional conflict at court. The country was paralyzed by bureaucratic inertia, litigiousness, and punishing commercial taxes. Spain's old religious absolutism—which had allowed for substantial individual and regional liberty—was being transformed into a system of French despotism. The architect of change, Godoy, was a centralizer and army reformer whose scheming personal ambition kept him close to the king and in bed with the queen. Godoy drove out rivals and antagonized both conservatives and progressives. His foreign policies brought constant war and defeat for the nation—but for himself, a favorite's privileges and royal designation as Spain's Prince of the Peace. By 1807 Godoy's many opponents placed their hopes in Charles IV's heir, his son Ferdinand—who was, for most Spaniards, a man of unknown character.

Spain's alliance with Bonapartist France was an unequal partnership. Napoleon had made it for his own imperial purposes, and gradually reinforced his armies in the Iberian Peninsula until they reached one hundred thousand men by the spring of 1808. The French soldiers came, ostensibly, as friendly forces preparing an invasion of Portugal that was intended to end that nation's long association with Britain, and to halt Lisbon's vast smuggling trade into Europe. That trade had grown after the Royal Navy shattered the French and Spanish fleets at Trafalgar (off the Spanish port of Cádiz) in the autumn of 1805. Napoleon's sole remaining means of pressure on the British enemy was to extend the continental boycott of her goods and impoverish the nation. The Continental System extended from France to Denmark to Russia and Austria; Portugal (and to some extent Spain) were the only weak points in the system. In December 1807, the gap seemed about to close when a French army under the command of General Jean Andoche Junot marched from Madrid, occupied Lisbon, and drove the Portuguese royal family into exile in Brazil under the protection of the Royal Navy.

After Trafalgar, the remnants of Napoleon's fleet had escaped capture and taken refuge far from home in the Spanish port of Cádiz, where they remained under British blockade three years later. But by 1808, French soldiers and sailors in Spain—while officially welcome as guests of an ally—were regarded with mounting suspicion by the local population. Napoleon's army now gar-risoned many towns and fortresses in the center and north of the country. In an instant, by Napoleonic whim, they could be trans-formed into an occupation force.

The French emperor had no respect for the monarchy of Spain; but until the Spanish Bourbons brought their domestic battles home to him, he had no explicit plans to depose them. In the autumn of 1807 King Charles and his son Ferdinand (who were by now deadly rivals) both appealed to the emperor for protection against each other. Napoleon ignored them, while reflecting on the benefits of installing his own regime in the peninsula. He sent more troops across the frontier. In March 1808, while French rein-forcements made their way to Madrid, the Spanish monarch and his son confronted one another in person at the royal town of Aranjuez just to the south. A mob directed by Ferdinand's faction seized the chief minister, Godoy, and delivered him as a prisoner to Ferdinand. King Charles, in panic, abdicated in favor of his son. Ferdinand VII was proclaimed king on a wave of popular enthusi-asm as Godoy's detested regime was swept from power. Across Spain, Godoy's political prisoners were released from their cells and liberals rejoiced.

When the feckless King Charles changed his mind and called on Napoleon to aid in his restoration, the emperor undertook an audacious act of perfidy. He summoned father and son to meet him inside the French border at Bayonne, and the Spanish royal family dutifully trekked northwards in their carriages. There a farce was played out, and the last pretence of Spanish independ-ence was destroyed. Once in France, the royal family were the emperor's prisoners. Napoleon induced Ferdinand's abdication under threat, restored Charles to his throne, and instantly deposed him in favor of his own brother Joseph Bonaparte (who was at that moment king of Naples by right of an earlier imperial edict). In the following month, a new Spanish constitution on the French model was decreed by a rump constituent assembly meeting under the emperor's eyes in Bayonne. Ferdinand was taken into comfortable French custody, a prisoner with his brothers at Viscount Talleyrand's estate of Valençay, where he would remain until Napoleon's downfall in 1814. King Charles and Queen María Luisa were rewarded for the loss of their kingdom with residence at the palace of Compiègne, where they were soon joined by the favorite Godoy.

Spain, like Portugal, had become a pawn in the emperor's global schemes. With British trade now excluded from Portugal and the last continental doorway shut, the rest of the Iberian Peninsula seemed an easy conquest: in the emperor's eyes it would be a fresh source of conscripts, cash, and a rebuilt navy; and it offered a gateway to Africa on the way to India, where Bonaparte dreamed of destroying Britain's trading empire through the back door. This was megalomania on a global scale; and in the peninsula its consequences were chaotic. Under the rule of the Bonapartes, Napoleon promised Spain reform and regeneration. Instead, the emperor was infected with his "Spanish ulcer," a wasting disease that finally proved fatal to the whole Napoleonic empire. In Spain, France bled to death.

The Spaniards—whose unified realm and empire had been a creation of the Catholic monarchs Ferdinand and Isabella three hundred years before—could tolerate an inept monarchy of their own. They could tolerate French armies camped on their soil. But they would not abide this Corsican coup. Discontent and suspicion against the French military presence had been growing for months. News of the royal family's departure for France, and rumors of its humiliation in Bayonne, fuelled popular anger during April. In early May 1808 there were spontaneous, violent risings in Madrid and across the provinces of Spain, put down ruthlessly by French armies under the command of Bonaparte's marshal and brother-in-law Joachim Murat (whom Napoleon had named "Lieutenant-General of the Realm" and effective head of government after the arrest of Manuel de Godoy). A toothless central administration, left in nominal power by Ferdinand on his departure for Bayonne, failed to challenge Murat and gave its allegiance to the new regime of Joseph Bonaparte. But the puppet government could not sustain its authority against the anarchic fury of the masses, and in the following weeks its power drained away to the regions. On May 25 Asturias became the first province to declare war on France, and called up eighteen thousand troops. Centralized Spain disintegrated as conservative provincial juntas (or governing councils) emerged on the shoulders of the mob to declare their independence, reassert their ancient liberties, and proclaim loyalty to the exiled Spanish king, Ferdinand VII. "The monarchy had fallen and broken itself to pieces," wrote Salvador de Madariaga, "and in Madrid and Coruña, Asturias and Valencia, these broken pieces of the monarchy were taking in hand the affairs of the nation."[1] Alongside the juntas, local Spanish garrisons and the church joined the revolt against Madrid and the French. By midsummer, Napoleon's regime found itself besieged throughout the peninsula. The emperor was committed to a war of attrition he could not escape. For Spaniards, the popular struggle became known as the War of Independence; for Frenchmen, it was the War in Spain; and for Britons, the Peninsular War.

In London, the British government welcomed the Spanish insurrection, made contact with the new provincial juntas, and quickly prepared to dispatch forces to Portugal to assist in the defeat of Napoleon's armies. "One month would probably be sufficient to ascertain the chances of advantage to be derived from the temper of the people in Spain," wrote Arthur Wellesley (later Lord Wellington) from Cork, where he commanded a British expeditionary force of nine thousand men destined for the peninsula.[2] That month stretched into seven years of war.

Almost half of Marshal Murat's French peninsular troops were stationed in Madrid; the remainder were scattered thinly at provincial outposts, mostly in the center of Spain, too dispersed to control the country as the regions declared their independence from Madrid. Suddenly the French forces faced hostile local citizens, rebellious Spanish garrisons, new provincial armies, and rogue brigades of peasants organized into terrifying guerrilla bands. French troops were generally better trained and equipped than the Spanish—and still buoyed, in 1808, by the powerful myth of Napoleonic invincibility. They easily triumphed in most direct encounters during the early days of war, at Torquemada, Cabezón, Santander, Logroño, Tudela, Mallén, and Alagón. But the territory of the Iberian Peninsula could not be easily—or permanently—pacified. It was too vast for that.

Murat believed that opposition to the new regime was focused in a few nuisance spots, which could be overcome when necessary with fast-moving French flying columns. For seven months General Junot had pacified Portugal while ruling the land as a reforming dictator. But after the Spanish risings the Portuguese, too, erupted in coordinated revolt, driving the French forces back from their outposts towards Lisbon. In May 1808, while Junot's isolated forces remained in Portugal, Murat dispatched another army south from Toledo, to occupy and secure the strategic port of Cádiz against attack by the Royal Navy. The force was led by General Pierre Dupont de l'Etang, a forty-three-year-old hero of Napoleon's victories at Ulm, Halle, and Friedland, who was in his first independent command. He expected an easy and unopposed march to Cádiz. Apart from five hundred elite seamen of the Imperial Guard, twelve hundred members of the Paris Guard, and thirty-three hundred Swiss mercenaries, Dupont's army was a motley crowd of young and untested conscripts (both French and foreign) led by "any officers who could be found in the depots."[3]

On June 5, after crossing the arid plains of La Mancha and the mountains of the Sierra Morena, Dupont and thirteen thousand troops reached Andújar, a dusty town 215 miles south of Madrid. To his west in the open valley of the Guadalquivir River lay the high road to Córdoba, Seville, and Cádiz. From La Carolina to Andújar on the road south, the towns and villages had been ominously empty of inhabitants as the French columns passed through; and here, in Andújar, Dupont learned that Andalusia too had risen against Napoleon and the new French monarchy. His advance would no longer be peaceful and his lines of communication to the north no longer secure. Three days later, in his first armed encounter at Alcolea bridge on the outskirts of Córdoba, Dupont's army easily routed an equal number of Spanish volunteers in open battle. As the Spaniards fled in disorder, the French general did not wait for an offer of capitulation, but stormed into the undefended city, where his forces engaged in a rampage of looting, killing, and rape lasting nine days. Henceforth, as news of these atrocities spread among Spaniards, French military stragglers and messengers faced brutal murder on the roads of Andalusia.[4]

In Córdoba Dupont soon realized his troops were isolated in a hostile land. For three days in mid-June, while his army waited to advance from the city, the new revolutionary junta in Cádiz bombarded and seized the French naval squadron that had been blockaded in the port since 1805, and imprisoned over three thousand French sailors. Cádiz would no longer be an easy prize for the advancing French army; and the ships of the French navy were already lost. Dupont had also received word that a large Spanish army was gathering to the south and east under General Javier de Castaños. If the French general proceeded further, he knew that his forces would gradually be decimated. The march to Cádiz was abandoned. Dupont might at that moment have moved his troops safely into the mountain passes to the north of Córdoba; but instead he retreated incautiously across the open plain back to Andújar, where he awaited reinforcement from Madrid while venturing no more than a destructive raid south to Jaén. On the road of retreat from Córdoba to Andújar the French were chilled to see dozens of mutilated corpses of their comrades. In Montoro, "they found the remains of more than two hundred men, some of whom had been torn to pieces, others crucified on trees or sawed between boards, and still others had been plunged into boiling oil." Fanatical hatred gripped the people of Spain. From Madrid, King Joseph Bonaparte wrote in pessimism to his brother the emperor: "You are making a mistake, Sire. Your glory will not be enough to subjugate Spain. I shall fail and the limits of your power will be exposed. Fifty thousand more men and fifty million francs are needed to set things right. Only this can save the country."[5]

At Andújar, Dupont waited with his army for a full month. Food supplies were short, the summer heat was growing intense, and many soldiers were ill. But the French officers put up a bold front, lighting up the camp at night, attending musical recitals and the theater. By early July two more French divisions under the command of Generals Vedel and Gobert had arrived in their support from the north. Dupont now had more than twenty thousand men under his charge in Andalusia. But rather than using them to secure his communications and line of retreat back to Madrid, or to take the offensive against Castaños in the plains, Dupont kept his main force idle at Andújar while concentrating the reinforcements separately ten miles to his east at Bailén, on equally open ground. Here he vainly nursed the hope of defeating Castaños or avoiding battle with him, renewing the march south, and winning his coveted promotion to marshal.

❖ ❖ ❖

SIX MONTHS EARLIER, in December 1807, the French quartermaster Louis Gille's Third Battalion of the First Reserve Legion had been issued cartridge boxes and ammunition at Bayonne, departed on foot for the border town of Irún, and crossed into

Spain. Here, the eighteen-year-old conscript determined to observe Spanish life as carefully as he could, to record the whole adventure in his notebooks, and to gain from his observations whenever possible. He could not imagine what was to come; but for seven years he kept his journals. Gille was an educated Parisian and a reluctant recruit, called up in the emergency levy of April 1807 to replace those Frenchmen killed at Eylau, where Napoleon had experienced his first great slaughter in indecisive battle with the Russians. Because he could read and write, Louis Gille was named as quartermaster or lodgings officer when his unit reached training camp at Lille, and relieved from regular guard and fatigue duties. He enjoyed the comforts of minor office, including "the most lively interest and desire to entertain me" on the part of his captain's wife.[6] Gille was a handsome charmer who, by his own account, made romantic conquests wherever he found lodgings as the First Reserve Legion marched south.

While the French emperor seized power in Spain and the masses revolted, Gille's regiment marched deeper into the peninsula to Segovia, Madrid, and Aranjuez. In Aranjuez, on May 1, 1808, Gille and his companions stood by warily as gunfire broke out during the first civil rising. Later they joined Spanish nighttime patrols seeking to restore order. Martial law was imposed, and French soldiers only ventured outside armed with bayonets. For the next few days Gille heard reports of savage carnage on the streets of Madrid, summary executions of hundreds of insurrectionists on the boulevards outside the Prado Museum, and indiscriminate acts of revenge committed throughout the city by undisciplined French soldiers. Soon the Spanish garrison of Aranjuez abandoned the town, marching south into Andalusia, where they intended to join the national armies being gathered for organized war against the French. But the French managed to hold on to the Spaniards' field guns.

In mid-June 1808 Gille's First Reserve Legion joined other French regiments under the command of General Vedel as they, too, departed for Andalusia in support of the increasingly isolated army of General Dupont. When they were joined a few days later by mercenaries of the Third Swiss Regiment, the nervous Frenchmen learned of attacks by bands of armed peasants—brigands, in French eyes, "for what other name can be given to rebels without discipline, without a leader, who rise without orders from their governments?"[7] The country had become too dangerous for the army to send out advance parties, so Gille and the other quartermasters (who normally moved ahead to find quarters and supplies for their units) remained with the main columns.

As they approached Manzanares in the plain of La Mancha, Vedel's men were met by a small French troop who reported that a group of Dupont's sick soldiers, left behind in the local hospital, had all been slaughtered. Louis Gille visited the hospital later in the day, where he saw fifty unburied French bodies, cruelly tortured, some of them plunged in pots of boiling oil. "There was only one cry from all our mouths: 'Vengeance! Vengeance!' The feeling seized all our hearts; even the general seemed to share it," Gille recalled.[8] But when General Vedel met the mayor, councillors, and notables of the town, they insisted that the crime had not been committed by citizens but by marauding peasants led by priests. The general promised no reprisals, and held his troops in barracks overnight. The next night, in the deserted town of Valdepeñas just to the south, the soldiers of the French division relieved their frustrations by raiding the wine cellars and drinking themselves into a brandy-soaked stupor.

As General Vedel's force moved on into the deep gorges of the Sierra Morena, the Spaniards who had reluctantly guided the carts and beef cattle of the divisional supply train suddenly disappeared. Before long, the columns of French troops came under fire from artillery and guerrilla sharpshooters on the heights above. They were routed by French riflemen scrambling up the rough slopes, and Spanish prisoners were summarily shot. The march continued. By the end of June, Vedel's units had reached the town of Bailén, already exhausted by the early summer heat, and short of food.

After two nights' rest, General Vedel sent thirteen hundred men of the First Legion (along with a baggage train) across the Guadalquivir River on a long twenty-four-hour march to Jaén, where they were ordered to requisition food supplies for delivery to General Dupont in Andújar. Instead they found thousands of Spanish regular troops and irregulars (or guerrillas) awaiting them on the heights surrounding the town. The two forces met in hand-to-hand combat, the Spaniards retreated in disorder, residents fled in panic, and the French seized the ancient fortress castle set high above the plain. The next day, facing a reinforced Spanish army, Vedel's men were forced to abandon both fort and town. For three days more the battle raged, the ground repeatedly changed hands, and Louis Gille witnessed terrible atrocities committed by both French and Spanish soldiers: a nine-year-old French drummer boy bayoneted to death by his captors; a four- or five-year-old Spanish child shot down by a French soldier as he presented the soldier with a loaf of bread; a group of French prisoners garroted by a Spanish guerrilla unit.[9]

On the fourth night in Jaén—their ammunition exhausted, their losses at 300 dead and 150 wounded—the French commander ordered a silent retreat in the darkness. Many of the injured had been burned in a vast powder explosion. Dying soldiers were left behind; wounded men who couldn't keep pace were abandoned in ditches along the way, sometimes pleading to be shot by their comrades. When a carriage of the wounded overturned in a ravine, Gille's commander prevented the lighting of torches to rescue those who could be saved. The starved and thirsty survivors reached the Guadalquivir River at Menjíbar at dawn, where they discarded the heavy bundles of silks, linen, and silver they had carried away in plunder from Jaén, and crossed over the water in disorder. In the following days Louis Gille and his fellow Frenchmen watched from the hills above the Guadalquivir as Spanish forces gathered in their thousands on the south bank.[10]

The Spanish army commander General Castaños, with thirty thousand troops, went on the attack against the French on July 14, crossing the Guadalquivir from the south two days later. Dupont responded defensively, marching his divisions fitfully back and forth between Andújar, Bailén, and La Carolina in the heat and dust of midsummer, engaging in a series of brief and bloody skirmishes. In one of these battles the French General Gobert was killed while leading a cavalry charge. By July 17 the Spanish army led by the Swiss General Teodoro Reding had occupied Bailén and

DUPONT'S ARMY AT BAILEN
(SECOND ARMY OF OBSERVATION OF THE GIRONDE)

Commander-in-Chief: Divisional General Pierre Dupont, Comte de l'Etang

First Division: Divisional General Barbou d'Escouvrières
   Chabert Brigade:

Seamen of the Guard	456
Fourth Swiss (Second Battalion)	608
Fourth Reserve Legion (3 Bns)	2,643

   Pannetier Brigade:

Third Reserve Legion (3 Bns)	1,763
Paris Guard (2 Bns)	1,246

   Schramm Brigade:

J. Reding's Rgt (Swiss) (2 Bns)	857
Preux's Rgt (Swiss) (2 Bns)	857
DIVISIONAL TOTAL	8,430

Second Division:
Divisional General Dominique Honoré Antoine Marie, Comte de Vedel
   Poinsot Brigade:

Fifth Reserve Legion (3 Bns)	2,318
Third Swiss (1 Bn)	1,010

   Cassagne Brigade:

First Reserve Legion (3 Bns)	2,589
DIVISIONAL TOTAL	5,917

Cavalry Division: Brigadier General Maurice-Ignace Fresia,
Baron d'Oglianico
   Privé Brigade:

First Provisional Rgt of Dragoons	667
Second Provisional Rgt of Dragoons	584

Boussart Brigade:	
Sixth Provisional Rgt of Dragoons	533
Duprès Brigade:	
First Provisional Rgt, Light Cavalry	477
Second Provisional Rgt, Light Cavalry	534
DIVISIONAL TOTAL	2,795

Artillery: 36 guns contained in:	
4 companies of Foot Artillery	
1 company of Horse Artillery	
Artillery train and sappers	
TOTAL	1,400

GOBERT'S DETACHMENT
(CORPS OF OBSERVATION OF THE OCEAN COAST)

Second Division: Divisional General Gobert (reinforced)	
Dufour Brigade (reinforced):	
Sixth Provisional Rgt (4 Bns)	1,851
Seventh Provisional Rgt (4 Bns)	1,872
Eighth Provisional Rgt (4 Bns)	1,921
Rigaud's Brigade of Cavalry (part):	
Second Provisional Armored Cavalry	621
DIVISIONAL TOTAL	6,265

TOTAL: 19,991 INFANTRY; 3,416 CAVALRY; 36 GUNS

Unit strengths are those reported by Oman; Reserve Legions and Provisional Regiments were made up from conscripts and depot batallions plus coastal and frontier guards; Schramm's Brigade consisted of Swiss troops in the Spanish service conscripted by the French before the Spanish rising as auxiliary troops.

(Adapted from Partridge and Oliver, 73–74)

ominously cut communication between the French armies of Dupont at Andújar and Vedel at La Carolina.

On July 18, Dupont decided to abandon Andújar: but the decision came too late for him to join Vedel in what might have been an orderly retreat towards Madrid. Dupont's forces set out from Andújar with five hundred oxcarts of booty and wounded men moving slowly in the midst of a six-mile-long column. (The gossip in Vedel's division, Louis Gille recalled, was that Dupont's wagon train, overburdened with "immense riches" in loot from Córdoba, could not be loaded in time to move north with Vedel.)

West of Bailén, Dupont's outnumbered vanguard confronted General Reding's divisions entrenched in the hills above, recklessly attacked them, and was repulsed with heavy casualties. With his main force now trailed closely by Castaños's army, Dupont chose to continue the vanguard's attack when he reached the front early next morning.

Fearing that Castaños might fall on his rearguard at any moment, he proceeded to send his troops forward in piecemeal assaults, as soon as they came on to the field. His troops, having marched all night along the hilly, sinuous road, were both exhausted and strung out, and to commit them in dribs and drabs was foolhardy in the extreme. Despite gallant efforts by his provisional dragoons and *cuirassiers*, the Spanish managed to beat off two more attacks and, by 12:30, with Castaños bearing down on his rear, Dupont was in dire straits. Grouping his exhausted conscripts around his last formed battalion, he led them in a final bid to break Reding's line. Again, the assault made considerable progress and parts of the Spanish force were soon on the verge of dissolution. However, the French had no reserves to exploit the breakthrough and, after another heated contest, they were again driven back down the slope. With his whole force demoralized and physically exhausted, Dupont was lost. The sound of Castaños's vanguard attacking his baggage column signalled the end and, with his Swiss troops deserting to the enemy *en masse*, the French commander sued for terms.[11]

The midday heat was stifling. Two of Dupont's Swiss battalions had gone over to the Spaniards; his men were exhausted and had no water; and Dupont himself was wounded. At Bailén his army of ten thousand men (now reduced to about eighty-two hundred) laid down their arms.[12]

Meanwhile General Vedel's force of eleven thousand was marching slowly south from La Carolina in relief. As he approached Bailén, Vedel confronted a Spanish brigade and routed it amidst triumphant French cries of "Vive l'Empéreur!"; but when news of the cease-fire reached him under a flag of truce, Vedel halted his attack to await Dupont's orders. In the following days he surrendered all his prisoners and marched northwards, undefeated and under arms, into the mountains of the Sierra Morena. There, on July 24, he received the news that General Dupont had formally capitulated with all the troops under his command, including Vedel's division, although they had hardly tasted battle.

By 1808 prisoners of war were no longer regarded as slaves or chattels. Their status had been altered in practice by the Treaty of Westphalia in 1648, when captives had first been released without ransom at war's end. In the eighteenth century Montesquieu, Rousseau, and other writers argued that prisoners taken in war should not be randomly punished, but only removed from the field of battle and held in a kind of quarantine where they could do no further damage as long as conflict continued. During the Seven Years' War (1756–1763), the British housed French prisoners in makeshift camps in southern England—including the grounds of Sissinghurst Castle—and on hulks in Portsmouth Harbor. Rough rules of fair treatment were slowly emerging, but they were uncodified, still heavily dependent on the humanity, sense of honor, and physical capacities of the captors. No international organizations existed to offer inspection or aid for prisoners of war.

At Bailén, the victorious Spaniards faced unprecedented problems in dealing with the French. The rapidly assembled Spanish armies under the command of General Castaños had no central government from which to take direction, and no obvious means of containing and caring for their captives. So it was not surprising that the instrument of capitulation signed by the French and Spanish commanders gave detailed promises, not just of protection, but of early repatriation to all the French forces. Dupont's army became prisoners of war; but Vedel's division—which had not surrendered—was excepted. They would not, technically, be considered as prisoners, although they would receive similar treatment. Both armies would march out of camp with all the honors of war, ceremonially depositing their weapons beyond the gates. French officers were permitted to keep their horses, their small arms, and their supply carts, without inspection, unless these had been seized in Andalusia. The wagons would be inspected for booty by one of their own generals. French officers undertook to recover any church silver seized by overzealous soldiers in the assault on Córdoba or elsewhere. All French troops were to be evacuated to the ports of San Lúcar and Rota (just west of Cádiz), embarked on Spanish transport ships, and repatriated to the French port of Rochefort. On the long cross-country journey from the battlefield, they would march by night to avoid the heat of day-time, under escort by Spanish troops of the line, preceded by French and Spanish commissioners who would arrange for their food and lodging; and during their march, the French would be supplied and paid according to rank "on the same footing as Span-ish troops in time of war." French wounded and ill would be cared for in a hospital, and returned separately to France "under good and sure escort." Civilian contractors to the French army (a sub-stantial train, in its hundreds, of traders, suppliers, and camp fol-lowers) were not regarded as prisoners and would retain all their rights during repatriation. (Since armies travelled on campaign for long periods and were expected to live off the land, civilian traders and suppliers normally moved with them, as did numbers of wives, companions, cooks, laundresses, prostitutes, and even chil-dren. Armies on the road were substantial travelling towns.)[13]

For the defeated army corps of General Dupont, this was gener-ous and face-saving treatment, promising immediate return to France on dignified terms. For Vedel's undefeated forces the capit-ulation seemed less attractive: one brigade officer briefly contem-plated revolt and—according to an eyewitness—"a large number" of cuirassiers, soldiers of the Imperial Guard and light infantry, dis-obeyed their officers and fled north to rejoin the French army in Madrid.[14] But the main body of Vedel's division obeyed the terms of surrender, and on July 26, 1808, they joined Dupont's forces in a formal ceremony of capitulation on the searing plains outside

Bailén. Seventeen thousand demoralized Frenchmen paraded out of camp to the sound of military bands, past the assembled Spanish armies of General Castaños and General Reding.

This impressive affair was, for many of the prisoners, their last experience of safety and order. As the captives marched through Bailén, they were taunted by the crowds; and in subsequent days, passing through other towns, they faced constant danger of attack. "When our march brought us to a town," wrote one prisoner, "the whole population swarmed at us, the men hitting us, the women spitting in our faces, the children crying out insults, as if they saw in each one of us a personal enemy."[15] Only their Spanish military guards prevented a slaughter. After several days, Louis Gille recalled that "several Frenchmen had fallen under the knives of enraged peasants.... I must pay credit to the troops of the line who escorted us: they knew it was their resolve that kept us alive; several of them were wounded in parrying blows meant for us."[16] The province of Andalusia seemed suddenly, through terrified French eyes, a realm of raging assassins.

Beyond the hostility of the crowds, the prisoners had to confront their own dark moods. As one of their doctors recalled, "victory and health go arm in arm; an army surmounts fatigue, peril, and privation as long as it is successful.... But in defeat, French armies fall into decline. The long lines of prisoners resemble processions of sick men leaving a burning hospital; they walk slowly, in complete disorder, without discipline; and if they fall, they are abandoned and killed by the locals."[17]

The defeat shocked all the French armies of Spain into sudden realization of their peril. Several thousand of Dupont's corps who remained further north, on the road to Madrid, decided to accept the capitulation and its unusual promise of repatriation. They marched south to surrender, raising the number of prisoners to about twenty-two thousand. For Napoleon, the defeat was a shameful humiliation. On August 3, he wrote to his brother Joseph in Madrid: "Dupont has stained our flags. What incompetence! What baseness!" The clear-eyed emperor put little faith in the terms of surrender. "I do not suppose," he advised his minister of war, "that it is necessary to make great preparations at Rochefort, because the British will surely not let these imbeciles pass, and the Spaniards will not give back their weapons to those who have not fought."[18]

Dupont's defeated army was marched west to Utrera and south to Puerto de Santa María, close to Cádiz—apparently in readiness for repatriation. But there the capitulation agreement began to fall apart as Napoleon had foreseen. The provincial junta in Seville expressed its disapproval; and at Cádiz the Royal Navy's influential commander in the Mediterranean, Lord Collingwood, informed Don Tomás de Morla, the captain-general of Andalusia, that he could not let the prisoners leave without consulting London. (In the absence of any central government representing the rebellious Spanish provinces, or any formal diplomatic ties between the Spaniards and London, Collingwood offered the only authoritative link with the British government in the summer of 1808. He was, in effect, both naval commander and ambassador.) On August 19 the minister of war, Viscount Castlereagh, delivered the British cabinet's response to Collingwood. It was phrased in the language of high diplomatic cunning, and intended to frustrate the return of Dupont's armies to France. "Looking... to the

mere tenor of the Capitulation," wrote Castlereagh, "it is impossible not to feel, and to regret, that an Army of sixteen thousand
men, nearly half of them fully equipped, is thereby permitted to
return to France, in order possibly to recommence, within the
space of a few weeks, a fresh attack on Spain—and that the Capitulation has produced nothing more than an exchange of position
of sixteen thousand men, in July posted in Andalusia, to thirteen
thousand men to be posted perhaps at Pampeluna [Pamplona]
before November."[19]

Castlereagh praised the courage and talent of Castaños' victorious army, noted the shame imposed on the French by the defeat,
and recognized that the surrender gave valuable time to the Spanish provinces to organize a central government. Nevertheless, he
insisted that Britain was not a party to the capitulation agreement
and could not be bound by it. His Majesty's government "has a right
to prevent any other Power, even a recognized Ally, from conveying
any Enemy of whatever description, and in whatever situation, to
the Enemy's ports, from whence that Enemy may immediately
recommence hostility against His Majesty or His other Allies."

Castlereagh threaded his way carefully through his ministry's
interpretation of the customs of war. While Britain would not
oppose a request from the Junta of Seville to repatriate the French
prisoners under the terms of the surrender agreement, Collingwood was ordered to impose a set of stringent conditions on the
transfer. The prisoners would have to be sent in a series of convoys, in unarmed Spanish ships, to a French port not under
British naval blockade (which ruled out the designated port of
Rochefort). Only one convoy could be dispatched at a time, and

each successor convoy would only be allowed to sail after the safe return of the previous one. Since the Royal Navy would provide escort ships of war for the prison ships, Collingwood possessed an effective veto on the operation. Castlereagh asked him to make clear to Seville, in the unusual circumstances of the time, that British interests must take precedence.

> It will naturally occur to the authorities who shall apply to you on the subject, that so long as no central government is formed in Spain, and before reciprocal arrangements are concluded between Great Britain and the Spanish nation, and a common system of conduct is agreed upon, by authority, for mutual interests; His Majesty is bound to consult His Own security, and maintain His Own rights, however He may be disposed to relax them in favor of Spain, whenever her real interests and honor are concerned—so far as the same can be reconciled with the permanent security and interests of the British Empire.[20]

This was even less than grudging support for the proposed repatriation: it was a blunt message to the Spaniards from their new and powerful ally. General Morla understood it. The Junta Suprema in Seville hesitated, claiming a lack of transport ships. When General Dupont protested the violation of the terms of surrender, the captain-general responded to him that the French could not expect consideration after their atrocities: "By what right can law demand the impossible fulfillment of a surrender agreement with an army that entered Spain under the pretence of an intimate alliance and union, imprisoned our king and his royal family, sacked his palace, killed and stole from his subjects, destroyed the countryside and seized the crown?" The terms of capitulation, Morla suggested, had been a convenient device for both sides, which the signatories never believed would actually be executed. Now "the overriding law of necessity" must rule. Morla promised to protect the captives from harm, but ordered them held in the scattered mountain towns to the south of Seville. He had repudiated the repatriation agreement. Neither Spain's British allies—who had guided his hand—nor Napoleon himself offered any protest.[21]

Vedel's division, moving behind Dupont's, followed more slowly toward the ports. After nine days' march on the back roads, some units reached the town of Morón, fifty miles south of Seville. There they were halted with reports that the ships were not yet ready to receive them. For almost three weeks they remained at Morón, camped in an olive grove; and soon a detachment of injured French soldiers joined them with tales of another group of the wounded from Jaén who had been slaughtered by Spanish irregulars at Villaharta.[22]

The fate of the French prisoners was now a matter of high politics. While they waited in the fields, Wellesley's British expeditionary force was coming ashore in Portugal to attack General Junot. The Junta Suprema of Seville—despite any considerations of honor arising from the surrender agreement—was in no rush to dispatch its captives back to France for reincorporation in Napoleon's invading armies. Soon, with the aid of their new ally, the Spanish patriots expected to drive the emperor's forces clean out of the peninsula. Then, perhaps, the prisoners from Bailén might be returned on foot to their homeland. In the meantime they could wilt in the olive groves.

On August 15 Wellesley's armies, with their wagon trains of

bullock carts creaking behind them, met the French advance guard on the Portuguese coast near Obidos and drove them south. Two days later Wellesley routed the French vanguard again. On August 21 at Vimeiro, Junot's main columns of thirteen thousand men took the offensive, attacking the British lines stretched out on the ridge above them. The columns broke under British fire and fled; but Wellesley's cautious superior commanders held off a charge that would have destroyed the French army. Instead, Junot offered the white flag. For the rest of the day, while Wellesley cursed, the senior British generals negotiated and signed the terms of surrender: "an extraordinary paper," in Wellesley's eyes, which provided for the immediate return of the entire defeated army to France—accompanied by its booty, and on British ships.[23] For Junot, the terms were as favorable as those negotiated by Dupont at Bailén—and more easily accomplished, since the ports and ships were nearby. They were also directly contrary to the instructions sent by the British cabinet to Admiral Collingwood just two days before on August 19, designed to frustrate repatriation of the French troops captured at Bailén in July.

On August 31 the Portuguese armistice accord was ratified by treaty in the Convention of Cintra. Days afterwards, a disenchanted General Wellesley left the peninsula, and in Britain found himself forced to defend the overly lenient terms of the French surrender in Portugal, which he had privately opposed. The London mob scapegoated him and threatened a lynching; the press demanded repudiation of the agreement; and through the autumn a military court of inquiry examined the scandal of Cintra. "Britain sickens, Cintra! at thy name," Lord Byron sneered,

> And folks in office at the mention fret,
> And fain would blush, if blush they could for shame,
> How will Posterity the deed proclaim![24]

In the end, the court of inquiry absolved the British generals and approved the Convention. But the British army was humiliated by the agreement and distressed by its consequences. The government itself had been blindsided by its negotiators in Portugal.

Junot's troops were repatriated as the Convention provided, and soon marched back into Spain. The soldiers of Dupont and Vedel, promised similar relief under the terms of their earlier surrender, became the unwitting victims of Cintra and a merciless war. Given the political atmosphere of London, after Cintra no British government could countenance the easy return of more defeated French soldiers to Napoleon's ranks.[25]

The Seville Junta, as it struggled to organize Spanish forces in Andalusia and to cement the military coalition with Britain, was unusually sensitive to the winds from London. While the British debated the merits of Cintra, Seville practiced further delay with the prisoners of Bailén. At Morón, General Vedel was ordered to divide his troops proportionally for lodging in a number of towns in western Andalusia. On August 22, as the French at Vimeiro signed their repatriation agreement, the prisoners in the south marched out again, to Campillos, Cañete la Real, Teba, La Puebla, Lebrija, Montilla, and elsewhere, their hopes of repatriation fading, their fears of massacre mounting. In Osuna the prisoners' columns were fired upon haphazardly; in Campillos "the crowds gave the sign of cutting our throats as we marched through the streets." When they reached their destinations, the prisoners were paraded before local officials and assigned to lodgings in homes, prisons, barracks, vacated convents, or inns. Their treatment varied from town to town and household to household: sometimes generous, sometimes brutal, sometimes indifferent. The French were forced to remain vigilant against random attack behind barricaded doors. In September the prisoners' pay was reduced; but in the friendly town of Teba (where Louis Gille was billeted with two companies of the First Legion), the mayor promised that supplies would be sold to the captives at the same prices charged to local inhabitants. Once a week, on Sundays, the prisoners were called out to inspection in the town squares by fanfares of drums and cornets, and paraded to mass, followed by mess with the officers. Gathered together in these weekly interludes, they briefly felt safe from spontaneous attack.[26]

The quartermaster Louis Gille, his Spanish rapidly improving, was befriended by the mayor of Teba, Don Florencio Altín de la Hinojota. Gille became the interpreter and intermediary for his fellow prisoners in the town—and on their behalf, rejected an invitation from the local magistrate for volunteers who would go over to the Spanish forces.

As summer passed into autumn and rumors reached the prisoners of changing fortunes on the battlefields, their hopes of return rose and faded. In September, General Dupont and 180 officers were repatriated to Toulon and Marseilles. For the general, that meant trial and disgrace at home. But these were the first and last of the prisoners of Bailén to depart under the terms of capitulation. Castlereagh's decree had resulted in the narrowest possible interpretation of the surrender agreement. The remaining captives in their thousands were never told of Britain's reluctance to support the agreement, nor of Morla's letter to Dupont denouncing it, nor of Napoleon's own contempt for it.

After Bailén and Vimeiro, as British armies advanced into Spain, the puppet King Joseph abandoned Madrid and took refuge at Vitoria, beyond the Ebro River. Now the French controlled only Navarre, Aragon, and Catalonia in the north. The war in the Iberian Peninsula might soon be over; King Joseph suggested timorously to his brother that the Spanish adventure should end, and that he should return to the relative comfort of his old court in the kingdom of Naples.

On the side of the insurgents, the various provincial juntas—more and more aware of the need for coordinated leadership in the war against the French intruders—agreed to create a Supreme Central Government Junta of Spain and the Indies, a confederacy consisting of two delegates from each regional government; and in September, the delegates swore their oath of loyalty to the exiled Ferdinand VII in the royal palace of Aranjuez.[27]

In November Napoleon curtly rejected his brother Joseph's defeatism, assumed personal command of the faltering peninsular armies, vastly reinforced his units in Spain, and began driving the allied forces back towards Portugal. When he reached Joseph's temporary capital in Vitoria, Napoleon bluntly lectured the puppet's royal court:

> I am here with the soldiers who conquered at Austerlitz, at Jena, at Eylau. Who can withstand *them?* Certainly not your wretched Spanish troops who do not know how to fight. I shall conquer Spain in two months and acquire the rights of a conqueror. Treaties, constitutions, and all other agreements cease to exist. I am no longer bound by them.[28]

Under Bonaparte's imperious command, the Spanish campaign had become a war without restraints. Spain was no longer an ally, but an enemy to be crushed. The country's revolutionary constitution, imposed from France only months before, evaporated in the autumn air. In early December Napoleon's Grande Armée entered Madrid, Joseph Bonaparte returned unhappily to the capital, and the rebel Junta Central retreated from Aranjuez to Seville. Within days the emperor violated the terms of Madrid's treaty of capitulation in a round of arrests, confiscations, and emergency decrees. And soon after that—apparently assured of his Iberian conquests—the emperor departed from Spain for the Austrian front. He would never return.

All this French success was, paradoxically, bad news for the prisoners taken at Bailén. As Napoleon's military cause prospered, popular sentiments hardened and the condition of the prisoners in the south suffered. In La Puebla, there were rumors of a plot to kill all the Frenchmen.[29] In Teba, the prisoners were told that the Junta Suprema in Seville, fearing an organized rising by the captives, had ordered all officers to leave for Cádiz within twenty-four hours. After the officers' departure, Spanish conscripts made a brief and ineffectual attack on the prisoners, who remained barricaded in their quarters. In Lebrija, local residents led (it was said) by "ferocious priests" attacked French officers and noncommissioned officers outside their barracks in what a survivor described as "a horrible carnage." The slaughter was eventually ended with the arrival of Spanish regulars.[30] In the absence of any firm central authority in the rebel provinces, the safety of the prisoners scattered through the small towns of western Andalusia rested on changeable local moods: and these were troubled by the rushing winds of hearsay about French atrocities, or travellers' gossip about the advancing Napoleonic armies. The news did nothing to calm the spirits of the captives.

When Napoleon's invading forces reached Toledo in their war of reconquest, the rebel Junta Central gave renewed orders for all French prisoners to be marched south to Cádiz. This was a double act of prudence: it would free them from the growing fury of the mob in their scattered places of detention, and it would keep them beyond liberation by the advancing French armies. In Teba the mayor provided funds to supply the departing units, and offered his good wishes. (But he warned Louis Gille: "I don't know where they are taking you," and urged him to remain in Teba as his interpreter. Gille refused to betray his country by accepting the mayor's generosity.) The French, in return, presented the mayor with a letter of thanks for his goodwill and protection. But as they moved, the prisoners were treated less tolerantly: taunted and stoned by crowds along the roadsides, or forced to cry "Viva España! Viva el Rey!" in fear for their lives. Behind the French columns, the lame and the weak were randomly murdered in the ditches. In Jerez, four junior officers were taken before a noble and his armed men, who stripped and searched them, stealing their watches, jewelry, and gold; even their drums and cartridge boxes were seized and given to the Spanish troops. Here the search seemed to be general. "The French," a prisoner recalled, "left Jerez with empty pockets."[31] From there, on Christmas day 1808, they marched in the rain toward the sea at Santa María, Puerto Real, and Isla León, where they were told that ships awaited them. The captives foresaw an immediate return to France, and "the joy of expectation... was in all hearts."[32]

❖   ❖   ❖

AS A YOUTH, Henri Ducor recalled being "transported by enthusiasm" at the reports of France's republican military victories. He conceived "an ardent desire to take part in the glorious work of our armies," and at the age of twelve, in 1801, he entered the navy as a cadet. After training he was posted to the warship *Argonaute,* which carried Polish legionaries to Santo Domingo and was later besieged by the Royal Navy in the friendly harbor of La Coruña in northern Spain. In August 1805 the *Argonaute* escaped from port to join the French and Spanish fleets under Vice Admiral Villeneuve at Cádiz, as Napoleon maneuvered his forces for an invasion of England. Off Cádiz, Admiral Nelson's squadron blocked Villeneuve's movements. On a reckless whim, Villeneuve embarked with his fleet to confront the English squadron, and on October 21 they engaged the English in the decisive naval battle of Trafalgar. The Napoleonic armada was routed, and in defeat the *Argonaute* took refuge once more, along with four other surviving French warships, at Cádiz.

For almost three years Henri Ducor and his companions lived on board ship in Cádiz Harbor, under protection by the Spanish shore batteries and within sight of the English fleet blockading the outer reaches. The exile was tedious but safe. That changed in June 1808 when the city joined in revolt against the imposition of the French puppet king in Madrid. The shore guns of Cádiz turned their sights inwards to the harbor and the French. While the Royal Navy stood neutral offshore, the French ships took fighting positions, refused a call for surrender, and endured several days of bombardment. But their plight was hopeless; they could not move, and Dupont's army was still far away to the north. On June 14 they surrendered, and Henri Ducor found himself a prisoner of the Spanish along with three thousand other sailors. For the next three years, the Frenchman applied his intelligence and ingenuity to schemes of survival and escape while he stored memories of his unanticipated adventures.[33]

After brief incarceration in the ancient Arab baths of Cádiz, Ducor and the other naval prisoners were transferred to prison ships, or *pontons* anchored in the harbor. These—like the British hulks of the same period—were battered and disabled ships of the line, shorn of their masts and unseaworthy. Three of the recently captured French ships, the *Argonaute*, the *Vainqueur*, and the *Vieille Castille*, were among them. The prisoners were at first forbidden access to the open rear decks, but instead were crowded into the darkness below, where the air was fetid and breathing difficult. When they were allowed on deck in daytime, the sailors were scorched by the merciless midday sun of summer. They were fed maggoty bread and biscuits, verminous rice, rotten vegetables, rancid lard, and sparse draughts of water "soaked up like drops falling on a hot fire." (The fortunates who still held cash could ease those hardships with purchases from floating merchants in the bay.) The prisoners' guards allowed them to wash only from bottles of sea water, and threatened to shoot them if they attempted to bathe in the harbor.[34]

Despair followed the news that Dupont's armies had surrendered; and soon, Ducor reported, "all kinds of illnesses erupted:

diarrhea, dysentery, typhoid, and scurvy overwhelmed these unhappy companions of misfortune." Those who were not ill fell into profound apathy.[35] For six months the horrors continued, the insanitary conditions grew worse, the local authorities remained indifferent. And then, in December, the ragged thousands from Dupont's armies reached Cádiz. Here their dreams of repatriation were dashed. The French sailors, Henri Ducor among them, were taken ashore to the prison of San Carlos on nearby Isla León (located in the salt marshes at the base of the long peninsular entrance to the city) while the soldiers and their camp followers replaced them on the dreadful hulks. Louis Gille recalled the warning of the mayor of Teba "that we were not departing to return to France: but to avoid violating the secrets of his government, he couldn't tell me of our destination."[36] Now Gille knew they would be kept on the prison ships.

This was an unimaginable experience for the weak and demoralized prisoners. They were "without hammocks, or mattresses, or straw," thrown aboard like corpses dropped into a common grave. That—they thought—was to be their fate. They would be left to die.

On the captured French ship *Vainqueur*, Gille was one of eighteen hundred prisoners, most of them crowded onto the gun deck without hammocks or supplies. Gille himself searched for sleeping space in the officers' quarters and found a safe and hidden corner, which served also as his office when he was named storekeeper for the hulk. The rest of his companions, without any privacy, were "plunged into the most disgusting improprieties, prey to the most frightful miseries." Gille found his close friend Golvin and brought him into his quarters; and with their hoarded cash, the two soldiers bought a few portions of dried figs, peas, almonds, and oranges to supplement their meager rations.[37]

Another prisoner taken at Bailén, Louis-Joseph Wagré, an eighteen-year-old apprentice baker who had, like Gille, been conscripted to the First Reserve Legion in 1807, used his talent for bargaining to gain a pass onto the hulk reserved for officers, the *Vieille Castille*. There he established himself as a laundryman. He was paid for his services with precious portions of his patrons' rations of food and fresh water. But after a few weeks Wagré fell ill and was taken to hospital on shore. Once recovered, he was placed on an overcrowded hulk, appropriately named the *Terrible*, where he lost his trade and his supplementary income.[38]

Food and bad water were supplied from shore every two days, but deliveries were unreliable. "Only twice in three months did we have all that we needed. When we had bread, we lacked vegetables; when we had one or the other, we lacked wood or water to cook them." Epidemics swept through the ships; the dead were dropped overboard into the harbor; and when the inhabitants of Cádiz protested at this filth to the military governor, the prisoners were forced to collect dead bodies on board for up to a week before their captors removed them. On hulks containing several hundred prisoners each, French deaths sometimes reached fifteen to twenty a day. Louis Gille reports an occasion when there were ninety-eight bodies piled on the forecastle of the hulk *Vainqueur*.[39] The Swiss officer Amédée de Muralt, on board the *Vieille Castille*, recalled that Spanish sailors on a longboat nicknamed "The Ship of the Dead" retrieved the bodies by tying them to a long cable and dragging them onto the beach for disposal.[40] The bodies decomposed; the stench filled the harbor. The sick cried out in pain, or hallucinated, or fell into unconsciousness. The healthy endured at their sides.

A medical observer noticed the curious fact that only the wives of the soldiers, and the canteen-women or provisioners, seemed to avoid illness. There were still several hundred of them among the prisoners, awaiting repatriation or remaining by choice with the men. The physician speculated that these women—like the medical staff—kept healthy because they moved about more than others in supplying the troops and because they were "born nurses," accustomed to living by a stern code of duty.

> The conviction that one will not be ill, and the determination not to be, are excellent hygienic qualities. Add to this the need to set an example by rejecting defeat—and thus one can understand why, in the midst of the most violent epidemics, doctors (and all those who must assist them) resist disease more than others. They are firmer in their stirrups. Among them, self-respect—the most powerful of stimuli—is at work.[41]

The physician believed that this kind of resilience was more common among officers and the better educated than among "the unfortunate peasants who brought with them the ignorance of their villages." Provincial conscripts, in their thousands, had to be watched and cared for like unruly children. The medical staff urged all prisoners to exercise and—once death had thinned the ranks on board the hulks—organized dances, games, and gymnastics on the crowded decks. The officers especially—many of whom were separated on their own prison ship—established a strict routine of activity and refused to lie down during the hours of sunlight, once the morning cannon salvo had announced each day.

Besides the advantages of self-discipline, the officers enjoyed other material benefits as the privileges of rank. Some of them still had substantial cash, with which they could buy fresh water, wine, bread, meat, and vegetables from local merchants who rowed out each day to the hulks. They kept changes of clothing, washed their shirts in fresh water, bathed, and shaved. A common soldier, by contrast, was lucky to have a torn cloak as a blanket and a single shirt that he could only clean in sea water. Few still had shoes. The officers reserved the military musicians for their own entertainment, while the men heard only the groans of the timbers, the insults of the guards, and the cries of the suffering around them. Although deference to authority restrained the common soldiers from revolt, their physical hardships inevitably affected their health and sapped their spirits.[42]

These deplorable conditions lasted until late winter in 1809. Then the local government—fearing epidemic, or the possibility of a French relief expedition—acted to clean and fumigate the prisoners' quarters, supplied camp beds on deck, opened pharmacies, and sent medical inspection teams on board. The sick were bathed in disinfectant and their clothes tossed overboard. Under proper care, they were miraculously revived, to dream again of victory and deliverance.[43]

Meanwhile, the French sailors, along with some of the soldiers of Bailén who could not be accommodated on the hulks, found a more comfortable life in the prison of San Carlos on Isla León. The building formed an arcaded square around a vast courtyard. In it more than four thousand captives slung their hammocks, while the officers settled into a separate pavilion "crowned by a magnificent terrace that served them as a promenade." On the day after their arrival, merchants set up stalls inside the prison, offering meat, potatoes, eggplants, tomatoes, figs, olives, raisins, and other supplies.

In the great halls of the jail, the sailors reorganized their lives to make the most of misfortune. They practiced fencing, attended dance classes, held balls where "the ugliest of the women merchants were sought out and fêted like the most beautiful of princesses." In the evenings there were boxing matches, boisterous gambling sessions, and elaborate spectacles. An entertainer created popes, cardinals, and dukes in grotesque masks and costumes; a doctor mounted a popular marionette show in which Pulcinella overcame the Holy Inquisition and, in a final halo of glory, the figure of Napoleon guarded by the genius of civilization appeared to offer benediction from center stage. The theatrical themes were comic and daring, a blatant affront to their captors. But after some initial challenges, the prisoners drove the Spanish guards beyond the bars of the main gate, where they could observe the revels without daring to intervene. Always, the prisoners honored Napoleon: "The Emperor! They thought always of him; in their minds, Napoleon and France were inseparable. Nothing could happen without him: for things to succeed, he had to be everywhere." "What a man!" the sailors exclaimed, when tales of his personal heroism were repeated. For the prisoners he was more God than emperor, still their savior and protector despite temporary defeat.[44]

By spring, the captives in San Carlos heard frightful reports from the doctors of conditions on the *pontons;* and in the rush to clean up the squalor, several hundred of the ill were brought ashore to be housed in the halls of the great prison. Marines and sailors gave up their hammocks to the sick. With modest comfort, fresh air, clean surroundings, and sufficient food, many of them quickly recovered their health.

The new threat to the prisoners of San Carlos came from the local population of Cádiz and Isla León. When a contingent of Swiss deserters from the French army arrived in Cádiz in March 1809, nervous citizens feared that the troops (who were now serving Spain) had actually arrived to seize the city. Angry crowds turned on the Junta Central's local representative; and when they were diverted from that target, they marched towards San Carlos. Rumors swept the prison that the mob was intent on a massacre. From the pavilion terrace the preparations could be observed. As the throng gathered, officers warned the inmates to prepare their defenses. Doorways were barricaded with furniture; bottles, pots, and paving stones were gathered as weapons. But what the prisoners most feared was fire. "We were not anxious to be roasted," recalled Henri Ducor, "and the idea of making an auto-da-fé of six thousand Frenchmen (for we were by then six thousand) could well have occurred to the Spaniards."[45]

The crowds reached the prison, crying "Death to the Frenchmen!" As they shouted for the gates to be opened, the military governor of Isla León turned two cannons on them and ordered their retreat. He promised to protect the unarmed prisoners with his Castilian honor, and was rewarded with further cries of "Death to the governor! Death to the lackeys of King Joseph!" While the mob hesitated, the governor repeated his threats—and made a diversionary appeal to Spanish prejudice:

> Do you think I can be intimidated? Why do you have gypsies among you—that perfidious, faithless, and lawless race, the dregs of humanity, hated by the nation that tolerates them? Aren't you Spaniards ashamed of mixing with these bastards of the world that no country wants to recognize, these thieves, these terrors of the highways and the countryside?[46]

In the face of renewed imprecations from the crowd, the governor challenged the agitators to join the Spanish army and kill Frenchmen gloriously on the battlefields. If they persisted in assaulting the prison, he warned, "you will pass over my dead body!" His cannons faced them down, and the mob gradually dispersed. The prisoners dismantled their barricades; but they feared more demonstrations, and prayed that they would soon leave San Carlos.

For two months petitions had reached the Junta Central, calling for removal of the captives from Cádiz. The most influential public claim against the prisoners was the danger to local health. Cádiz's prosperity as an international trading center depended, among other things, on its freedom from contagion—or from rumor of contagion. The hulks were no credit to the city's reputation. But for the British and the Spanish military, the overriding concern was the protection of Cádiz as a safe fortress within free Spanish territory in the peninsula. With French armies on the move across Spain, thousands of their imprisoned compatriots and the captive French ships in Cádiz Bay might well be the object of a relief expedition. As early as December 1808, the new British minister to Spain, John Hookham Frere, reported to London that orders had been given to remove the ships and prisoners from the strategic port as a contribution to its security.[47] But the administration of independent Spain was chaotic, and decisions were not easily implemented. For three months after that, complex diplomatic wrangling between the shaky Junta Central and the British government over the terms of a treaty of alliance, the size and conditions of British financial aid to the impoverished rebel regime, and Spanish sensitivity over the defence of Cádiz by British forces, meant that the immediate fate of the prisoners was ignored while they suffered on the hulks. Finally, the prisoners in San Carlos and on the *pontons* were told at the end of March 1809 that they were about to embark on two sea-going convoys. The sailors would go to the Canary Islands, and Dupont's soldiers to the Balearic Islands of Majorca and Minorca. The long-delayed order came from the Junta Central in Seville, with the compliance of the Royal Navy. The local explanation was that the move was necessary to protect public health; but the dictating reason was military. The prisoners were to be removed from mainland Spain where they might be freed by the advancing French armies.

As the two allies assembled a transport fleet, they gave little thought to the captives' fate after reaching the Balearics and the Canaries. No one was thinking of repatriation. The prisoners, on the other hand, wished to believe that they would re-embark for France from the Mediterranean islands in fulfillment of their terms of surrender eight months before. They did not know that the local government in Cádiz and the Junta Central in Seville had limited authority beyond their ability to ship the prisoners out of range. On the Balearic Islands, the French would fall under the influence of another semi-autonomous regional government—

with the Royal Navy and its London masters always close and decisive in the background.[48]

The sailor Henri Ducor, who was anxious for repatriation and eager for further service in Napoleon's campaigns, gambled on fate. Rumor among the prisoners was that the land forces sailing for Majorca and Minorca had a better chance of repatriation than the sailors bound for the Canaries. So the young man Ducor traded his naval uniform for that of a dying cavalryman, and was accepted as a soldier of Dupont's army as the departure from Cádiz was prepared.

For many days the prisoners on the hulks could see ships gathering in the outer roadstead, their masts "like an immense forest." At last, the exultant captives from Bailén were moved out to sixteen transport ships at anchor beyond the harbor, and on Easter morning, April 3, 1809, the prison fleet destined for the Mediterranean sailed from Cádiz, escorted by four Royal Navy ships of the line (HMS *Bombay*, *Grasshopper*, *Norge*, and *Ambuscade*) and the Spanish frigate *Cornelia*—twenty-one ships in all. The British convoy commander, Captain William Cuming of the *Bombay*, reported tersely in his log: "Convoy consists of sail of transports having on board between five and six thousand French prisoners."[49] About half the prisoners were left behind on the hulks.

2
A DISGRACEFUL AND REPULSIVE IDEA

DON JOSÉ RODRÍGUEZ DE ARIAS, captain of the Spanish frigate *Cornelia*, received his orders from the Junta Central on March 25, 1809, in Cádiz Harbor. He was to sail with the convoy of transport ships to Palma de Majorca, where the prisoners would be divided "among all the Balearic islands including Cabrera" in proportions to be decided by the junta of Majorca. The prisoners' destination was the archipelago of the Baleares, a straggling chain of four principal islands (Ibiza, Formentera, Majorca, and Minorca) located in the western Mediterranean a few hundred kilometers off the Iberian Peninsula.

Islands are safe refuges from continental disorder. But they can also be prisons. The main islands of the Baleares were long-inhabited outposts of the province of Catalonia. The largest among them, Majorca, had a population close to 150,000. About 30,000 of those were residents of the capital city, Palma, which was distinguished by its vast, honey-colored gothic cathedral dominating the harbor, narrow streets and grand houses, and massive medieval walls encircling the old city.[1] Aside from Cádiz, Palma was the only major city of Spain remaining free from French siege or occupation. Majorca's fields produced olives, oranges, lemons, figs, dates, almonds, cereals, and market crops, and its major port had been a thriving commercial center when sea trade centered in the Mediterranean. Cabrera, by contrast—the only island specifically mentioned in Captain Rodríguez's orders—was a small and rugged outcropping from the sea, desolate and unoccupied, just to the south of Majorca. The specification in the orders was a strange one.

Because food storage on the transports had been "reduced to accommodate the largest number of prisoners," and because the cost of supplies was high, Rodríguez was instructed to warn Palma in advance so that there could be a rapid disembarcation on arrival. By that time no food or water would remain on board. The transports were commercially chartered ships, and calculated underprovisioning meant increased profits for the owners. Their passengers on this journey deserved even less care than usual. Captain Rodríguez would carry with him one million reales as a contribution from the Junta Central towards maintenance of the prisoners in the Baleares.[2]

The transformed cavalryman Henri Ducor found himself on transport number nine—a ship, he reported, just as crowded as the *pontons*. "But what a difference! What a future opened up! We were going to be returned to our country...." His shipmates included General Dufour, a group of seamen of the Imperial Guard, many noncommissioned officers, and about thirty canteen-women.[3] (Most of the other camp-following provisioners, who were not being held as prisoners, seem to have been left behind at liberty when the troops were put onto the transports.) The young quartermaster Louis Gille was placed on transport number ten, *El Príncipe Real*, along with 507 other captives crowded into just a third of the ship's quarters. The rest of the space was reserved for officers and crew.[4] The conscript Louis-Joseph Wagré, also from Vedel's division, was assigned to transport number two. General Privé and other senior officers enjoyed the relative comforts of the commanding Spanish frigate *Cornelia*.[5]

The ships beat southward to the Strait of Gibraltar, while the escorting British men-of-war regularly fired their guns alongside the transports to keep them obediently in line. On the night of April 6, after passing through the Pillars of Hercules into the Mediterranean, the convoy met a violent storm. Mountainous waves broke over the troopships and terrified the occupants. The convoy separated in darkness. Masts went down and pumps could not handle the intake of water. Transport number ten was driven onto a reef on the African coast, but floated off on the next gigantic wave. By five the next morning HMS *Bombay* had only seven sails of the twenty-one-ship convoy within sight, and signalled them to close up and run in for Gibraltar Bay. Others sought refuge as they could, in Gibraltar, or Málaga, or further east at Almería. For twenty-four hours transport number ten was alone and out of sight along the Barbary shore. On April 8 one of the Royal Navy warships approached, fired a shot that shattered its mizzenmast, and took the transport under tow for Málaga, where half the fleet was recovering in harbor. For five days the convoy remained in disarray while urgent repairs were made to the battered transports; but the captives could only gaze hopelessly towards shore from their prison ships. On transport number ten, where Louis Gille lay in his hammock suffering from a heavy fever, a French medical officer arranged for small rations of wine and quinine to be brought on board for the sick. Gille's friend Golvin cared for him with "indefatigable zeal"; and at last, after a week in the darkness below decks, the convalescent was able to hobble on deck on Golvin's arm to catch a few longing glimpses of tropical Málaga. On Henri Ducor's ship, the prisoners— believing that they would soon be returned to France—bartered pieces of clothing or equipment for bottles of the excellent local wine. By April 12 the guardships had reassembled the fleet off Cabo de Gata, bound for Palma de Majorca and the Royal Navy base at Port Mahón in Minorca. Once more at sea, Louis Gille's high fever returned, and the prisoner was only saved from throwing himself overboard in delirium by his faithful friend Golvin. On all the transports the suffering and illness continued: the fleet, in one captive's eyes, was "no more . . . than a floating hospital."[6]

A night or two out of Málaga, in the darkness off Cabo de Palos, seamen of the Imperial Guard on transport number nine staged a revolt, seized control of the ship, and broke off from the convoy. By dawn she was well away and under chase by two of the British men-of-war. The lumbering transport was no match for the speed and firepower of HMS *Ambuscade*, which soon recaptured her. To humiliate the French rebels (and perhaps, especially, the shaken Spanish crew) the ship was taken in tow for the rest of the voyage.

In the Mediterranean the prisoners were under the ultimate control of Vice Admiral Lord Collingwood, the Royal Navy's regional commander-in-chief now based at Port Mahón, in Minorca. (Although Minorca was a Spanish possession, the acquiescent island was under the dominant influence of the Royal Navy throughout the war.) According to one contemporary observer, Collingwood had the authority of a viceroy in the Mediterranean: he was "the prime and sole minister of England, acting upon the sea, corresponding himself with all surrounding states, and ordering everything upon his own responsibility."[7] Since early March Collingwood had consulted over the prison expedition and noted the prospects in his journals.

Monday 6 March 1809.... To Mr. Frere His Majesty's Minister at Seville acquainting him I have been informed the Spanish Government intend sending the French Prisoners from Cádiz to the Islands of Majorca and Minorca, a measure which would be likely to put those Islands in great danger.... To Rear Admiral Purvis on the same subject....

Wednesday 29 March 1809.... a Letter for the Captain of the *Bombay*,... acquainting Captain Cuming of the State of the Baleares Islands, —and directing him to make such arrangements with the Governor General at Palma, previous to the French Prisoners being landed, that they may be confined in the strong holds in Majorca and to the Islands of Ivica [Ibiza] and Fromentera [sic]—Minorca not being in a State either with respect to Prisons or Forces to Secure them. —Having seen the Prisoners landed the *Bombay* and *Grasshopper* are to join me and the *Norge* & *Ambuscade* to proceed to Gibraltar.[8]

Collingwood said nothing of repatriation. The terms of surrender at Bailén had been forgotten. As the intermediary who had done most to scuttle them months earlier, he had no interest in reviving them now.

By April 17 the convoy lay off Majorca, at the wide entrance to the Bay of Palma. But instead of landing the prisoners, the British escort ships engaged in a busy exchange of messages—onshore, among themselves, and by fast sail with Collingwood on Minorca. Collingwood's journal continues:

Thursday 20 April 1809.... To the Secretary of the Admiralty.... that I have heard the Majorquins are determined not to allow the French Prisoners ... a landing.

At dawn the next day, HMS *Bombay*, with the whole prison fleet in company, arrived unexpectedly off Port Mahón. Captain Cuming—frustrated by his inability to disembark the prisoners in Palma de Majorca—was forcing the hand of his commander. Now, in their thousands, they were here before Admiral Collingwood's eyes. The commander responded decisively.

> At 7 the *Bombay*, *Norge*, and *Ambuscade* appeared off the harbor with a Convoy of vessels from Cadiz having French Prisoners on board, —Sent orders for them to remain off the Port. The *Grasshopper* and a Spanish frigate which had come up with the Convoy anchored.... Having consulted with the Spanish Governor of this Island as to the expediency of receiving the French Prisoners, —it appeared that not more than four or five hundred could be put in places of security, —which Number came in, in two vessels. —Sent orders to the Captain of the *Bombay* to proceed with the remainder of the Convoy to Majorca, —and having landed the Prisoners he was to join me off Toulon, —sending the *Norge* and *Ambuscade* to Gibraltar.... The Convoy... at Sunset stood for Majorca.[9]

Simultaneously with the convoy's return to Palma, Collingwood asked for cooperation from the local government.

> Friday 21 April 1809.... To the President of the Supreme Junta of Majorca and to the Captain General of that Island on the necessity there is of receiving the French Prisoners... on that Island—Minorca being inadequate both with regard to Prisons and Forces to secure them—and that those which have been left here are not thought to be secure without a Ship of War being left to guard them—and requesting they will make the necessary arrangements for precluding the Danger which the Inhabitants apprehend from the Prisoners forcing their Liberty.[10]

Collingwood knew that the inhabitants of Majorca and Minorca shared the same fears about the prisoners: that they carried infectious disease, that they might escape and overwhelm the islands, that their presence might provoke a French naval attack. What distinguished the two cases for the British commander was that Port Mahón was a vital strategic base responsible for blockading the French navy at Toulon and sweeping the entire western Mediterranean for French ships—especially troop convoys moving reinforcements from Toulon to Barcelona to reinforce Napoleon's armies on the peninsula. Collingwood needed the convoy's escort ships for other tasks, and could not afford to tie them up in guard duties at Mahón or Palma. Nor would he allow large numbers of prisoners onshore near his Mediterranean headquarters. His first priority was to disembark the prisoners from the transport ships—somewhere—and thus to retrieve his ships-of-war. Responsibility for the unfortunate Frenchmen would be thrust upon the local authorities of Majorca whether they wanted it or not.

In Palma, the government of the Balearic Islands was in the hands of the Junta Superior, "governing the Kingdom of Majorca in the name of His Majesty Ferdinand VII." The junta consisted of twenty-seven persons representing the traditional elite, the church, and the military. It had evolved from the local military government created after the nationwide risings in the spring of 1808.[11] By early 1809 the Majorcan regime (like the junta in Cádiz) was subject to direction in the war against France from the Junta Central, now resident in Seville after its retreat from Aranjuez. What had emerged in rebel Spain was a vaguely confederal system; but the division of authority was uncertain and contested. While the disposition of French prisoners rested ultimately with the Junta Central (and with its ally the British), once the captives had been moved, their daily maintenance and protection lay with the local authorities. The arrival of thousands of prisoners on Majorca meant that substantial costs of provisioning, lodging, health, and supervision would fall suddenly on the unsteady, inexperienced, and impoverished administration of the islands. But there was potential advantage in that prospect as well—for it might give Palma bargaining power in its negotiations with the central government over wartime tax transfers and the supply of troops, horses, arms, and foodstuffs demanded to fight the war on the mainland. The fear of residents over the health of prisoners of war in their midst was just one of the factors faced by the local government as it debated the fate of the soldiers on the transports. Beyond the plea of common humanity, nothing encouraged a quick or automatic decision to bring the prisoners ashore. For another ten days of quarantine, the captives endured their uncertainty on the transports.

Majorca's reluctance to take French prisoners was no surprise: it had been obvious to the Junta Central from the beginning. Island society was divided among a dominant elite of landholding nobility, clergy and military, a bureaucratic and commercial middle class, and a majority of rural and urban poor. The dominant class was itself split between an active, progressive minority of liberals inspired by the eighteenth-century enlightenment and a reactionary majority, an outward-looking merchant community and an inward-looking gentry, all living warily with an insular multitude, traditionally fearful of invaders, contagion, or siege. As the war on the mainland intensified, the island was inundated with thousands of refugees fleeing the violence. Palma was crowded with insecure temporary residents, and the junta was nervous over the local population's wartime mood. Only two months before the arrival of the prison convoy, in February 1809, a battalion of the provincial regiment ordered to the mainland for service against the French had mutinied in protest and randomly sacked the Jewish quarter of Palma known as the Sagell.

Almost everyone on the island feared the French. Majorca had been a favored place of exile for refugees from the French Revolution, clergy, military officers, and civilians; these expatriates in their hundreds were suspect aliens now that France was an aggressive enemy. Forty merchants of French nationality were taken into custody in Palma in January 1809, and fifteen resident French priests were listed for observation by the junta in February. In early March 1809, the island grudgingly accepted 120 French prisoners arriving from Alicante. But when the first rumors of preparations for a major prison convoy reached Palma at the same time (along with a report from the *Gazette* of Tarragona that 50 to 80 of the prisoners on the hulks of Cádiz were dying daily), the Junta Superior in Palma echoed local anxiety that they would bring contagious disease and disorder to the islands. As one writer noted, the Junta Central had inevitably created its own dilemma: "Having accepted contagion as the reason for removing the prisoners from Cádiz, it had to hide the situation from the Baleares."[12] But that could not be done. Twice the Majorcan junta sent formal messages to the central government pleading with it "to revoke any order that had been given to transfer these sick prisoners to these islands." The Baleares were unsuitable "because we lack both the means to provide for them or the armed men to keep them in custody, and also because their only suitable destination—the quarantine hospital in Mahón—cannot now serve since it must take a thousand wounded from our army in Catalonia.... It would be a cruelty to expose these islands to the contagion Cádiz wants to free itself from." If the prisoners nevertheless arrived, Seville was warned, "they would not be admitted."[13]

The news in April only hardened Majorcan resolve. The central government informed Palma that the convoy was about to sail from Cádiz (in fact it had done so days earlier), that the local government would receive a subsidy of one million reales to support the prisoners, and that fifteen hundred to two thousand of them could be removed by exchanging them for an equal number of Spanish soldiers detained by the French in Barcelona. The numbers remaining after such an exchange were still more than Palma was prepared to accept; and the price was not right. On April 11 the local junta called on Seville to stop the convoy en route, or, if it could not do so, to send the ships directly to Minorca for medical observation. If the captives should arrive in Majorca despite all these appeals, Palma demanded "a quick and abundant subsidy" sufficient to match "the overwhelming nature of this affair." According to the junta, the support offered by Seville would last barely a month. Majorca did not want the prisoners; but it wanted the benefits to be wrung from Seville in return for taking them. Was there some means of squaring the circle?

The next day an official ordinance from the central government confirmed that the prisoners were on their way, and formally proposed—if there was disease on board the transports when they arrived—that the Frenchmen could be landed on Cabrera, the tiny and barren island just to the south of Majorca. That action—the Junta Central explained—would not only prevent the spread of infectious disease to the inhabitants of the islands but would restrict the "pernicious influence" of the prisoners' revolutionary opinions, and limit the troubles and anxieties of keeping them in safe custody. That, the dispatch concluded reassuringly, had been Seville's sole purpose in moving the captives from the hulks in Cádiz to the Baleares.[14]

This ordinance seemed to be the first the Majorcans had heard of the Junta Central's proposal to use Cabrera as a prison camp (although the captain of the *Cornelia* had known of it for three weeks). The early twentieth century Majorcan writer Miguel de los Santos Oliver laments the thought.

> In this document the fatal name and the disgraceful, repulsive idea —the origin of so much evil, of so many deaths, of so many miseries—appeared for the first time. Such a solution had occurred to no one in Majorca, and perhaps never would have. But from that day it was launched to the four winds, permitted and even approved by the national government. Thus the people and the authorities—who suffered an immense avalanche of refugees from the mainland, who cared for the wounded and ill from almost all regions of the Levant, who knew the horrors (whether by instinct or terrible experience) of a single immigrant suffering from contagion—resigned themselves to the idea.[15]

For the next three weeks, the local Junta Superior and its commissions met in almost daily session in Palma to debate how to avoid the inundation—or how to make the best of it in negotiation with the central government. The prisoners, it was agreed, would be sent first to the quarantine hospital in Mahón; afterwards they would be divided equally among Majorca, Minorca, and Ibiza.

But public panic could not be calmed once the prison convoy actually came into view. In this situation cool reason and generous humanity lost their force. On April 21—the very day that the convoy sailed away to Minorca—the Junta Superior, meeting in extraordinary session, altered its previous decision and agreed, by a plurality, that once the prisoners had been released from quarantine in Mahón, they would be taken directly to the island of Cabrera "without contact with anyone." The junta went to unusual lengths in its record of debates to offer an official explanation and apology for the choice:

> The Junta considers it harsh to send these unfortunates to a desert island where the only habitation is a miserable little fort,... but it accepts this necessity as a means of avoiding contagion on these islands. Despite all that the health inspectors of Mahón could do, they could not carry out all the observations required to certify the health of these prisoners and to remove any danger of communicating with them. The news received from various ship's captains, who have come from Cádiz to this island, on the illnesses they have suffered and what has been publicly reported, especially in the *Gazeta de Sevilla*, repeated by the *Diario de Cartagena* of 14 March, demands that this Junta take the most extraordinary measures to prevent all danger of contagion. Thus it has taken the decision to move the prisoners from Mahón to Cabrera, a measure proposed by the Junta Central in its Royal ordinance of 22 March as much to prevent contagion as to avoid other dangers....[16]

By the time the convoy returned to Palma on April 24, the destination of the prisoners had been decided. Admiral Collingwood was the enforcer of the Junta Central's decision to leave the prisoners on the Baleares, and the Majorcan junta knew it could not defy him: the island's safety from the French was in the Royal Navy's hands. But the ultimate decision to drop the prisoners onto a desert island was theirs alone. The danger of contagion gave them the pretext. The junta had no clear evidence (and never would have any) of grave infectious disease on the transports: the captives suffered from illnesses of malnourishment, exposure, bad hygiene, and occasional venereal disease. The compelling but unstated factor in the junta's decision was the public mood, fed by rumor and overcome by fear. Cabrera was to be the prisoners' place of internment, not of temporary quarantine. Local anxieties would be calmed, and Majorca would seek its benefits from the central government: substantial relief from tax levies and military service, and cash subsidies to maintain the prisoners. The fate of the prisoners would be settled by appealing to "the law of necessity" or reason of state—an option beyond the dictates of law or common humanity.

The offer of a partial French-Spanish prisoner exchange remained open. On April 22 the Spanish commander in Tarragona warned the junta in Palma that unless it immediately dispatched two thousand French prisoners to the mainland for exchange, the French army might send its Spanish prisoners into internment in France and cancel the understanding. The Majorcan government accordingly asked the Spanish convoy commander to send transports containing that number of captives to Tarragona, on the coast of Catalonia, with the first favorable winds. For the rest, the junta prepared to supply the remaining prisoners with tents and building supplies for their new life on Cabrera and to arrange for regular shipments of food to the desert island. Their precise numbers remained unknown in Palma, and may have been underestimated. Meanwhile the captives, anxiously floating offshore, knew nothing of their fate—although there was gossip about an exchange and a spell of quarantine somewhere on land.[17]

Members of the local government remained genuinely troubled by their decision to send the prisoners to Cabrera. A special commission composed of two members of the junta was quickly appointed to study how the operation could be implemented. After visiting the barren island, they reported on "the great difficulty of executing the plan," proposed that the prisoners should instead be kept on board the transports, and called again for more financial aid from the central government. But on April 26, despite this sceptical report, the Junta Superior in Palma reaffirmed its intention to send the prisoners to Cabrera.

The next day one member of the Junta Superior, Don Francisco March, presented a written motion describing the proposed Cabrera policy as "inhuman and costly… exposing Majorca to many dangers," reporting public dismay, and calling for rejection of the decision. The old city of Palma was still encircled by its great medieval walls and a deep but dry moat, and March proposed that part of the empty moat should be transformed into enclosed barracks for the prisoners. Another critic, Don Juan Dameto, offered the alternative suggestion that Majorca should receive as many prisoners as it could accommodate in its towns, while the rest should be returned to Cádiz. But after tense debate, both motions were defeated and the original decision was reaffirmed. The dismay mentioned in March's resolution was shared—wrote the historian Santos Oliver—by only "a small enlightened minority... but not by the great majority, dominated by the fear of epidemics, which was the origin and basis of the draconian resolution."[18] The minority repeated its dissent from time to time, but the junta would not alter its decision.

The Junta Superior was advised by a health commission made up of medical doctors, who saw their immediate task as both to assess and promote the health of the prisoners. Their initial inspection of the transports convinced them that the captives were free of contagious disease, and that the greatest sources of illness were the very overcrowding and lack of sanitation on the ships. Their advice was to vacate the wretched transports as rapidly as possible. Since there was no danger of contagion, the commission added that the prisoners could be more easily and more cheaply cared for on Majorca than Cabrera. But that was a political decision already taken. Their advice was ignored.[19]

As the weeks passed, conditions on the transport ships deteriorated. Appeals for food supplies and medicines grew more desperate. For a few days more the proposed exchange of prisoners in Tarragona was delayed in haggling over the terms for hiring the transport ships. By the end of the month, the Junta Superior received unconfirmed reports that the Spanish prisoners to be traded in the exchange had already been moved to internment across the French border. With that news, the commander of the Spanish escort ship *Cornelia* demanded positive confirmation that the exchange would take place before he would accompany any prison transports to Tarragona or Barcelona. A fast ship was dispatched to the mainland for the purpose; and in the interim, the civil and naval authorities in Palma agreed that all the prisoners would be landed on Cabrera.

On May 7 Admiral Collingwood noted the junta's plans to exchange prisoners in Catalonia and to confine the remaining captives on Cabrera. The junta had also requested that he provide a Royal Navy guardship "to cruise near it to prevent their being taken off." Collingwood responded with a qualified offer ("...when I could appropriate a Ship to guard the prisoners on Cabrera, one should be ordered to that service") and accompanied it with a warning of "the Evils likely to result to the Spanish Cause if any of the Prisoners were sent to Barcelona at this moment, and recommending the Measure to be reconsidered by the Junta."[20] For the junta, this combined display of British support and steely prudence was decisive. Collingwood's advice was accepted. The plan to exchange prisoners was abandoned, and the promise of a guardship was welcomed.

Meanwhile urgent preparations to establish the new prison camp continued in Palma. On May 2 the junta refined its policy in a way that revealed its troubled counsels, its inconsistency, and its awareness that contagious disease among the captives posed no real problem. French senior officers from the rank of captain upward, the junta decided, would be confined in Palma rather than on Cabrera. At the same time regulations were published prohibiting all unauthorized contacts with the port, coasts, and bays of the designated prison island under pain of death, and requiring all ships sailing in its waters to keep a distance of one league from shore. Once on the island, the prisoners would be registered and allowed to keep only a few possessions for their personal use such as blankets, tobacco, and watches. All the rest, including cash, jewelry, small arms, and any remaining booty from the Andalusian campaign would be confiscated for the benefit of the junta of Majorca. Thus the conscripts would be deprived of any means of trading or bargaining for escape. The officers to be imprisoned in Palma, on the other hand, would be exempt from this act of confiscation—and senior officers would be allowed to keep from fifty to one hundred duros in cash in addition to their regular pay. As the Majorcan historian Miguel Benássar Alomar notes, the distinction allowed the officers to buy the food and clothing they needed—and benefited the local merchants who supplied them.[21] Yet letting even a limited number of officers ashore in Palma risked the wrath of the local population, whose prejudices had dictated the original sentence of exile on Cabrera.

By early May, amidst reports of French privateers near the Baleares, Admiral Collingwood moved to disengage his ships rapidly from escort duty with the convoy. The command ship HMS *Bombay* sailed from Palma to rejoin the British squadron in Minorca, while the *Cornelia, Ambuscade, Norge,* and *Grasshopper* remained off Majorca with the prison transports until the prisoners could be landed on Cabrera. Rodríguez de Arias, the *Cornelia's* captain, was as anxious as Collingwood to complete the mission, since Palma had refused permission for his crew to come ashore on Majorca. Unlike the British sailors, they were quarantined along with the prisoners, and showed signs of revolt. Finally, the impatient guardians sailed away from Palma Bay, the great buttresses of the cathedral fading in the distance as they conducted the prison ships safely south to Cabrera in three convoys between

May 5 and May 11, 1809. With their mission completed, the *Cornelia* and the empty transports made their way back to Cádiz, while the British men-of-war returned to regular duty at Gibraltar and Mahón with Collingwood's fleet. Just one of them would remain on station off the prison island.

Before the convoys set sail from Palma, ninety-nine senior officers, two officers' wives, and a handful of camp followers were taken ashore into restricted confinement in Majorca. As the fleets departed, the remainder of the unfortunates on the transports—about forty-five hundred French, Polish, and Italian conscripts, Swiss mercenaries, soldiers of the Paris Guard, seamen of the Imperial Guard, gendarmes, dragoons, and twenty-two women followers—had no idea where they were being taken. The diarists Henri Ducor, Louis Gille, and Louis-Joseph Wagré were among them.[22]

After a few hours in the choppy passage beyond Palma Bay, the prison ships approached the low, craggy chain of islands to the south of Majorca, and passed through a high-walled gullet into a calm harbor on the largest island of the group. Before them the prisoners saw the ochre rocks and scrublands and empty beaches of Cabrera port.

Most of the soldiers had not stood on land for four months, since they boarded the hulks in Cádiz on Christmas Day, 1808. Now, as they waded ashore from the ships' launches, they had neither guards, nor instructions, nor knowledge of the island to guide them. They could see no dwellings and no signs of human life. Majorca was behind them and out of reach, a low line on the northern horizon. The Elysian prospect of safe refuge there had vanished in the wind. They were alone on Goat Island.[23]

3
CABRERA

T HE FIRST PRISONERS to touch shore on May 5 were in a state of near delirium. Many were ill, and all were weak, light-headed from the lack of food, and unsteady on their feet. They were relieved to be off the transports, but confused and disheartened by their presence on this bleak and unknown island. Beyond the calm turquoise waters of the bay, what confronted them in the dusk was a forbidding prospect of rock, broken shale, and scrub brush rising into the hills on all sides. The men gathered on the strand according to their units, and began to explore in search of inhabitants and shelter for the night. Some of them made their way up the slopes of the central valley, scrambling anxiously over shale and brush. Unusual blue-black lizards dodged into hiding as they approached. Other prisoners climbed to the castle above the harbor entrance, where they discovered signs of recent habitation, and space for perhaps thirty residents. By nightfall, as the temperature fell, the soldiers met grimly at the base of the valley and built bonfires. Henri Ducor recalled "a thousand fires" burning throughout the makeshift camp, "a strange and moving spectacle, that must have amused our guards in the fleet.... For us, they were funeral torches that illuminated our graves!"[1]

Next morning, in the harbor, the prisoners retrieved the cooking pots and utensils they had used on the ships, which had been left onshore before the transports departed. The materials were divided among the regiments; but for the moment they were useless, since their captors had left no food. On the second day, a barque arrived from Palma carrying basic supplies: hard biscuit, rice, lard, and bread. But the crew treated the prisoners "as if we had the plague": while the provisions were unloaded on the beach, the Frenchmen were kept at bay by armed guards. With this first shipment, the Majorcan authorities established the prisoners' basic rations: for enlisted men, a pound of bread and a handful of beans or rice, a little oil, and a little salt each day; for the higher ranks, double the basic ration plus occasional supplies of raw vegetables, meat, sugar, coffee, oranges, and wine. For the common soldiers, this was a starvation diet whose suspension, even for short periods, would result in many deaths.[2]

On its second trip the barque delivered tents intended for the junior officers who remained with their units, or for the sick. Soon, a longboat also arrived offering "a mixture of merchandise" for sale to those with cash or valuables to trade. But the merchants, too, avoided direct contact with the captives because they feared contagion. Coins offered in payment had to be dropped into a jar of vinegar for retrieval before the soldiers' purchases were dumped onto the beach.[3]

The routine for supplying and guarding the prisoners was now apparent. Onshore, there was no supervision. At the harbor mouth, the Spanish frigate *Lucía* lay at anchor with its launches. Beyond it in the gut stood a Royal Navy brigantine, on rotation from the Mediterranean squadron in Mahón. Supplies arrived every four days from Palma on one of two small three-masters, or *jabeques*, the *Santo Cristo de Santa Eulalia* and the *Beata Catalina Tomás*, privately contracted from their owners in Palma. On the island, supplies were brought ashore for immediate distribution to the military units by the prisoners themselves.[4]

Meanwhile the marooned captives continued their explorations. From the harbor the prisoners could see only "a shapeless mass of almost inaccessible crags."[5] Cabrera rose from the sea in a jagged outline of low, brush-covered hills and valleys, with forested stands of white pine in the east. One of the soldiers described the island:

> It is a vast rock covered by a thin and sterile layer of soil. There are no fruit trees, no green plants, nothing that will supply the necessities of human life.... There is no foliage, aside from a few miserable pine trees fringed by briars. Its arid mountains shelter no wild animals.[6]

The island measured about two miles across from north to south and three miles from east to west. Its highest point, on the peninsula just west of the harbor, was 550 feet above sea level. Most of the coast was rimmed by steep slopes falling away precipitously to the sea. The explorers found two springs, only one of them supplying fresh water. The medieval castle, containing a number of dark rooms accessible only by a constricting spiral staircase encased within the stone, stood sentinel on the heights above the port. There were no other buildings on the island.

Cabrera was, in Ducor's eyes, "a horrible solitude... populated only by lizards." And yet, up the main valley from the port there was a small field of wheat. Was there a resident hermit? The castaways, encouraged by this discovery, called out and searched for him. No one responded. What they found instead was a donkey, "or the shadow of a donkey," approaching and braying. "Was all this a dream?" wondered Ducor: "For there was something fantastic in this apparition, something we could not quite believe." The animal was tethered and taken back to camp, named Robinson by some and Martin by others, and used as the island's beast of burden, carrying water and firewood to the camps. It had apparently been abandoned by shepherds or goatherds who had rapidly vacated the island just before the arrival of the prisoners. The donkey became the spoiled child of the inmates: "... everyone catered to him, gave him grass, caressed him. He was aware of this; he was intelligent, affectionate, our friend Robinson."

To avoid conflict over the ownership and use of the animal, it was put into the hands of a sergeant's widow, one of the brave canteen-women, transformed into nurses and companions, who had accompanied the prisoners from Bailén to Cabrera. On board the transport to Majorca she had given birth to twins that she was still nursing.[7]

As the explorations continued, a few goats, and more rabbits, were also discovered on the island; but these were soon wiped out in the prisoners' desperate search for food.[8]

The days grew warmer under the brilliant sun, the nights more temperate. Some prisoners slept in the open, or made crude dugouts in the hard ground; others began to build primitive shelters with brush walls and roofs—but nothing very solid, recalled Louis Gille, "because we didn't want to believe that the Spanish government would leave us for long in such circumstances."[9] In his weakened condition, Gille built a puny shelter: "My lodging was only the length of my body. I wove a few branches together for cover, with a kind of door made of foliage brought to me by riflemen of the company. The house served me for seven months."[10] The pathways and slopes stretching outwards from the port took on the untidy appearance of a temporary shanty town, dotted with clusters of crude dwellings. Some of the noncommissioned officers and their women companions took up more sheltered residence in the castle.

The fresh water supply was limited, and its distribution was disorganized. In the first days prisoners sometimes waited two days and nights in lines at the spring to fill their canteens; and in the early summer drought the source dried up entirely. The thirsty prisoners turned to the other, brackish spring for their supplies. Already weakened by their ordeals, some died from drinking bad water.[11]

By the end of the first month, the Palma authorities reported 62 dead on the island, or a projected annual death rate of almost 20 percent. On June 3 an additional 162 men were being treated in the island's makeshift hospital.[12] They were cared for by six surgeons and five apothecaries (who were themselves French prisoners), but suffered from the virtual absence of shelter, sparse medical supplies, and only minimal supplements to their starvation diet.

A delegate of the Majorcan junta, Don Jerónimo Batle, was initially appointed as a temporary commissioner responsible for monitoring and reporting on the condition of the internees, both those on Cabrera and the officers who had been permitted ashore in Palma. Under the junta's direction, Batle called on the prisoners to appoint an official spokesman who would be responsible for receiving and distributing food supplies, reporting on the captives' health, and transmitting the formal requests and complaints of the prisoners to the Junta Superior. Batle's first instructions to the captives were limited to a request for regular health reports, an order to bury bodies rather than throwing them into the sea, a request that the soldiers should refrain from insulting the good name of Spain, and a warning that letters between prisoners in Cabrera and Palma should not contain any coded messages.[13] The commissioner had no conventional rules for the treatment of war prisoners to guide him. Palma, it was evident, had no intention of actually governing the prison island: that would be left to the inmates themselves. But the junta was sensitive to possible complaints that the prisoners were being treated inhumanely—and fearful that they might be plotting against the Majorcan regime.

The captives, for their part, had already established an informal administrative council made up of junior officers representing the major units, which was intended to ensure a state of minimal internal order and to represent them in their dealings with Palma. That arrangement was disrupted at the end of May, when all the junior officers originally sent to the island (aside from a few volunteers) were evacuated to Palma, and the original council evaporated. A few weeks of disputed authority and confrontation followed among the disorganized troops, until a new, self-constituted council gained Palma's tacit approval in restraining two dissidents, Pajadon and Richard, who had rallied supporters in an effort to take over and monopolize control of the food supply. On June 25, a wounded career officer, Lieutenant de Maussac of the Fourth Reserve Legion, was chosen as replacement chairman of the council, and an uneasy equilibrium returned. Maussac was assisted in his duties by two more French Lieutenants, Carbonnel-d'Hierville and Degain de Montagnac; two Swiss officers; and six medical officers.

"Why did these officers remain on the desert island," the Swiss historian Geisendorf-des-Gouttes wondered, "when so many others were eager to leave?" The answer, he guessed, was to be found in their names. They were survivors from the Old Régime, minor provincial aristocrats whose commitment to duty lived on. "The truth was that all the valuable officers in the armies of Napoleon were not the sons of grocers or stable-boys. Some... despite their relationships to the provincial nobility, or to the thousands who left in the great Emigration, lived for military campaigning. Knowing that denial [of the revolution] was useless, they chose to make their careers under the imperial eagles, and did so successfully." Maussac was just one of several noble officers who volunteered to stay with their men on Cabrera in the summer of 1809. What Geisendorf failed to notice was that all those who joined him on the reconstituted council (like Maussac himself) were either apothecaries or surgeons, whose professions gave them an additional source of commitment to their men. Maussac's regime as chairman of the council lasted for nine months, until the arrival of more senior officers from Palma in March 1810. During that time he was assiduous and courteous in his many dispatches to the Spanish authorities in Palma, while his own followers called him "kind and compassionate," "more like a father than a governor."[14]

The council's legitimacy rested on Palma's formal recognition, its control over distribution of the food supply, its imposition of a crude regime of criminal justice (dealing mainly with the theft of food), and the prisoners' residual habit of obedience. Councillors met regularly as a court to try thieves and persistent troublemakers, and a few dozen soldiers acted as enforcement officers.

Convicted miscreants were detained on reduced rations, tied naked to a stake or pillory near the settlement's center for up to twenty-four hours, flogged, or occasionally, garroted, stoned to death by angry onlookers, or thrown from a cliff into the sea. Sentences were without appeal and were executed at once; and the prisoners generally "offered no resistance to the punishments inflicted on them." Punishments seemed to be most severe in the early days of settlement when order and authority were still uncertain.[15] The council never extended its authority beyond this elementary role. There was no effort to establish firm military discipline. On arrival of the supply ship every four days, council members supervised the distribution of food to the military units with "a kind of solemn and religious gravity"; but apart from this initial division, they did not police any rationing system. That was left to the units and their subgroups according to their own differing preferences.

In most aspects of their lives the prisoners remained free and unregulated, forming casual and shifting groups among friends or regimental companions, cooperating where they saw immediate mutual benefit, establishing their own daily routines, settling quarrels by their own (sometimes rough) means, trading and bartering food and clothing without explicit rules. Cabreran society, as it evolved in these early days of seclusion, was outwardly anarchist, governed by little more tangible than the residual dignity and sense of mutual restraint that Frenchmen and servants of the emperor had brought with them to the desert island. To this veneer of civil order was added the passivity of prisoners of war, and the fatalist conviction that they would soon be dead. "From stoical," wrote Miguel de los Santos Oliver, "they became misanthropic, and from misanthropic, suicidal." Henri Ducor recalled "a certain insouciance" among the captives in the early days, an indifference to all efforts to save their lives. "To die today or tomorrow, when there is only suffering: the sooner the better," some of them lamented. The officers, Ducor thought, might have ordered them to cooperate in conserving food or building shelters, "but the extremes of shared misfortune had virtually destroyed subordination, and [the prisoners] refused such efforts to help them."[16]

During the first weeks of endurance on Cabrera, more prisoners arrived to share the fate of the original inhabitants. On Minorca, the local authorities and Admiral Collingwood agreed that the Frenchmen taken ashore in April should be transferred to Cabrera (with the exception of a few officers who were allowed to remain, and others who were sent to Palma). Their transport ship was escorted to Cabrera in late May by a British brigantine. In early June another 450 prisoners arrived in the Baleares from Tarragona and were quickly dispatched to Cabrera. By mid-June there were about 5,400 people in detention on the island. The Junta Superior wrote urgently to the captain general of Catalonia to report that Cabrera could take no more prisoners because of its scarce water, that Palma had difficulty sending sufficient food to the detainees, and that further subsidy from the mainland was required at once. The commercial provisioner appointed to buy and manage regular food shipments to the island, Don Nicolás Palmer, bombarded the junta with demands for more generous funds and more supply contracts from Valencia. Despite his efforts, the flour, vegetables, and rice arriving on Cabrera from Palma every four days were often of poor quality. Palma kept up regular appeals to the Junta Central for additional funds to maintain the prisoners and periodically received emergency grants to subsidize its own contributions.[17] But budgets were always strained, and payments to suppliers fell into arrears.

The prisoners' council delivered its own stream of petitions to the junta's commissioner, Don Jéronimo Batle, for repatriation, clothing, medicine, tents, utensils, axes, and saws; and he in turn passed the requests upwards to the junta with his support. Once approved, they were conveyed to the provisioner, who did what he could to fulfill them within his inadequate financial means. But on May 19 Batle received a spiritual rather than a worldly appeal from the prisoners, requesting the dispatch of a priest who could offer consolation to the dying. A month later, the bishop of Majorca and the military vicar-general appointed a parish priest from the island town of Porreras, Don Damián Estelrich, as chaplain to the prisoners. Estelrich was in his forties, spoke French, and had freely volunteered his services. He arrived on Cabrera on July 18 with an assistant and was installed by the prisoners in an apartment in the castle. Later, to avoid the steep climb to the fortress, a small house was built for him in the main encampment at the harbor.

The priest lived in relative comfort on his military salary of eight hundred reales per month. He evoked mixed reactions among the captives: his multiple role as pastor, intelligence agent for the authorities, and intermediary on behalf of the prisoners made such reactions inevitable. In the beginning, especially, the priest's authority was ill defined: while the prisoners had asked only for a spiritual guide, Father Estelrich assumed (in the absence of military guards or a resident commissioner) that he had a worldly role as well, and acted on that assumption. The Majorcan writer Jaime

Garau described him as "the true governor of the island." Louis Gille felt that Estelrich was always ill at ease among the prisoners: "There was nothing agreeable in his appearance, and one could read dissimulation in his behavior." For Henri Ducor, the priest was "this nasty man with a pockmarked snub nose, tiny eyes, and the expression of a weasel." Because he spoke French so well, there were rumors that he was a Frenchman who had fled the country during the revolution. But that was a canard. Ducor described the priest as "living among us with the happiness of a holy man on an apostolic mission," who was (despite his appearance) essentially a good man, but ignorant and something of a fanatic. The noncommissioned officer Robert Guillemard, who arrived on the island in 1810, wrote that Estelrich "was not a priest, but a true Spanish monk, chokeful [sic] of fanaticism, gluttony, and the most shameful ignorance." The prisoner Sébastien Boulerot dismissed him as "a wicked and fanatical being, mixing faith and irony in everything that he said, preparing his blows against us with a devilish cunning."[18]

Sometimes those blows were real. Father Damián admitted this in a letter to the Majorcan commissioner in November 1809:

> One day the insolence of a prisoner, who declared in my presence that Spaniards were more cruel than the most barbarous and inhumane savages, led me (because I was unable to stand for such an insult to my nation) to strike him full in the face. He returned the punch, and we would have fallen into a real brawl if others hadn't pulled us apart. Even though we were later reconciled, I can see that unless things improve, I will have other stories of the same kind....[19]

But more often, the priest antagonized his dependents with a cascade of insulting quips, which were soon reported throughout the camp. He talked of planting flax on a small plot, and boasted that the crop would eventually provide shirts for the whole colony. When a soldier responded by asking: "Father, do you think we will be here for a long time?" Estelrich was said to have pointed to the tiny shoots of new fig trees and proclaimed: "You'll leave when these trees bear fruit!" To others, he insisted with "brutish pleasure": "You'll depart when my walking stick bursts into flower!" Witness after witness repeated similar stories. "These were the words of hope," wrote Louis Gille, "that this minister of God offered to these unfortunates."[20]

Despite his temper and unruly tongue, Estelrich managed to gain the grudging trust of the prisoners' council, supported their petitions, and often succeeded in his interventions on their behalf. Twenty-four of his letters to the Cabrera commissioner (which survived in Palma in the collection of Desbrull family papers) demonstrate his persistence in defending what he saw as the interests of his parishioners. From the moment of his arrival, he reported to the junta on the shortage of fresh water and the prisoners' health, recommended the removal of women and sick prisoners from Cabrera to Majorca, and indicated the willingness of some prisoners to transfer into the Spanish forces. Apart from a few short interludes of absence, he remained with the captives on Cabrera throughout their five-year ordeal. The Majorcan writer Miguel de los Santos Oliver, writing a century later, judged him generously:

If we reflect carefully on the acts of the Junta and its records, elementary justice and impartiality require us to recognize in the priest Don Damián Estelrich a true—and almost the only— benefactor of his parishioners, a constant and effective defender of the unfortunate prisoners.[21]

Benefactor and defender he may have been; but the priest's good works were too easily obscured (above all in the eyes of the many sceptics and radicals among the captives) by his stern insistence that their worst sufferings were nothing but divine punishment for their sins—and by his transparent desire for worldly power.

That desire brought him into conflict with the chairman of the prisoners' council, Lieutenant de Maussac, who complained in a letter to the Cabrera commissioner in October 1809. Maussac could not abide Estelrich as a man who abused his pastoral authority:

If the priest were a sociable man, he would have dealt with me in a more honest way. But this man is worse than the lowest peasant; he intrudes on the island into an infinity of things completely foreign to his ministry. I speak to him rarely; and far from consoling the unfortunate prisoners, he seems to mock their misery. He argues with soldiers who complain to him, saying: "We will have to cut off your head!" In short, this man is an idiot with whom one cannot come to terms. You will understand, sir, how it mortifies me to take orders from him. I ask that you end all these difficulties by ordering the priest to exercise his functions as a priest, to be good, charitable, and discreet if he wishes to be respected and to gain the confidence of the unfortunates here on Cabrera.[22]

The new Cabrera commissioner, Don Antonio Desbrull, replied with reassuring words a few days later: "I grant that the priest is hardly capable of offering consolation. I was wrong to take him so seriously; from now on I will take your advice, and do as the council wishes."[23] Late in 1810, when Father Estelrich sought formal recognition from the junta as chief administrator and commander of the island, his request was summarily denied on the ground that it might provoke disturbances among the prisoners.[24]

The first complaints made to the priest concerned the island's shortage of water. Estelrich at once made two attempts to relieve it—one of them at the suggestion of the enterprising prisoner Louis-Joseph Wagré. One day, as the priest explored close to the upper spring where fresh water collected in a small pool beneath a rocky vault, Wagré showed him how the reservoir was regularly dirtied and exhausted by impatient soldiers struggling to fill their canteens. He suggested the need for limited and controlled access, which would assure sufficient water for those who were ill. The priest agreed and sought direction from Palma. The junta quickly ordered the erection of a locked entrance gate, and appointed Wagré as one of two "guardians of the spring." A formal order, in four imposing articles, was printed and posted at the gate directing prisoners to respect the authority of the guardians, who would allow access for five hours each morning and four hours each afternoon. For this inspiration, Wagré received the nickname "Corporal of the Fountain" from his fellow prisoners, and a double ration of beans at every four-day distribution. (He claimed in his own memoir that he had to share this bonus with the priest.) In the mountains on nearby Majorca, it was said, the freshwater springs were guarded by water sprites who had once planted the woods with flowers and taught the waters and winds and birds to speak. On Cabrera the worldly Corporal Wagré took their place.

Given his new-found power as protector of the waters, the amiable corporal was confronted with desperate pleas for extra rations of water, and tempting bribe offers. When he succumbed ("What would you have done in my place?") and was denounced, Father Estelrich threatened his removal—but lacked the authority to order it. The Spanish guardship commander settled for a mild warning, and sent the guardian back to his duties at the spring.

The prisoner prospered. "Louis-Joseph Wagré," commented Geisendorf, "is living proof that in any society—even the most rudimentary—the man who gains a privilege tends naturally to become a bourgeois." Nearby, Wagré built a modestly comfortable shanty with the aid of several prisoners, and planted two small garden plots where he reported growing cabbages and a few tobacco plants. For a time he revived his trade as a laundryman; later, he baked bread for sale, but the enterprise faded when he could no longer buy flour from the priest; and then, briefly, he became a basket maker. When he found a gold coin at the harbor, Wagré surprised his friends by renewing his wardrobe and growing fat with food purchased in the market.[25]

The summer of 1809 was drought stricken throughout the Balearic Islands. Despite Wagré's imposition of order at the spring, Estelrich knew that the situation on Cabrera remained dangerous, and pleaded for help in a letter to the junta sent with the returning supply ship. By the next barque the junta replied that the prisoners' appeal for water would be satisfied; and during the next ten days, fresh water was delivered from Palma—only once, in the memory of some prisoners, or possibly three times, in the memory of another.[26]

On August 4, 1809, when a small ship arrived with forty barrels of fresh water, the Royal Navy guardship (usually anchored close in at the mouth of the harbor) had inexplicably joined a Spanish frigate at sea—perhaps in pursuit of an unidentified sail coming in too close to the island. As the Frenchmen gathered on the beach to receive their precious rations of water, a group of fifteen seamen of the Imperial Guard planned to seize the ship and escape northwards to the French coast. When the water had been unloaded, the guardsmen forced their way on board, took control, and set sail as most of the Spanish crew leapt into the sea. "We were immobilized with surprise, and they were quickly in mid-bay," wrote one of the observers on shore. The air rang with the French seamen's cries of "Vive l'Empéreur" and the astonished cheers of their supporters.

The priest and the marooned Spanish sailors stumbled up the hill to the castle and watched in dismay as the sloop departed. From the signal platform on the castle ramparts, Estelrich waved his cassock and lit a fire in a vain effort to warn the British warship of the prisoners' escape. After two hours the guardship returned to port, learned from the curé what had happened, and sailed out again in pursuit, its cannons firing wildly with what must have seemed comic effect to the captives who cheered the flight from onshore. But the escapees had too great a lead to be overtaken.

For those who remained on the island, the consequences were

grave. Henceforth Cabrera received no more supplies of fresh water; and after a trial undertaken by the junta in Palma, the owners and crew of the water ship were conscripted into the Spanish navy; the value of the ship (which was estimated at 350 Majorcan pounds) was charged to the provisioning accounts deducted from the prisoners' wages; the captives were forbidden from approaching within firing range of the beaches during the unloading of all supply ships; and Spanish soldiers accompanying the suppliers were encouraged to shoot any transgressors. From then on—according to one diarist—Father Damián never hesitated to express his aversion towards the prisoners. He had arranged for the supply of water, and the Imperial Guard had betrayed his trust. But he continued to act as an intermediary on the captives' behalf.[27]

The plight of the Frenchmen still nagged at the consciences of the Majorcan governors. On September 12, the junta resolved:

> ... in order to assure that the French prisoners on the island of Cabrera may live through the inclement winter weather without affecting their health, and to see that they receive what humanity demands, ... the Cabrera commission should name a competent person to go at once to the island to inform himself on housing the prisoners, on the hospital created for the sick, on the tools and clothing that they possess, and on all else he considers necessary to report to the Junta about the true situation and enable it to provide the necessary assistance.[28]

The task was given to a member of the junta, Don Joaquín Pons, who travelled at once to Cabrera, observed conditions with care, and remained as one of the commissioners for the island until early December. In response to his inquiries, the prisoners' council told the junta on September 18 that seven hundred shanties, each to house six soldiers, would be necessary to protect them from the winter cold. These would require a total of 350,000 roofing tiles. "We pray that this great expense will not deter you from preparing for a harsh winter in a place men have found too frightful to inhabit. But if it is only the fury of the mob that keeps us isolated, we insist that the soldiers would prefer death in Palma to dragging out their unhappy lives here."[29]

On September 26 Pons made a "somber and pessimistic" report that sparked an emergency debate in the junta on the following day. A resolution supported by a minority of members (described as "Auroristas," to reflect the name of the liberal Palma newspaper, the *Aurora Patriótica Mallorquina*) called for an appeal to the towns of Majorca to take groups of prisoners proportionate to their populations for work in the fields. But the obdurate majority rejected it, and voted instead for a resolution declaring that Palma had done what it could for the prisoners, noting that the public was indifferent, appealing again for financial support from the Junta Central, and—in the absence of that—disclaiming any further responsibility for the fate of the prisoners. "At no time," the junta concluded, "could anyone say that we have disregarded the dire misfortune of these individuals...; on the contrary, the Junta has always done more for them than it could afford to do."[30]

For most of the next year, the junta's chief commissioner responsible for liaison with the prisoners of Cabrera—replacing Don Jéronimo Batle—was Don Antonio Desbrull y Boil de Arenós. Desbrull was one of Majorca's landed nobility, the Marquis of Villafranca, commander of the police force of Palma, a leader among the island's enlightened liberal minority, and a man of elaborate courtesy, fairness, and goodwill. Initially he refused the office of chairman of the Cabrera commission because of his "hatred for the French nation"; but the junta ignored his protests and he accepted the appointment. Desbrull's actions in office suggest that his show of reluctance owed as much to humane fellow feeling for the prisoners as to any antipathy towards France: an attitude that could not easily be admitted before he took up the task. During that year he received over eight hundred petitions from the prisoners, about half of them dealing with requests for repatriation, the provision of food and clothing, removal of the sick to hospital in Palma, or appeals for transfer into the Spanish forces. In response Desbrull offered help—often in small ways—whenever he could do so.[31]

The commissioner's first initiative in office was a final humanitarian call to the junta to abandon the prison island and bring all the French prisoners to Majorca. Adequate housing on Cabrera for the captives or a decent hospital for the infirm, he insisted, was no more than a dream, since they could not be adequately financed from the central government's donations. But winter was approaching and the works would have to be undertaken on the island with materials from Majorca, shipped "at infinite expense and over a long period of time." He knew from the debate of September 27 that the junta would not provide sufficient subsidy for that to happen. Desbrull appealed instead to the council's sense of Christian obligation and political prudence. These "miserable people" should be relieved of their terrible discomforts; and the French enemy should be deprived of the temptation to send ships and arms to liberate the prisoners. The commissioner asked the junta to place the prisoners, under sufficient guard, in various quarters in the towns of Palma and Pollensa. But the cautious junta—still alarmed by Majorca's vulnerability to French attack, and ever sensitive to popular fears and prejudices—rejected Desbrull's petition.[32]

The specter of a French raid constantly haunted Majorca's governors in these early months of the captivity. During the summer the junta and the Royal Navy received warnings that two ships were taking on powder, cannons, and pistols in Barcelona, probably headed for Cabrera. For whatever reasons, they did not appear near the islands. In September, the junta was alarmed by rumors that a French squadron loaded with supplies had left Toulon; and again in October it heard that a large fleet of twenty warships and two hundred sails might be approaching. There were even reports from the mainland that twelve ships had set sail from distant Rotterdam to assault Majorca.[33] If the enemy high command was indeed monitoring the fate of its compatriots and intending to rescue them, the junta preferred to keep the prisoners on the barren island to the south of Majorca, where a naval attack would offer no direct threat to Palma. The truth was that there was no chance of a French attack.

Instead of responding directly to Desbrull's appeal, the local government had already taken another step to reduce the numbers of prisoners on Cabrera. About the time of commissioner Pons' inspection of the island, the exiles were informed that any of them who wished to go over to the enemy would be offered service in the Spanish forces. According to one memoir, seventy-four Italian and Swiss soldiers accepted; according to others, one hundred and thirty-one non-Frenchmen left the prison island by that choice over the next two months. In the following year another two hundred Italians made the same decision. For foreign conscripts or mercenaries, this was a means of escape to be taken without guilt or dishonor; their service involved no patriotic commitment, and their captivity was an unlucky accident of fate. As the penitential years stretched out, Frenchmen too were tempted by the same promise of liberation. Before the end of the war about twelve hundred French conscripts, their Napoleonic fervor dulled by hardship, had volunteered and been accepted for service in the Spanish army.[34]

The prisoners' medical staff began the confinement on Cabrera by setting up a makeshift hospital, under tents, on the lower slopes of the central valley a few hundred yards beyond the harbor. They could not offer much relief to the suffering: a canvas roof, a bed of straw, fresh water, an occasional dose of salts or quinine or laudanum, a little reassurance. Most patients believed fatalistically that the field hospital was a way station on their last journey, both bodily and spiritual: for just two hundred yards further up the valley, at the top of a primitive trail, a cemetery was laid out on the rubble slope. The ground there was hard, and the graves were little more than shallow mounds hacked out among the rocks.

In mid-September the medical staff gave Palma a long list of demands for hospital supplies, divided among the needs of the administration, the surgery, and the pharmacy. Their profession made them realists, and their appeal was suitably modest. The material requests included such basics as two hundred straw mattresses, blankets and bedsheets, one hundred water jugs, fifty chamber pots, a large cooking pot and ladle, two hundred yards of rope, and a second donkey along with forage to keep it alive. For the surgery, the staff asked for lint, thread, metal pins, and simple operating instruments; and for the pharmacy, a month's supply of sulphuric acid, quinine, salts, herbs, emetics, antiseptics, and laudanum. Few of the necessities arrived.

At the same time, as illnesses and deaths mounted alarmingly, Maussac and Carbonnel appealed on behalf of the prisoners for a permanent hospital of three hundred beds on the island. Father Estelrich made a similar and equally urgent request. Palma's commissioner Don Joaquín Pons responded by recommending to the junta the immediate construction of thirty hospital buildings, each to contain ten beds. When members of the junta protested that the funds would have to be drained from the prisoners' daily food budgets, others pointed out that the hospital could be financed from a cache of six thousand gold francs found in possession of Colonel de May, a Swiss officer interned in Palma. The project was duly authorized; a master mason, Tomás Abrines, was appointed by the junta; plans were approved at an estimated cost of 40 pounds or 531 reales per building (if prisoners supplied the labor); and by mid-October, construction was ready to begin.

From the start the scheme was doomed by haphazard planning and the simmering contest of power between Father Estelrich and the prisoners' council. On October 15, fifteen Majorcan workers arrived on the supply ship to supervise construction. Estelrich ordered that half a dozen French officers should be ejected from the castle to provide living space for the Majorcans, but the prisoners refused to move on the ground that the priest had no written eviction order from Palma. The Spanish guardship commander came to Estelrich's support, but the Frenchmen stood firm in an exchange of threats and raised fists; and on their first night ashore the builders camped in a stable below the castle. The next day, after the priest pleaded to the ship's captain that his authority as the lone Spaniard on the island would be destroyed unless his order could be enforced, the captain gave notice that he would fire on the port in half an hour unless the space was evacuated. Under this threat the officers relented. Estelrich told the story at length in his next letter to the Cabrera commissioner, insisting that "this is the whole truth against as many as may lie."[35]

Twenty-four prisoners were recruited as laborers on the project with a promise of extra rations from the priest, and on October 19 work began. Over the constant protests of Maussac and the prisoners' council, Father Estelrich assumed the unlikely role of construction superintendent, assigning workers and supervising the distribution of extra bread and wine. Both Estelrich and Maussac claimed to act on the authority of the Cabrera commissioner; but the priest's supply of bonus rations gave him the edge on this occasion, and the work went forward under his supervision. Abrines had offered only the most primitive plans, and as the windowless clay walls rose, the builders worried that they would not support the weight of the roofs. When the rains came in early November, the buildings sagged and collapsed before they could be occupied. The general superintendent of the project apparently made no visit to the island until the walls already lay in shapeless heaps.[36]

Meanwhile, the sailor Henri Ducor fell ill in October 1809 and was placed in one of the hospital tents on the sloping ground. The inhabitants suffered all the diseases previously known on the hulks: typhus, dysentery, scurvy, gastric upsets—and eye strain from the harsh light of the sun. The doctors offered rest, a supplemented diet, and few remedies. But in their immediate preoccupation, they had not thought much about the changing weather. The autumn storm season had come. Three nights after Ducor's arrival at the hospital, in the darkness, terrible winds and rain fell on the island. Dry gulleys became torrential rivers, and great cascades of water swept through the encampment. Afterwards there was an ominous silence; and when the morning light returned, Ducor could see that his was the only hospital shelter that remained. "The tents, the mattresses, the sick, all had been swept far away in the debacle: it was a heart-rending spectacle." Down the slope the dead and dying lay in the mud and gravel, the wounded agonizing over their torn and broken limbs. Some of the bodies, it was evident, had been swept down the valley from the exposed graveyard above the hospital. Prisoners from elsewhere in the shattered colony searched among the dead for their friends, or offered relief to the living. Father Damián moved among them, "crucifix in hand in this frightful scene, like an angel of the last judgment, the messenger of heavenly vengeance." In his "lugubrious and inanely prophetic voice" he insisted that God had punished the impious: "he spoke of Sodom, Gomorrah, the Philistines, the Moabites, the Ammonites; he went through all the chastisements of Genesis." The desperate prisoners rebuked him, and Estelrich pleaded with Palma to order them not to insult him "for the evils that I share with them, that I have not caused and cannot remedy." Louis Gille counted fifty dead among the patients.[37]

Gradually the tents were gathered up and restored in a relocated but still makeshift hospital site on more level ground near the harbor shore. Some of the ill were moved into dry quarters in the castle. Father Damián—despite his claims of divine punishment for the Frenchmen's sins—appealed to Palma more practically, but in vain, for the crumbling hospital barracks to be rebuilt with solid brick and timber imported from Majorca. The junta had other preoccupations, and no cash to spare. "The hospital," lamented the memoirist Turquet, "vanished like a castle in Spain."[38]

The storm set back the efforts of the harassed physicians to care for their patients, and in the weeks afterwards—through most of November—the death rate on the island sometimes reached ten or a dozen each day.[39] The bodies remained unburied. To prevent contagion, they were burned. But the sight was horrifying, since combustion was not always sufficient and the remains sometimes had to be burned a second time. Burials were thus recommenced in the old graveyard, now a mile distant from the new hospital in what had been christened the Valley of the Dead. The grave diggers toiled in the hard gravel, reburying cadavers exposed in the deluge and adding the fresh daily toll to the expanding site. Officers from the British guardship, viewing the chaos after the storm, had supplied them with pickaxes to ease their labors.[40]

In the wake of the tempest and the collapse of the hospital project, the junta agreed with Don Antonio Desbrull that the sick should be transferred from Cabrera to Palma; and in late November 120 prisoners were evacuated from the island to the new Palma hospital of El Sitjar. The first medical report to the junta on these soldiers, delivered one week later, indicated that many of them had been quickly restored to health by a "nutritious and tonic diet." The rest suffered from various complaints, the most threatening of which was chronic diarrhea, "the effect of bad water drunk on Cabrera; this illness alone is what has sent so many to the grave. Nevertheless," the doctor concluded, "I am confident that with the methodical plan we have established, and with the appropriate diet they are now receiving, most of them will be cured. I have found no contagious or suspicious illness among them."[41] From then on, for several weeks there were regular transfers of the sick from Cabrera to Palma, despite the priest's paradoxical anxiety that if they continued "there will soon be few [prisoners] or none left on Cabrera...."[42] Estelrich was wedded to his little imperial domain.

Henri Ducor—who had already proven himself an ingenious opportunist by his change of uniform in Cádiz—now conspired with a friend, Lestrade, to slip in among the officers' servants before the ill were removed from Cabrera. In fact he remained sick and was placed in the prison hospital on arrival in the city. He must have been one of those who recovered quickly, and after forty days both he and his companion were shipped back to Cabrera, where Lestrade had the energy for one more escapade. On their return, Ducor and Lestrade gained lodging among the prisoners in the castle, close to the priest's apartment. Lestrade managed to break into Estelrich's quarters, where he found a gourmand's supply of fresh food, stole it, and shared a delicious meal of sweet biscuits and pâté with his friend. After discovery of the theft, the two were expelled from the castle and returned to the discomforts of common prisoners in the harbor below.[43]

❖ ❖ ❖

THE AUTUMN WEATHER—and especially the violent November storm—forced the captives to think of more permanent housing. The priest reported to Palma that the rains had penetrated virtually every hovel and extinguished every fire. The men were wet and cold. More than two hundred shelters had been completely destroyed while another two hundred were badly damaged; and all the rest were in danger of collapse if the rains continued.

The prisoners understood at last the full implications of their terrible situation: this was no temporary exile, and Palma would provide no housing. While some set off despairingly in small groups to live as hermits in caves discovered across the island, others formed work parties to build the semblance of a town. The first permanent houses were built for the canteen-women in a ragged little square at the base of the central valley, wryly christened Palais Royal to remind the exiles of Paris's revolutionary gathering place. Suddenly there was great activity in and around the harbor, as the military units organized their men to build dwellings in their own distinct quarters. The First Regiment of Dragoons and the First Provisional Legion claimed sites on "Dragoons Hill," in the central valley. The 121st Regiment built their settlement up a trail on the western peninsula, giving the pathway their own name; the Fourth Legion chose a site to the east of Palais Royal, on the slopes of the hill called Bellamirada; the Gendarmes settled near the main beachfront; and the seamen of the Imperial Guard built their shelters just below the castle on the narrow lip at the northern side of the harbor. Louis Gille reported soldiers carrying stones for walls and foundations, mixing cement, cutting timbers for roofbeams, and hauling them painfully over the slopes. The diarist and four other noncommissioned officers from the Fifth Legion made ambitious plans for a stone house large enough for six. They built on the ruins of an old dwelling, where they found cornerstones a yard square and the white marble capital of a Corinthian column, probably Roman in origin. A solid stone house emerged, the envy of other builders. It was imitated, but in the occupants' prideful view it could not be matched because "we had used the best stones." (On this rocky island, that claim could only be made in the absence of quarrying tools.) To furnish the house, a sergeant-major built chairs, footstools, a dining table, and beds with mattresses of leaves. Louis Gille hoped to invite his friend Golvin, a common soldier, to occupy the sixth place in the dwelling; but his housemates, all corporals, jealously rejected the suggestion. The place remained empty.

By the end of the year there were hundreds of dwellings close to Palais Royal: Louis-Joseph Wagré reported more than a thousand around the harbor. Lacking glass, their facades were largely windowless; but some had roofs of stone, and others of wood topped with turf. From a distance at the harbor entrance, the settlement had the appearance of an established town; but on closer sight, it was clear that tolerably decent houses stood next to hovels "that elsewhere might have been taken as pigsties." A new prisoner arriving early in 1810 described the huts as "pretty much like those we are wont to have in our camps, but neither so regular nor so clean." Without help from Palma, that was the best the prisoners could manage.[44]

Palais Royal became the central market and gathering place for the community. Every morning those who had objects to sell found their customers there. Bread, wine, salt fish, needles and thread, twine, wooden forks and spoons, clothing, carvings, and hoarded valuables were on offer. For a while two hussars who had discovered an area of rabbit holes—and made snares to trap their prey—had a monopoly on this precious trade, and sold their catch each day in the market. Soon others discovered their source of supply and destroyed the monopoly; and before long the animals too were entirely wiped out. In the evenings soldiers met their friends to promenade and gossip on the square at Palais Royal or along the path to the spring, now christened the Street of Sighs.[45]

After a year of imprisonment since the surrender at Bailén, and with no hope of rescue, the prisoners' council and medical staff knew the importance of diverting and entertaining the captives. That was as much taken for granted as the need for adequate food, clothing, and housing. As on Isla León, the Frenchmen turned naturally to theater, and by midsummer of 1809 a raised platform was under construction near the harbor. Under the supervision of noncommissioned officers from the gendarmes, volunteer laborers erected a backstage wall from interwoven branches garlanded with heather, producing a pleasingly rustic proscenium stage. The construction crew was rewarded with extra rations of bread.

Just four months after their arrival on the island, on September 8, the theater opened with three productions whose texts had been recalled by the performers: *Monsieur Vautour, Jocrisse's Despair* (*Le Déséspoir de Jocrisse*), and *The Soldiers' Quarters* (*Le*

Billet de Logement). The performances concluded with freshly composed rhyming couplets about life on the desert island, and were greeted with enthusiastic approval. For both audience and actors, wrote Gille, "the times passed more agreeably than for those who had never lived in cities and were strangers to this kind of entertainment." But the autumn winds and rain closed down the theatrical season.[46]

During the winter the original performers were joined by a new arrival, Robert Guillemard (or the officer who later published under that name), whose theatrical knowledge, entrepreneurial spirit, and desire for escape combined to inspire a new and more elaborate venture. He arrived on Cabrera in late February or early March 1810 and, as a noncommisioned officer, was at once coopted to the prisoners' council. From the moment of arrival his first object was escape. He saw in the stage a means of acquiring equipment, finances, and comrades directed to that goal. In his memoir, Guillemard took more credit for the idea of a theater than he alone deserved:

> I was astonished that no one had thought of it before. Indeed some scenes had been performed, but that was done in the open air, and without planning as a profitable venture. My ideas were quite grand compared to such things. I resolved on being at one and the same time, if necessary, author, actor, director, and machinist, and to make my companions partners in my labors and the fruits of it, which were to be employed in accomplishing our favorite object.[47]

Father Damián ("the hypocritical") would not permit theater to be performed within the castle. But not far below it on the steep hillside was a large, abandoned cave reservoir, the roof half collapsed, the walls rotting away, the floor coated deeply in mud. Guillemard and his companions lowered themselves into it on ropes and determined that, with one side opened out, there would be space enough for a stage and an auditorium. They paid the priest to buy four leather buckets from Palma, and hired prisoners to clean and dry out the cistern and build a stage of stone. With paint also purchased from Palma, the walls were colored ochre and bordered in red. The auditorium was decorated all around with garlands of leaves. Guillemard reported that the stage front was painted with the motto "Castigat ridendo mores" ("Manners are changed by laughter"), while Gille recalled that the proscenium bore the legend "Obliviscitur ridendo malum" ("Laughter banishes misfortune"): both of them familiar theatrical epigrams from eighteenth-century France.[48]

In this relatively elegant locale, Guillemard's company opened with a production of La Harpe's *Philoctète,* a classical tale of Hercules' friend, who lit his funeral pyre and carried his poisoned arrows into the siege of Troy. Once again there was no printed text and the verses had to be recalled; and where there were blanks, the directors improvised. Two of Guillemard's colleagues played the parts of Ulysses and Pyrrhus, while a conscript "with a stentorian voice, and no small portion of feeling, assumed the character of Hercules." Three hundred spectators (at two sous a head) crowded into an amphitheater lit with pine torches for that first night. When the play opened with the lines, "Here we are on Lemnos, in this savage land/Where never any mortal has set foot upon the strand" ("Nous voici dans Lemnos, dans cette île sauvage/Dont jamais nul mortel n'aborda le rivage") there were shouts of recognition; and more applause greeted the line, "They have done me every wrong; may the gods punish them." ("Ils m'ont fait tous ces maux; que les dieux le leur rendent.")[49]

Guillemard's theater was a triumph. Soon "the whole colony took an interest in our dramatic success; for after the second performance, I always allowed twenty of those who had not the means of paying to receive free admission." Guillemard wrote out several more plays from memory, and they too were performed. The company prospered. "Our funds increased amazingly, as well as our general comforts. We gave half our profits to the general fund, and divided the rest." Costumes, a theater curtain, ropes, nails, a hammer, and a hatchet were purchased—all the accessories, as the thespians intended, for dual use in the theater or as aids in an escape. The actors also tried to buy sabers from their captors, but in vain: they were forced to use wooden swords on stage. For months in 1810 the entertainments continued, including works by Molière, Regnard, and Beaumarchais. When a new group of officers arrived from detention in Mahón early in 1810, they brought with them the elements of an orchestra, and combined their talents with the existing theater company to mount a series of operatic performances. Officers from the Royal Navy brig anchored in the harbor sometimes attended productions, "admiring us for our ability to create pleasure in such awful conditions."[50]

Guillemard and his fellow entertainers Chobar, Darlier, and Ricaud stockpiled supplies while awaiting their opportunity for escape. It came later in 1810, during a performance of Destouches' *The Spendthrift* [*Le Dissipateur*]. During the last scene, Chobar suddenly appeared in the prompter's box to whisper: "News!" The actors rushed their lines to the final curtain, and Chobar told them that a boat had come ashore on the other side of the island. Its crew of three had built a fire and were asleep. In the darkness Guillemard and his companions set out, carrying ropes, provisions for four days, and a keg of fresh water. They ambushed the sleeping crew, tied and gagged them, forced them to the bottom of the boat, and set sail for the nearest islet to the north, Isla Conejera or Rabbit Island, where they landed. Here the hijackers explained themselves to their prisoners and left them to be rescued. Before re-embarking, the Frenchmen took "their cloaks, their thick pantaloons, and Catalonian caps. In exchange for their clothing, we dressed them in the fragments of our uniforms; we left some provisions, seventy francs in cash—which was more than the value of their boat"—and sailed away. With the aid of Darlier's small compass, the escapees headed southwest towards the Spanish mainland. By morning they were on the open sea, with the heights of Cabrera disappearing behind them. That evening they came ashore north of Valencia, found a French military post, and were reunited with Napoleon's peninsular armies.

The theater-in-a-cistern had lost its artistic manager. Guillemard the adventurer soon found himself participating in the siege of Tortosa, where he was promoted to sergeant and received the cross of the Legion of Honor. Later he was captured in the Russian campaign of 1812 and imprisoned in Siberia until 1814. He returned to further swashbuckling service as an officer during the Hundred Days, and finally left the army in 1823.[51]

❖ ❖ ❖

FOR THOSE WHO REMAINED on the prison island as members of the community of Palais Royal, life had begun to assume the settled patterns of a civil society distinguished only by its unusual isolation, the absence of law and government, a huge imbalance of the sexes, remnants of clothing that grew more and more ragged, and food supplies always dangerously close to starvation levels. The prisoners still depended for their subsistence on shipments from Palma every four days. But individual rations gradually increased because for months Palma failed to reduce shipments to coincide with the high rate of death on the island. According to Henri Ducor, the mortality rate was intentionally hidden from the Spaniards—although this seems unlikely as an explanation for the junta's behavior, since its agents were frequently on the island, and Father Damián continued his regular reports. More likely, sympathetic officials turned a blind eye as one means of reducing suffering among the prisoners; or they were unwilling to face the brutal facts. When periodic censuses were at last undertaken, some prisoners managed to keep the official numbers higher than justified by reappearing in the census lines to have themselves counted twice. Father Estelrich recommended to Palma that such cheaters should be summarily shot, but his proposal was ignored. By December 1809, when deaths on the island had reached about seventeen hundred, only seven hundred were reflected in Palma's calculations.[52]

The primitive settlement became a center of bustling activity. Hidden cash made its miraculous appearance, and when it was scarce, beans from the four-day stock supplied from Palma served as a medium of exchange. Majorcan day traders established several shops in the port, selling hardtack, wine, vegetables, and pottery. Scarcity allowed for high prices, but "those with money were happy to spend it." A cottage industry of wood sculpture developed, for sale to the crews of the guardships or in the markets of Majorca. The island community boasted bake ovens and metal forges. "But the most abundant articles with us," wrote Robert Guillemard, "were teachers of all kinds. One half of the prisoners gave lessons to the other half." Literate soldiers taught reading and writing to the illiterate, and purchased food or clothing with their earnings; others taught languages, and mathematics, and swimming. With advances on his income from teaching reading, writing, and arithmetic, Louis Gille clothed himself "from head to toe," buying his outfit from others who preferred nakedness to starvation. A Masonic lodge was created, offering mutual help to its members. A group of Parisian prisoners created a newspaper in manuscript, entirely composed from fictitious dispatches, which reported that the emperor had not forgotten the prisoners, took a personal interest in their plight, and was sending an expedition to save them. No one believed such fantasies for long, but the reports were a source of harmless distraction. One of the surgeons, Dr. Thillaye, undertook a topographical and botanical survey of Cabrera; Louis Gille and a friend (perhaps the same Thillaye) also toured the island to map its features, completing the project "with all the accuracy possible for engineers who lacked graphic instruments." (After the war, Thillaye submitted his botanical studies of the island for a doctorate at the University of Paris.)[53]

On their expeditions the amateur mapmakers explored two massive caves, one on the western tip of the island and the other on the eastern shore. They approached the eastern cave on a precarious path that entered into the rock, to discover a vast cavern with walls covered in crystals, ceilings draped in tall stalactites, and floors thick in stalagmites. Gille suggested that the eighteenth-century French writer Lesage had described this cave in his picaresque *Histoire de Gil Blas de Santillane*. (That was quite possible. The island could have been known to the Spanish writer Vicente Martínez Espinel, whose autobiographical adventure story *La vida del escudero Marcos de Obregón* was Lesage's source.) The western cave— with a honeysuckle and a fig tree marking its entrance, as Lesage had described it—could be reached only by descending thirty feet or more by rope into similar, dramatic halls decorated with giant pillars, arches, and beams. When torchlit, the vast space became a glimmering cathedral, christened "the Bishop's Cave." Below on its distant floor was a fresh water basin, too isolated to be of any use to the prisoners. Elsewhere on Cabrera there were more accessible and dry caves, now inhabited by reclusive groups of soldiers. In one, the surveyors saw thirty men living in complete nudity after discarding their tattered uniforms: "These unfortunates, grouped round their fire, their skin blue, their cheeks hollow, their bodies blackened by the smoke, looked more like the fabled Cyclops than like French soldiers." No one seems to have recorded how long they remained, or survived, in these primitive conditions.[54]

The topographers identified olive trees growing wild, some juniper and box trees, iris flowering among the rocks, and various unknown bushes and root plants. One laurel-like shrub produced a small fruit similar to a strawberry—but less tasty. A tuberous root with an unusually sour taste, christened the "Cabrera potato" in the first days on the island, was identified by the medical officers as poisonous, and a probable source of many early deaths. Another rapidly growing plant with large leaves and a thick, spongy stalk proved, when dried in the sun, to be light and buoyant. Pieces of the trunk, cut into short lengths, served as floats for those learning to swim.

Rabbits, which were found in abundance in the early days, had been wiped out. More were trapped by prisoners who could swim the short distance north to Rabbit Island, but these, too, quickly disappeared. Lizards were common but indigestible. Thrushes, sea swallows, and gulls nested on the cliffsides as they do today, but their eggs were accessible only by precarious descent on ropes from the heights above—and thus were mostly ignored. The sea offered sparse rewards: sponge, squid, mullet, and small fish—probably anchovies, the Majorcan favorites known as "boquerones"—were caught and sold in the market by Spanish fishermen. But the prisoners themselves, forbidden the use of boats, could not harvest this local resource.[55]

During the winter of 1809–1810, regular food shipments across the windy channel from Palma were sometimes delayed by calm or storm; and just before Christmas, one supply ship failed to arrive on schedule. The prisoners endured eight days before new supplies arrived, their stocks disappeared, and for four days most soldiers had nothing to eat.

That experience was troubling enough. But in mid-February the weakened captives faced a more serious crisis. Because of heavy winds, the regular supply ship could not make harbor in Cabrera port, and anchored instead in the neighboring bay, Cala Ganduf, beyond view of the British and Spanish guardships. Only a few supplies had been disembarked when a group of prisoners went on board in an attempt to seize the ship. As the winds began to sweep the jabeque offshore, those remaining onshore pelted the hijackers angrily with rocks. Some of them jumped into the sea. Simultaneously a Spanish sloop arrived, firing towards the Frenchmen on shore with rifles and cannon, and sharpshooting at the helpless soldiers in the water. The supply ship was boarded, recaptured, and escorted away from the island with most of its essential provisions still on board. In his formal report on the incident to the Spanish naval commander, Lt. Carbonnel of the prisoners' council insisted that the attempted seizure was so inept "that it couldn't have been planned in advance.... I myself was present, as is my custom, at the time when the supplies were unloaded.... I was wearing my uniform that day, and you would rightly consider that if this rising had been premeditated, I would not have allowed myself to be recognized by my uniform." A French quartermaster was killed in the affair; according to Carbonnel's testimony, he was the only casualty.[56]

Four days later, the next regular supply ship did not arrive. The captives interpreted this as a deadly act of vengeance on the part of the Majorcan owner or the provisioner. Famine inevitably followed. As the days passed, groups of prisoners mounted watch on the castle heights for signs of a sloop coming out from Palma. Others scoured the rocks for thistles and roots, which could only be eaten after hours of boiling. A sergeant cooked a sheepskin overcoat that had been donated for use by the sick, sharing the soup and skin among his camp-mates: Louis Gille pronounced them excellent fare. The daily death rate climbed. When the captain of the new Spanish guardship came ashore with a telescope to join in the search for a sail, he emptied his pockets of ship's biscuit to the first prisoners he met, and ordered his crew to sell all their food to the captives. The supply was insufficient, and provoked a riot (wrote Louis Gille) in which "only the strongest could approach. We got two or three biscuits and made a bit of soup among the five of us." The guardship departed for Palma, and the despairing men once more believed they had been left to die.

By the eighth day without supplies, after long argument, the prisoners' council made the reluctant decision to kill Robinson the donkey and divide the body among the military units to be boiled into soup. The killing and apportioning (about three-quarters of an ounce per person) became a somber little ceremony; and the thin gruel that resulted, according to Gille, "gave a little tone" to several thousand starving stomachs.

Gille recalled his discovery, on the same day, of the "frightful spectacle" of two soldiers in Swiss uniforms, hidden among the rocks, tearing apart and roasting the limbs of a dead comrade. But they ate nothing, because they saw that the body was diseased. By evening one of the two was dead of malnutrition. Louis-Joseph Wagré told a similar story of a Polish recluse preparing to cook the body of a comrade. In Wagré's version, the offender gave himself up for execution by Spanish soldiers and was granted his request for a meal of beans, bread, and wine before being shot. Gille does not mention any punishment, but clearly regards the event with equal horror. Of the two writers, only Gille offers a firsthand account; perhaps Wagré recalled, or was given, hearsay reports of the same incident.[57]

In an era when tales of shipwreck, starvation, and survival were familiar fare, it may seem surprising at first sight that the stories of cannibalism on Cabrera were so infrequent, and that those reports stimulated such uniform abhorrence. By contrast, just a decade later the crew of the shipwrecked Nantucket whaleship *Essex* practised cannibalism *in extremis* and were regarded with indulgence for it after their rescue.[58] The reasons for the contrast are probably straightforward. The Cabreran captives living in the main community of Palais Royal never considered themselves totally isolated and alone: the guardships stood in the harbor within view, the daily market offered a limited source of fresh provisions, and Palma was only a few hours away just over the horizon. For those prisoners, authority, external judgment, and potential relief were always at hand. Restraint and taboo, it seemed, could only lose their civilizing power for the demoralized hermits who had fled the community to live or die in isolation in the island's caves. For others they maintained a compelling grip.

The next day the Spanish frigate returned in convoy with a supply ship, and normal four-day rations were at last distributed to the soldiers. In some units, prudent noncommissioned officers gave out small portions of bread, along with further rations every few hours. In others, the entire four-day suppy was distributed holus-bolus and eaten at once in a mood of frantic euphoria—but with the most dire results. Gille estimated that eight or nine hundred prisoners died during or in the immediate aftermath of this period of famine; Santos Oliver estimates the death toll at five to six hundred. No one kept exact count.

The memoirists Ducor, Gille, and Wagré describe the crisis of starvation in similar terms, but cannot explain why the food failed to arrive. Was it retribution for the attempt to hijack the supply ship? Had the jabeque been becalmed, or seized by a French corsair? Were there difficulties of some kind in Palma? Curiously, the records of the junta make no explicit reference to these terrible events—which indicates to the Majorcan writer Jaime Garau that the prisoners must have suffered no more than minor privation, a spell of hardship that was massively exaggerated by the former captives.[59] What the records do show is a previous six-month history of disputes among the junta, the wholesale suppliers, and the provisioner over cash, credit, payments, and deliveries of food, leading to a standoff among them by the end of February. The junta had difficulty covering the monthly budget of 400,000 reales assigned to feed the prisoners; the commercial provisioner, Nicolás Palmer, bought his goods on credit; and when he could not pay his debts to the suppliers, food was eventually withheld and the supply ship could not be loaded. While the authorities argued over the accounts, the captives went hungry and died. Before shipments to Cabrera were resumed, Palmer was forced to offer his resignation. He was replaced by a salaried agent of the junta, and henceforth the supply of food was maintained on a regular schedule every four days. The intricacies of this imbroglio (and the varying motives of the antagonists in Palma) have been lost in time. Whether or not the members of the junta appreciated the full horrors of the episode, those who wished to know understood enough to realize that the lives of the captives were sustained by a fragile and easily severed thread.[60]

In April 1810, General Privé (who remained a relatively privileged prisoner in Bellver Castle in Palma) complained to commissioner Desbrull that his compatriots on Cabrera were still "perishing in the most frightful misery." He asked for clothing for those who, "against the good faith of treaties and all the laws of war, had been stripped and plundered in the prisons of Andalusia." Privé offered to buy clothing for his own units with a credit note drawn on the French imperial treasury in Paris. Desbrull apparently rejected the suggestion—perhaps, as Jaime Garau speculates, because he knew that Napoleon's regime would do nothing to assist the disgraced soldiers of Bailén if it were to be asked.[61]

About the same time, in the early summer of 1810, officers from the Royal Navy brigantines *Espoir* and *Alacrity* came ashore to tour and examine conditions among the captives. The British observers agreed that starvation was no longer a critical problem. Like General Privé and Lieutenant Guillemard—who had arrived a few months earlier—Captains Mitford and Palmer were appalled, instead, by the prisoners' state of undress. Guillemard wrote that many of the captives "were quite naked, and black as mulattos, with beards fit for a pioneer, dirty and out of order [sic]; some had pieces of clothing, but they had no shoes, or their legs, thighs, and part of their body [sic] were bare." On arrival he had seen only three soldiers "with pantaloons and uniforms still almost entire."[62] When Mitford and Palmer saw the cave occupied by thirty naked and blackened men, they recoiled in horror. For months they had been telling the junta in Palma that the greatest need on the island was for clothing to cover the prisoners' nakedness; but Palma replied that its treasury was empty. Now the captains made appeals for clothing (or "slops," in naval language) to the English flotilla off Toulon. The new British commander-in-chief for the Mediterranean, Admiral Sir Charles Cotton, reported his actions to the Admiralty:

> The distresses of the French prisoners on the island of Cabrera... have induced me to collect what Slops can be spared from the ships off Toulon, and to forward the same for Captain Palmer's distribution among them: —many not having a vestige of clothing to cover their nakedness!
>
> I have done this no less on account of the Spaniards, whose prisoners they are, than on the score of humanity, —And as such I trust the same will meet the approbation of the Lords Commissioners of the Admiralty.[63]

When the *Espoir* returned to Cabrera in July, it brought Royal Navy shirts, undershirts, and trousers for the prisoners: enough to outfit perhaps five hundred men, or a fraction of those on the island. The clothing was distributed by lot—and frequently bartered away to other prisoners, or to sailors on the Spanish and British guardships, in exchange for cash or food. Louis Gille—who was still adding to his wardrobe—recalled that he bought a new blue British shirt in exchange for a few rations of bread. The guardian of the waters, Louis-Joseph Wagré, acquired one as well.[64]

The prisoners' council offered formal thanks to the British for their assistance; and for a few months Royal Navy crews made regular trips ashore to fish and cut wood, probably sharing their take with the destitute captives. Friendly contacts with the guardships gave some prisoners the chance to write letters, giving their families the first news of their survival after Bailén. Louis Gille wrote a short note home, which arrived several months later via

Italy. But for Louis-Joseph Wagré, an English shore visit stimulated less genial memories. One of the officers was "a milord whose breadth and obesity contrasted starkly with our pallor and meager bodies. As soon as he landed, he began eating and drinking in front of us, and one unfortunate Cabreran, without thinking of the disgrace he created, threw himself at the officer's feet and ate the small portions of food that the milord threw to him."[65]

The navy's distressing reports of conditions on the island were disturbing enough to merit the attention of the British ministry, and in September 1810 the foreign secretary conveyed its complaints to the British ambassador in Spain:

> The situation of these unfortunate French prisoners on the Island of Cabrera is deplorable, and demands the immediate interposition of your good offices, to prevail upon the Regency equally from motives of humanity and policy, to succour their immediate wants, and to make a suitable provision for their maintenance, as long as they shall remain unexchanged.
>
> You will take the first opportunity of representing to the Spanish govt. the urgency of the case, and the extreme impropriety of their being abandoned, without other clothing than what His Majesty's Ships on that station were accidentally able to supply.[66]

The diplomatic protest was futile. The government of independent Spain was perennially empty-handed, dependent on British loans or cash from its colonies in the new world for survival from month to month. Majorcan budgets were inadequate. And there was no rescue in sight.

The Family of Charles IV by Francisco Goya, 1800
(by courtesy of the Museo del Prado)

At the center, María Luisa and Charles IV; at front left, the heir Ferdinand.
Goya himself appears at the easel in the left background.

Napoleon Bonaparte
by Robert Lefèvre
(by courtesy of the V&A Picture
Library)

Fernando VII in Camp
by Francisco Goya
(by courtesy of the Museo del Prado)

The Second of May by Francisco Goya, 1808
(by courtesy of the Museo del Prado)

The Third of May by Francisco Goya
(by courtesy of the Museo del Prado)

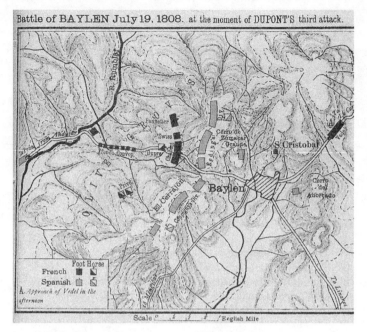

Battle of Baylen, July 19, 1808, at the moment of Dupont's attack
(from Charles Omar, *A History of the Peninsular War,* by courtesy of the
napoleonseries.org)

General Dupont (by courtesy of the
Bibliothèque nationale de Paris)

Cuthbert Collingwood, baron,
vice-admiral, and Royal Navy
commander-in-chief on the
Mediterranean, 1805–1810,
by Henry Howard
(by courtesy of the National
Portrait Gallery, London)

The Surrender at Bailén by Casado del Alisal
(by courtesy of the Museo del Prado)

Officer and Grenadier of the Guard of Paris
(by courtesy of the Anne S.K. Brown Military Collection, Brown University Library)

Tanto y mas (*So Much and Even More*) by Francisco Goya
(from *The Disasters of War,* by courtesy of the Museo del Prado)

Se aprovechan (*They Equip Themselves*) by Francisco Goya
(from *The Disasters of War,* by courtesy of the Museo del Prado)

Grande hazaña! Con muertos! (*Wonderful Heroism! Against Dead Men!*)
by Francisco Goya (from *The Disasters of War*, by courtesy of the Museo del Prado)

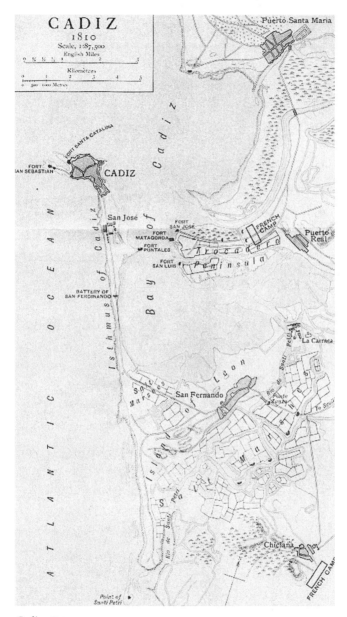

Cadiz, 1810

(from John Fortescue, *History of the British Army,* by courtesy of
the napoleonseries.org)

Majorca and Cabrera, 1765, from the *Mapa del Reyno Balearico*
by Francisco Xavier de Garma y Duran, Barcelona
(by courtesy of the Servicio Geográfico de Ejército de España)

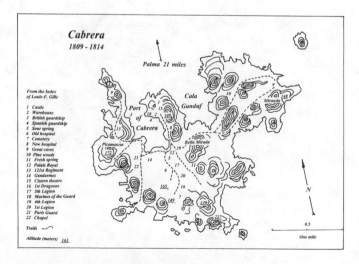

Cabrera, 1809–1814 (map by Denis Smith)

The castle as seen from the port at Palais Royal, Cabrera (photo by Denis Smith)

The port of Cabrera from the castle with Palais Royal in the center background, Cabrera (photo by Denis Smith)

The castle from the Cabrera harbor entrance (photo by Denis Smith)

Ruins of the cistern theater, from the castle, Cabrera (photo by Denis Smith)

Prisoners' graffiti on the castle wall, Cabrera (photo by Denis Smith)

Prisonniers français, détenus dans l'île de Cabrera

Revue du Mois
de Décembre
1809

Revue du mois de Décembre 1809.

Désignation du Mois	Officiers Présent	Sous off.ers Présent	Caporaux Présent	Soldats Présent	Effectif à la fin du Corps	Effectif Général
Du Premier décembre	54.	425.	833.	2581.	3859.	3859.

Certifié Véritable, Cabrera le premier décembre 1809.

Census of prisoners on Cabrera, December 1, 1809,
certified by the chairman of the prisoners' council, Lieutenant de Maussac
(by courtesy of the Archivo Municipal de Palma)

N° 3.

Demande Particulieres Pour le besoin
de Messieurs les officiers Prisonniers a Cabrera

Messieurs les officiers Sont Depourvus
d'objets Necessaires Pour Se Coucher.
Ils demandent que la Junta Veuille bien
leur Procurer les Moyens a set Egard

Objets de toute Nécessité
Pour le Couchage
des officiers

36 Paillasses
36 Couvertures
36 Oreillers
36 Pains de Draps
36 Couchettes

Certifié Véritable Cabrera le 17 septembre 1809.

Request for beds
and blankets for the
officers on Cabrera,
September 17, 1809
(by courtesy of the
Archivo Municipal
de Palma)

4

A REMOTE AND FLEETING HOPE

WHILE PALMA IMPROVISED and the prisoners languished on the desert island, the Spanish war of liberation on the mainland faltered. Through 1809, Napoleon's reinforced armies in Spain, toughened by the infusion of war-hardened units led by his most distinguished marshals, beat back the English and Spanish armies and their citizen-guerrilla irregulars with heavy casualties and suffering on both sides. The emperor had ordered his officers to drive the enemy into the sea. General Arthur Wellesley, commanding combined British, Portuguese, and Spanish forces, retreated to the safety of Portugal after a cautious victory at Talavera in Spain. In November 1809 the Spaniards suffered a major and demoralizing defeat at Ocaña, on the southern outskirts of Madrid, which opened the road south for France's imperial armies. Three months later in February 1810, after a rapid advance through the Sierra Morena and across the plains of Andalusia, the puppet King Joseph led the invaders into Seville. The rebel Junta Central retreated to Cádiz, where French forces under Marshal Victor began a long siege of the new capital from the shores of Cádiz Bay.

After sixteen months of existence as the confederate government of the rebellious Spanish provinces, the Junta Central was increasingly weak and uncertain about its legitimacy. Its military record was unimpressive. In Cádiz, its first decision was to abandon power to a new, five-member Council of Regency acting in the name of the exiled king, and charged with preparations for a meeting of the Cortes, the old parliament of the regions and principalities of Spain. Until the Cortes could meet, the Regency Council governed the unoccupied areas of Spain by decree, in uneasy tandem with the newly elected Junta of Cádiz—who provided the Regency's sparse funding from local taxes, duties, and cash from the colonies of Spanish America. After interminable delays in the election of deputies, the Cortes finally met in September 1810. This was the first meeting of a representative national parliament since the achievement of Spanish unity in 1515. On its convocation, the Council of Regency was transformed into the executive of the regime, owing responsibility to the new Cortes and loyalty to Ferdinand VII. Within eight months, unoccupied Spain had experienced three distinct working constitutions as it struggled unsuccessfully to overcome the will of Napoleon and the massive armies of the emperor. By the summer of 1810 there were more than 350,000 French soldiers in the peninsula.

From Catalonia in the east, refugees and ragged units of the Spanish forces continued their flight to Majorca and Minorca, placing ever heavier burdens of supply and maintenance on the governors of the islands. In its search for credit, the local junta sequestered savings, disposed of cash seized from the prisoners, and decreed an unpopular wartime confiscation of gold and silver from individuals and the church. Rumors of defeat and a potential French invasion of Majorca—perhaps to be reinforced from the vengeful hordes of prisoners on Cabrera—heightened the anxieties of the local population. (In the febrile atmosphere of war, the absence of evidence to sustain such fears meant nothing. The starved and weakened prisoners were in no condition to attack anyone.) As in Cádiz a year earlier, the prisoners of war became the easy targets of panic: the collective mind of the mob was gathering force again. The island's governors feared it.

The junta in Palma—having already declared that it could take no more responsibility for the captives—agreed in principle that all the prisoners on Majorca, Minorca, and Cabrera should be transferred to the mainland; but in the absence of cooperation from the new central government and the Royal Navy it could do nothing to achieve that goal. Popular protests against the continuing presence of French officers in Palma and Mahón grew more frequent; and the authorities sensed that the smallest spark might ignite an explosion.

About one thousand French officers and civilians, including Generals Dufour and Privé, had accumulated in Palma after the common prisoners were moved to Cabrera in May 1809; and late in the year a further 120 soldiers had been brought from Cabrera to the hospital in Majorca. Among the detainees in Palma, only a half dozen, including a general's widow, a woman servant of General Dufour who dressed as a man, two secretaries, a doctor, and a thirteen-year-old boy, were identified as noncombatants and granted safe passage to France by way of Barcelona. The remaining officers made an honorable request to be transferred to Cabrera to share the fortunes of their men; but the petition was denied.[1]

Once they were confined in military barracks in Palma, the officers made persistent complaints to the junta over their unhealthy quarters, inferior food, and inadequate compensation. When those protests brought insufficient result, one of the officers threw a list of grievances from a prison window into the street, asking that it be circulated and read to the junta. Members of the junta received it, judged the petition to be moderately and justly phrased, and treated it with consideration; but rumor immediately spread, suggesting that the complaint contained blasphemous and subversive language. The cautious junta—always nervous about the effects of any campaign to arouse the populace against the prisoners—called for a judge to examine the facts of the case. In July 1809, Judge Nicolás Campaner reported that the French officer's paper "contained nothing contrary to our holy religion, nor anything insulting to the Spanish nation." The junta endorsed Campaner's judgment that two priests, a doctor, and a layman had falsely maligned the French author of the petition, with the obvious purpose of disturbing public order. The priests were sentenced to two months of monastic detention, the doctor was condemned to eight days of spiritual exercises in the Capuchin convent of Palma, and the layman to eight days of prison. Three of the sentences were duly applied; but the doctor managed to evade acceptance of his summons by moving about Majorca in defiance of the junta. The episode illustrated the deliberate even-handedness of the junta once the bulk of prisoners had been dispatched to Cabrera, a certain chivalry in its treatment of military officers— and the decidedly fragile state of popular sentiment.[2]

For months the Cabrera commissioner was deluged with letters from the French officers in Palma, seeking assistance for their men on Cabrera, requesting repatriation, the provision of books, the arrangement of lines of credit through French bankers, enclosing letters for mailing to France, or asking for back pay.

Beyond offering his sympathetic ear and forwarding their mail, Don Antonio Desbrull could do little to help them.

The officers' complaints, and public annoyance over their continued presence in Palma, mounted during the autumn of 1809. For better security against both escape and the menaces of the mob, Generals Dufour and Privé, along with some other officers, were moved to greater isolation in Bellver Castle (the medieval home of the kings of Majorca), located on a high hilltop dominating the city. Small groups of citizens began to confront individual members of the junta to protest about taxes, shortages, the fear of invasion—and always, about the dangerous presence of foreign prisoners in their midst. More than once, threatening crowds gathered at the doors of the officers' prisons. "Far from inspiring compassion for the French prisoners," wrote Santos Oliver, "all things conspired to damage them in the public's eyes: the prosperity of the foreigners, the advances of the imperial army in Valencia, the state of decomposition and anarchy of the nation." For a week in early March 1810, Majorca was suddenly flooded with hundreds of refugees fleeing from the mainland, bringing fresh reports of French atrocities and renewed panic to the island.[3] Xenophobia infected the air of Palma.

On March 12, the latest rumor brought the anticipated explosion: someone spread word that prisoners in the Lonja barracks on the harborfront had thrown rocks at nuns passing along the wall below. "Hatred of the enemy," Santos Oliver reflected, "impatient religious sentiment, the desire to make trouble, the weakness of the authorities... came together to precipitate a riot." A howling crowd approached the doors of the barracks armed with knives, hatchets, and sabers, calling for a massacre. The mob grew; the militia at the doors nervously brandished their arms. The new military governor of Majorca—another Swiss mercenary, General Nazaire Reding, brother of the victor of Bailén, General Teodoro Reding—elbowed his way into the barracks alongside the city's chief of police and commissioner for Cabrera, Don Antonio Desbrull, and Judge Campaner, all of them pleading with the crowd to remain calm.

But the appeal was fruitless. Stones rained against the doors and windows of the prison barracks, falling back on the surging mass below. The prisoners armed themselves with chair and table legs, knives, razors, scissors, anything that might serve as a weapon. One of the besieged officers, Charles Frossard of the Imperial Guard, recalled their courage:

> We were like lions; we wanted to go out and fall on our assassins; armed in this way we believed ourselves strong enough to throw them back. On a field of battle we would not have been impressive; but in barracks where there was only one entry gate, we knew we could kill anyone who entered. We sustained one another; it was only a question of who would be the first to assault our enemies.[4]

The crowd drew back from the doors when they saw the officers preparing to defend themselves. In futility the militia shot blanks into the air to clear the square and then, in panic, fired into the gathering, killing one of their own grenadiers and wounding several civilians. Rage mounted, and units of the urban police arrived, apparently intending to defend the crowd against the militia.

A state of general emergency was declared. To appease the rioters and protect the lives of the captives, Reding and Desbrull (who had by now left the barracks) offered to transfer the French officers at once to Cabrera, and during the afternoon the local naval commander requisitioned the necessary ships and moved them to the docks nearby.

According to Lieutenant Frossard, the governor promised to arm the French officers before leading them to the port for embarkation. But when the first fifteen officers emerged from the barracks—still unarmed—their compatriots saw them cruelly struck down by the mob. Despite these blows, a single officer reached the harbor and swam toward the ships. When he reached one of them, he was beaten back and left to drown by members of the Spanish crew. On shore, the prisoners observed these murders with frustrated anger. They were prevented from breaking out of the main entrance to engage their assailants by the fifty guards who barred the doors.[5]

As the disturbance intensified during the day, the bishop of Palma (who was also president of the junta) made his way to the Lonja barracks accompanied by a phalanx of ecclesiastics and members of the religious orders, chanting the rosary, raising the image of the Holy Virgin above them, and pleading for public restraint. Fresh units of the urban guard followed them. A few moments of calm ensued, and the authorities took the decision to bring the prisoners out by the main doors, instead of leading them to the ships along the city wall and beyond reach of the rioters. When a group of prisoners appeared, the tumult erupted once more. "In vain," wrote Santos Oliver, "the bishop, the canons, many monks, soldiers, and aristocrats, forming a veritable cordon and linking their hands, tried honorably to lead the captives safely to the boats. Stones, viciously thrown, rained on many of them; the mob spat on everyone. Two of the unfortunates who fell unconscious and were left behind were barbarously murdered within sight of the holy images."[6]

As disorder continued, Reding and Desbrull made their way back to the barracks through the violent crowd to escort the remaining prisoners to the boats. Once inside, and able to assess the immediate danger, they decided not to take the Frenchmen out by the same doorway, but rather to break an escape hole through the city wall facing the harbor. The demolition was quickly accomplished, and up to two hundred officers scrambled through the rubble, along the walls and onto the ships before this humane ruse was discovered by the angry mob. Their rage intensified, but their force was divided as they pursued prisoners emerging from the barracks in two separate places. Under armed escort, the remaining officers reached the harbor and swam to safety on the ships—sometimes followed into the water by their raging pursuers.

Once past the gauntlet and resting on the transports as they nursed their wounds, the prisoners offered their praises to General Reding and commissioner Desbrull for their quick wit and courage in leading many of them to safety. On shore, the protest faded away. The dead were gathered up and buried, and within days the mob's leaders were arrested, summarily prosecuted, and deported to the mainland. Desbrull's police investigation showed that the disturbance arose from a malicious lie. There had been no precipitating incident. But the objective of the rioters had been gained: the French officers were gone, aside from a dozen senior officers left behind in Bellver Castle. The Majorcan Jaime Garau commented a century later that "these barbarous and unchristian events were a proof of human ferocity when no authority contains people, and they act without thought or fear of God. Majorca, in other times, was a place of calm that respected law and justice; but now the population had become tumultuous, disobedient, and cruel. The result was bound to be disastrous."[7]

❖ ❖ ❖

NEXT MORNING THE PRISONERS of Cabrera saw a mass of sails approaching from Palma. Many of them felt "a remote and fleeting hope of liberty": so many ships must be coming to take them back to France. The internees gathered expectantly at water's edge, until forced back by gunfire from the marine guards on the approaching ships. Then they recognized their officers, who came ashore to tell them of the troubles in Palma and the courage of those who had saved their lives. "What a spectacle for us," wrote Charles Frossard, "to see these poor unfortunates in such condition on our return to this island! They were all virtually naked, pale, and gaunt: left so long without provisions, they resembled skeletons."[8] After putting the officers ashore the convoy departed empty for its return to Majorca.

The officers rejoined their units in the makeshift housing of Palais Royal. As the most senior officer among the new arrivals, a seriously wounded fifty-three-year-old naval captain named Duval assumed chairmanship of the prisoners' council. Duval had served forty-four years in the French navy, since the age of nine. At the battle of Trafalgar, as captain of the warship *Pluton*, he had been crippled in both arms; and now he suffered bouts of internal bleeding as well. In better times he would have been an obvious candidate for inclusion in an exchange of wounded prisoners, but his pleas from imprisonment in Cádiz and Palma had been ignored. Duval was already on good terms with Don Antonio Desbrull in Palma, and now sought Desbrull's good offices on behalf of all the prisoners. He complained about the reduced officers' rations available on the island, and eagerly endorsed Father Estelrich's hope that the infirm would soon be repatriated to France (while pleading again for his own inclusion in that company on the grounds of his age, weakness, and battle wounds).[9] Other officers wrote to the Cabrera commissioner seeking to recover their meager personal belongings, all of them abandoned in the sudden flight from the Palma mob. In two commonplace reminders of life among the captives, a certain Captain Richard asked Desbrull to retrieve his clean laundry from a Palma laundress: a pair of blue trousers, two shirts, two undershirts, and five handkerchiefs; and General Privé's aide-de-camp pleaded for the return of his guitar, "my only source of distraction in this unhappy situation." Another officer objected to the indignity of being placed on the island among insubordinate common soldiers.[10]

Charles Frossard found only seventeen of the seventy-five members of his Imperial Guard unit who had arrived on the island in 1809; but he encouraged the survivors to keep their hopes of deliverance alive. The officers told their men that the Palma Junta had recently agreed to a mass transfer of all prisoners from the islands and continued to proclaim that it would fulfill that decision. Spirits on Cabrera briefly revived.

Many prisoners remained sceptical of all promises. They had been betrayed too often and looked elsewhere for relief. Beyond the daily struggles to keep alive, escape offered the boldest means of seizing destiny by the throat. At least two successful breakouts had occurred, and members of the Imperial Guard and the seamen of the Guard constantly sought fresh occasions for escape. Once when the supply ship arrived late in the day and anchored overnight, thirty seamen imagined a daring escapade. Henri Ducor was in their company that night. In darkness, they would cut the lines of the ship's launches, bring the boats silently ashore to take on prisoners armed with knives and truncheons, attack and seize one of the guardships, overcome the second guardship, search the coast for fishing boats, return to Cabrera port with this squadron to offer freedom to more prisoners, and make off in a triumphant convoy towards the occupied shores of Spain. The plot blossomed and flowered in a few evening hours. Alas, it was all a dream. "Twenty times we were on the point of entering the water, but always we heard the hum of voices on the supply ship; the sounds continued all night, and at last we abandoned the attempt and retired to bed."[11]

This elite cadre from the Imperial Guard grew obsessed with the thought of freedom. In June 1810, a Guard officer, Lieutenant Gérodias, took the lead in supervising two boatbuilders and twenty or more prisoners, working two shifts night and day in a grotto, to build a longboat. The conspirators labored in secret, with watchmen posted to avoid detection by other members of the colony. But as the craft neared completion, they were discovered by a wandering prisoner who escaped unidentified back to the camp and betrayed his fellows to the Spanish naval commander. The next morning an armed patrol arrived at the grotto, arresting Gérodias, his fellow officer M. Boniface, and two shipbuilders as the other prisoners escaped over the hills. The gunship commander reported to Palma that the unfinished boat, along with all the prisoners' tools, materials, and supplies had been seized, while the French officers were questioned and shipped off to Majorca for further interrogation.

There are conflicting accounts of what happened next. The memoirist Méry recalled that Gérodias made a brilliant legal argument before the junta, claiming that prisoners of war who were improperly held (as the French soldiers from Bailén had certainly been) were justified in exercising their natural right to escape without any threat of punishment. In this version, his judges were persuaded and Gérodias was granted his freedom. The junta's records, on the other hand (including letters from Gérodias himself), reveal that despite his plea, Gérodias's gold watch, ring and chain, and eighteen Spanish reales in cash were confiscated while he was detained on reduced rations in Bellver Castle. The prisoner complained of his treatment in a courtly exchange with commissioner Desbrull, requesting proper food and the return of his belongings. When the appeal was granted, Gérodias offered thanks for Desbrull's goodwill. Soon afterwards, when a transfer of officers to England was imminent, Gérodias asked that he be permitted to take with him his young domestic servant, and that his accomplice in the escape attempt, Lieutenant Boniface, should be accompanied by his elder brother from the prison island. The benevolent Don Antonio Desbrull apparently granted both requests. Meanwhile the unfortunate Frenchman who had betrayed his comrades' escape was allowed, as his dubious reward, to save his life by transferring into the Spanish army.[12]

While Gérodias and Boniface were treated with chivalrous respect in Palma, on Cabrera the community suffered collective punishment for the failed escape. The commander of the Spanish guardship *Lucía* ordered the captives to give up all their iron tools (such as knives, daggers, and scissors) under threat of immediate bombardment from offshore. Captain Duval and his council conceded. The junta also ordered an intensive search of the island for further evidence of boatbuilding; and in early July the commander and his party discovered another boat and its equipment, apparently supplied to the prisoners from one of the English brigantines in a clandestine gesture of sympathy for the exiles. "They were notable always for giving aid to the captives," Santos Oliver drily noted, "but it would have been impolitic to pursue such suspicions against Spain's all-powerful ally."[13]

❖ ❖ ❖

BY EARLY 1810 the French minister of war, the Duke de Feltre, learned what had happened to the prisoners taken at Bailén after their removal from the hulks of Cádiz in the previous year. In February, he was informed that fourteen sailors of the Imperial Guard had arrived in Toulon from Barcelona after their escape from the island of Cabrera. (These were the prisoners who had seized the water ship in August 1809.) In June, the minister received more detailed intelligence from General Morand, the commandant of French forces in Corsica.

All the soldiers of two divisions that capitulated at Bailén can be found on Cabrera, a small desert island located eight leagues from Majorca, amounting to as many as 4,500 men; these soldiers are naked and exposed to the open air; food is brought to them from the island of Majorca every two days consisting of a pound and a half of bread, dry beans, and a little oil. In summer water is rare on the island, since there is only one spring and a brackish well. The prisoners are guarded only by two gunboats with forty men each, anchored in the small harbor.[14]

Relying on information that was now three months outdated, Morand told the minister that the French officers and general staff taken at Bailén were billeted in Majorca and Minorca. In Majorca they occupied a barred prison; in Minorca they had spacious quarters and few guards. Minorca was not garrisoned, but a British naval squadron of twenty ships of the line was frequently anchored in Mahón Harbor. Morand indicated that the citizens of Minorca were "very peaceful" and supported the English for commercial reasons, while the residents of Majorca were strong partisans of the British alliance.

Within days of this report, the minister received similar information in a letter from the Dutch city of Maastricht, written by an escaped prisoner from Majorca, Lieutenant Cosme Ramaeckers. The letter's wording—which is almost identical to the report from Corsica—suggests that Ramaeckers was the source for the earlier intelligence. Le Feltre at once informed the Emperor Napoleon of the prisoners' situation and the forces guarding them. At the same time he wrote to the Corsican commander requesting the source of his information and asking "if it would be possible to establish communication with these islands if that were to be judged useful?"

In Napoleon's vast and detailed military correspondence, there are just four brief letters from the emperor's hand that refer to the prisoners of Cabrera. The first of these, in July 1810, instructed the navy minister to determine "if there is some means, without launching the squadron and exposing it to a major battle, to send three good ships…to recover the prisoners.… I don't suppose there are more than two thousand of them." The others, written intermittently through 1811 and 1813, are progressively milder inquiries about the chances of rescue. The minister knew—given Britain's total command of the seas—that a rescue convoy would never survive departure from Toulon or Corsica. The emperor did not press the case.[15]

The possibility of a limited exchange of officers seemed more likely. It was pressed by the government of the satellite Swiss confederation, which had known since the autumn of 1809 about the fate of soldiers from the Third and Fourth Swiss Regiments taken prisoner at Bailén the year before. Two officers of the regiments, Colonels Freuller and Louis de May, wrote in October 1809 to the Swiss governor from imprisonment in Palma pleading for his help in freeing them after fourteen months of captivity under "painful and difficult" conditions. Freuller and May made a specific proposal.

> Several Spanish officers, natives of this island, are prisoners of war in France, and we think that the Junta of Majorca would agree to discuss their exchange.…
>
> We are the only two senior Swiss officers held prisoner in Majorca, and the number of officers of our two regiments found here amount altogether to only six captains and fifteen subalterns.[16]

The following April, after the disturbances in Palma and Mahón leading to the transfer of officers to the prison island, a Swiss delegation from a passing ship was allowed to visit Cabrera to observe conditions in the camp. (No similar right was ever granted to the French.) The mission reported the names of twenty-one Swiss officers under imprisonment; and soon afterwards the Swiss governor and chancellor wrote to the French minister of foreign affairs.

Your Excellency knows that at Bailén two Swiss battalions from the army of General Dupont were made prisoners of war. The officers transported to the Balearic Islands have been detained there for a long time. On 13 March last, they were victims of a riot which broke out in Palma. The public marched in a rabble to the castle to massacre the prisoners. But thanks to the firmness and generous unselfishness of the Governor (M. de Reding) who risked his life for them, they escaped the popular fury. The Governor placed them in safety for the time being by taking them to the wild island of Cabrera; but soon they received news through one of the officers, M. de Muralt of the Third Regiment, announcing that they would be taken to Cádiz. I suppose the intention of the Spanish authorities is to turn them over to the English who dominate this city, which has become the principal seat of the insurrection.

There is general sympathy in Switzerland for the extended misfortunes of these brave officers. Their circumstances have made a profound impression here—so much so that we do not know for certain whether they are protected by the law of nations relating to the treatment of prisoners of war, and if the Emperor, influenced by their condition, would extend his goodwill to them.

Today negotiations for an exchange of prisoners have begun; an English commissioner has arrived in France to treat with the

government. The moment to request freedom for my
unfortunate compatriots has come, and I plead that my
entreaties should be conveyed to the minister of war or the
minister of foreign affairs, as may be appropriate.

If it were possible to include them in the first exchange, this
would be regarded in Switzerland as a great act, and would
have a very beneficial effect on the military service in general.[17]

Before the end of June 1810, the French minister of war responded
by assuring the Swiss that their appeal was reasonable, and promising to "busy myself when circumstances permit in giving effect
to such exchanges."[18] For three years exchange negotiations
between the English and French continued; but none of the Swiss
officers reached home before the end of the war in 1814.

❖ ❖ ❖

MOST OF THE MEMOIRISTS OF CABRERA treated the subject
of the island's twenty-one women with tact or virtual silence.
Charles Frossard, however, attempted a group portrait.[19] He
recalled that five or six of the women were legitimately married to
officers, and exempted them from his story. Of the remaining fifteen, Frossard described six, whose lives he considered representative of the others as well. They were all merchants or canteen-
women, camp followers of the French army who maintained their
roles after the surrender of Bailén, accompanying the prisoners
onto the hulks and ultimately to the desert island. Among them,
apparently, was the mother of one soldier, the sister of another,
and the Spanish mistress of a prisoner who chose to join him from
the mainland. The limitations of commerce on the prison island
meant that for most of them life centered on prostitution and the

wine trade. The women received the attentions of an overwhelmingly male and military community, and "several of them," Frossard wrote, "had rather strange adventures." Predictably, the canteen-women found themselves making bargains with "the capitalists of the island, that is, those who were able to accumulate funds: some of them voluntarily, others by arrangement with their so-called husbands, who agreed to surrender their marital rights in return for a share of their income."[20] But despite the flesh trade, the memoirists agree that the prisoners generally treated the women with consideration, as they had done when they were companions in the field. The camp followers were known on the island by their nicknames.

Marie, a brandy merchant, lived with a noncommissioned officer of the First Legion while offering amorous attentions to her clients in return for better clothing. But she was old and stout, could win no hearts, and ended up toiling thanklessly as a laundrywoman. "I remember no more than her name," Frossard recalled.

Her neighbor, "La Jacquette" (who lived with a gunner named Jacquet) was more fortunate. She was young and pretty, a wine and coffee merchant, and a seamstress as well. La Jacquette distributed her affections widely in the camp.

> She carried on many affairs and was sought by many officers, all of whom she tried to satisfy. She had such a good heart that one day she tried to jump into the sea and drown herself because one of her lovers had left her for another woman. Despite the efforts of all those who would save her, she kept sinking back into the sea.
> Afterwards, the most remarkable thing was that she demanded to see the one she said she loved best and insisted

on going with her husband to persuade him to return to her shop. She fell into his arms and overwhelmed him with the most tender caresses. Finally, under her renewed threats of drowning, he promised to take her back. After this unusual demonstration of affection, the officer showed his gratitude by taking his sweetheart away with him to England. She left her Jacquet on Cabrera.

"Marie-in-tight-pants" ("Marie-culotte") was not content with her companion, a corporal who made her wear rough canvas breeches, while other women sported dresses of cotton. She abandoned her corporal for Lieutenant Vidal of the dragoons, took on airs and a new wardrobe, and sent her trousers back to her husband. Still he desired her, and went every day to her lover's quarters to shower the dragoon with insults.

But this didn't stop Lieutenant Vidal from keeping his new "bride." What's more, he refused to go to England with the other officers, preferring to stay on the desert island in order to hold on to his conquest. I don't know what happened later to this officer. Shame forced him to separate himself from his fellow officers, because they all despised him.

"La Denise"—a pretty brunette wine supplier whose husband, Sergeant Denis of the light infantry, kept her under close guard—acted with discretion in rejecting the advances of many officers. But sometimes her wine sales required her to go out alone, when she was propositioned and took gifts from her suitors. Finally she responded to their advances. As a result she was repeatedly beaten by her husband; and once, covered in bruises, she remained hidden in their shelter for two weeks. "The best part of this story,"

Frossard reflected mordantly, "was that her husband never learned the names or the number of his wife's lovers." (This was the only recorded account of a woman being beaten on the island.)

For Frossard, the most beautiful of the vintners on Cabrera was Angélique, the widow of an infantryman who died on the hulks in Cádiz. She was taken up by a sergeant of the horse artillery, who regarded her as his wife and treated her well. The sergeant had cash, and on Cabrera he set her up as a wine merchant. Angélique ran the most popular canteen in Palais Royal.

Eventually a warrant officer of the dragoons promised to marry her if she would leave her artillery sergeant. She accepted the offer and left the sergeant; but he would not abandon her, and forced her to return to him—and to the lucrative business. For a long time, Angélique managed to keep both her partners, leaving the sergeant periodically for the warrant officer; but each time she returned to her source of income at the tavern. At last, the sergeant proposed an intriguing business arrangement with another prisoner:

> Angélique was sold to the Baron de Schaunburg for the sum of three hundred francs in cash, and a promise of three thousand francs payable on their return to France, in return for which the Baron could marry Angélique.
>
> These arrangements satisfied all three of them: one had a partner, the other had money, and Angélique expected to become a baroness! For a short while all went well. But about fifteen days later, Angélique demanded to be married at once to the baron. It was not easy for the officers to halt this alliance, for the baron had already consented, and had spoken to the island's Spanish priest.... I must say that we did not wish the

wedding to occur, because it was not appropriate for a young officer to marry someone whose conduct was so despicable. But finally this young woman made the baron the unhappiest among all the officers: he finally left her and she joined another junior officer for the transfer to England.

Frossard never learned what became of Angélique; but the disappointed baron fared badly. After the war, he became a sergeant-major in a regiment of dragoons, was dismissed for bad conduct in 1817, and remained penniless and without friends.

Another woman too, Frossard reported, was traded as a piece of property on Cabrera. She was a Polish widow whose husband had also died in a Spanish prison camp. She was young, blond, and attractive, and lived with a Polish noncommissioned officer; but in Frossard's eyes she lacked the calculating wiles of a Frenchwoman. She was sold by her countryman to a dragoon sergeant for eighty francs. (For other writers, gossip priced her at sixty francs, and identified her buyer as an artilleryman, a lancer, or a rifleman.) Louis Gille reported that another Polish canteen-woman was offered in a lottery, at four sous per ticket.[21]

The prison memoirists tolerated "the promiscuity of men who had reverted to a state of nature," admired the women of Cabrera for their courage in joining their countrymen on this barren rock—and damned the Spanish authorities for their cruelty in sending them there. For Father Damián alone the presence of the canteen-women on the prison island was a shocking offence to decency. His letters to Palma repeatedly demanded their removal from the island. Two of those letters provide the only catalog of women's names, laid out like a theatrical cast list:

Tiny Maria Murviosa, of Versailles.

Madame Bela, calling herself the wife of Guimé.

Maria, calling herself the wife of sergeant Martin.

Cristina, calling herself the wife of sergeant Cosin.

Cristiania, German, calling herself the wife of grenadier
sergeant Carvet.

Sofia, a German widow.

Maria, sergeant Galiaco's woman.

Maria, sergeant Dionisio's woman.

Fat Maria, a sergeant major's woman....

Rosa the Pole, Antonio Bordange's whore (who she abandoned
to join another prisoner).

La Jacqueta, after a certain Jacquet (who did the same and left
him to live with her first love).[22]

On October 15, 1809, Father Estelrich wrote to Don Antonio Desbrull demanding that "the officers and sergeants who occupy the
governor's rooms in the castle" should be removed to other quarters because four women lived with them, "serving no purpose
but the diversion of their masters and the scandal of others."
Once they were gone, "my home would not be, as it is at present, a
theater of games and recreation, dance and hijinks, but rather a
school of virtue and a shelter for the unfortunate." The hovels of
the women Frossard described could not compare with the governor's rooms in the castle; but wherever they lived, the priest
wanted the women deported unless they could prove they were
married to their companions. When Palma gave Estelrich permission to expel the women, the officers refused to obey. The priest
wrote despairingly to Desbrull:

... after having given your orders to M. Monsach [sic], I warned him to order the appearance before me of all the women of the island, in order to determine by their documents which are the legitimate wives, and which are the widows or celibates so that I can deliver them to the captain of the Spanish guardship who, according to your order, must take them on board for Majorca. Despite the source of this order, not one of them appeared; and what is more, some fled into the hills while others refused to move, with the exception of one who dared to present herself directly to the ship's captain. Since the ship was unfortunately stranded here, she eventually came back on shore.

The outraged priest lectured the prisoners' council for its disobedience.

They replied that, while none of the women could prove that their marriages were legitimate because their papers were lost, all had lived permanently with their spouses from the moment they joined them in the army. On the strength of their word and that of their partners, the officers insisted on regarding them as married unless there is proof to the contrary.... I offer this information to the Junta so that it may take the necessary measures.

When Palma made no reply, Estelrich took another futile initiative. On October 26 he wrote to Desbrull:

As for the women, I took care to say at mass last Sunday that they should all present themselves to me to give documentary proof of their marriages or be prepared to go to Majorca. If they refused, they would be imprisoned under Spanish guard for eight days and be fed only bread and water. Once again they paid no attention and disobeyed me. Three days later I appealed to Members of the Council, who replied again that the women had no papers, but were recognized as wives by the various units; they said further that they would not present themselves without their commanders' orders, that no one could force them and no power could separate them. That is how they replied to Your Lordships. I wish, then, to resort to force to carry out my decree, with the help of the guardship commander. . . .

The Junta can be certain that the Officers have a great interest in the women's presence, since their absence would deprive them of their greatest pleasures; but Your Lordships have a greater interest in the good of the State, which could save what the women cost it; what is more, the State is concerned with the well-being of the poor soldiers, and the women diminish the rations available to them; still more, you have an interest in the Holy Church, which is outraged by these scandalous abuses; and finally, Your Lordships have an interest in my honor and authority, which will be reduced to nothing if I fail in an enterprise that excites my zeal solely for the greater glory of God.

Don Antonio Desbrull's answer was deafening silence. Father Damián repeated his unheeded demands. Even in the wake of the terrible November storm, as he faced more immediate problems, the priest could not desist:

As regards the women, I cannot see the possibility of avoiding fornication and abortion, beyond all the inconveniences I have already warned about; I can't see any means of leading them onto a better path unless the Junta separates them from the others.

By December, Estelrich was pleading only that Rosa the Pole and La Jacqueta be forcibly removed—but other testimony suggests that this appeal failed like the others. The women remained.

The stubborn camp followers would not leave the island for an uncertain fate in Palma at Father Estelrich's command; but that did not mean they found life on Cabrera pleasing. When the chance came, most of them departed for England with the officers in the summer of 1810. Their places were taken by new female arrivals throughout the period of captivity, and life among the prisoners must have been as precarious for them as it was for the first arrivals. Finally, in March 1812—in what seemed to be the junta's first explicit display of concern for the canteen-women— the local government decided that any penitent women on the rock could be evacuated to a hospice created for them in Palma. At least three of them accepted the offer.[23]

❖ ❖ ❖

IN PALMA, the March riots of 1810 intensified the junta's efforts to free itself from further responsibility for the French prisoners. A fresh manifesto was despatched to Cádiz, documenting the history of the entire affair for the new national government. Emissaries set off for Cádiz and Mahón to argue the Majorcan case directly to the Council of Regency and the Royal Navy. In Mahón, the British regional commander, Admiral Hood, took a neutral position, defer- ring to the authority of the Spanish Council of Regency. From Cádiz, the Majorcan delegate Don Miguel de Victorica reported a partial victory at the end of May. The Council of Regency had agreed to remove from the Balearic Islands "the French officers— that is, generals, subordinate officers, sergeants, unit commanders, and sailors that have been prisoners on Cabrera; and in addition to send three million reales to the islands for relief in place of the two million previously promised...."[24] The officers, it appeared, would be moved first to Cádiz and then to Gibraltar, where British ships would take them to England as prisoners of the Crown. Ordinary soldiers would remain on the prison island.

There was no explanation from the Council of Regency for this proposal to divide the prisoners, and none was necessary. The normal assumption was that relief for military officers must come first. Behind the scenes, however, the decision seemed to be the chance outcome of a game of maneuver and high diplomacy. The British knew that Spain lacked both funds and facilities to maintain the growing numbers of French prisoners under its care. In Cádiz the detention centers were full; and in the Baleares, the junta struggled unsuccessfully to finance the Cabrera operation or to dispose of its captives. Rioting against their presence had occurred, or was threatened, in Cádiz, Mahón, Ibiza, and Palma. On all counts political, economic, and moral they were a dangerous and embarrassing inconvenience. The Spanish government implored the British to take the Frenchmen off its hands. (Probably underlining, by this very appeal, that the British were the ones who had vetoed repatriation of the prisoners under the surrender agreement of 1808.)

In February 1810 the Majorcan junta made a desperate plea of its own to Lord Collingwood: a plea made orally, it appeared, because of its outlandish nature. Collingwood, who was dying and had already asked to be relieved of his command, received the request but was in no condition to report it to London before his death on March 7. The Admiralty Board heard of the matter in the following month, when Admiral Purvis forwarded a paper "which was I believe intended to have come officially from the late commander-in-chief." It was written in a fine hand, and unsigned:

When Lord Collingwood arrived at Minorca about the 26 February (so ill as to be unable to apply to business but of the last moment) a Spanish Lieut. Colonel de Lanti was waiting here, with a representative from the Junta of Majorca, stating that they had come to the resolution of getting rid of the French Prisoners about 4300, who were confined in the Balearic Islands, principally on Cabrera—the reason,—their inability to maintain them, having already advanced upwards of 100,000 Dollars above the remittance some months since sent from the Central Junta.

The Junta of Majorca were desirous of Lord Collingwood taking charge of these Prisoners, and send[ing] them to Malta or England, —in short to do what he pleased with them, provided they were taken away. Symptoms of discontent bordering on revolution had appeared among the Majorquins and the Junta could not think of levying further Taxes for the maintenance of the Frenchmen, and had therefore come to the above decision, to get rid of them.

Lord Collingwood replied that it was a subject of great moment, and exclusively came within the cognizance of the Government of Spain, as the prisoners belonged to the Nation, but that as a representation relative to the disposal of the French Prisoners at Cadiz similar to this from the Junta of Majorca had been submitted to His Majesty, his Lordship apprehended that decision would equally apply to those in the Balearic Islands, and as soon as he was in possession of it their Excellencies should be immediately informed.

Colonel Lanti's oral communication was to enter into an arrangement for the Prisoners being put into the possession of the British, by embarking them ostensibly for some place with Flags of Truce, and then to be met and seized by the English.

Since prisoners of war could not properly be transferred from one nation to another, the Spaniards—Lanti suggested on behalf of the Majorcan junta—would simply launch the prisoners out to sea in transport ships to be captured by the Royal Navy. The British commander replied with a show of scepticism.

> Lord Collingwood informed him of his reply to the Junta, and at the same time stated it to be an extremely delicate affair, as establishing a precedent of practice at present unknown among European Nations, that of turning Prisoners made by one Power over to another, and by way of example drew a case.
> —Suppose from any circumstance France and Turkey or one of the Barbary States should coalesce against Great Britain, and by the chance of War the former got possession of a number of British Prisoners, the French in such event might deliver over men to their ally for slavery,—and adduce our own example as a sufficient justification.[25]

This kind of folly might end with Englishmen enslaved at the oars of Algerian galleys! Collingwood's example was far-fetched, but the reply was also respectful and gently ambiguous: it meant discouragement and delay, certainly, but not outright rejection. The admiral promised to inform the British minister at Cádiz of the indelicate Majorcan proposal, and subsequently did so. It was a signal of Majorca's desperation.[26]

Meanwhile the new British ambassador in Spain, Henry Wellesley, confronted another strategic dilemma. (By this time Britain's relations with the besieged Spanish government were an unusually close family affair. The military field commander in Spain and Portugal was General Arthur Wellesley—now created Viscount Wellington for his victory at Talavera—while the British foreign secretary was his elder brother Richard, Marquis of Wellesley. Richard had enjoyed a brief term in 1809 as the first ambassador to wartime Spain before returning to London and handing over the ambassadorship to his youngest brother Henry.) The Spanish regular armies in the peninsula were near collapse, and the remnants of the Spanish navy remained idle in harbor, dangerously accessible to capture by the French occupiers at the gates of Cádiz and Cartagena. The Spaniards insisted on keeping several of their best fighting ships in Cádiz prepared to evacuate members of the government and state property to Spanish America in the event of a complete French victory in the peninsula. And despite the efforts of March and April 1809 to clear the Cádiz hulks of French prisoners, the prison ships had filled up again. Henry Wellesley and the local British commanders believed that imminent military danger required the removal of the prisoners and the Spanish fleet from the Bay of Cádiz; and Wellesley, stretching the limits of his broad discretion, informed the Council of Regency that Britain would accept half the Cádiz prisoners in England if they could be transported there in the Spanish ships of the line, which would afterwards return to the Royal Navy base in Minorca "where they will be secure from falling into the hands of the Enemy."[27] (Wellesley was not constrained in the least by Collingwood's "extremely delicate" precedent. If a transfer of prisoners from one power to another assisted the war effort, he would undertake it.)

The Council of Regency appeared to agree to this bargain, but hesitated for two months as it faced public criticism in Cádiz over the potential departure of Spain's ships of war from the port. Late in May, French prisoners on two of the hulks managed to cut the anchor cables, allowing the vessels to drift across the bay to the opposite shore, which was under French occupation. Wellesley wrote that "I should not have considered it of any material consequence, if a large proportion of the prisoners on board one of the pontoons had not consisted of officers, of which the enemy is probably in want." He renewed his urgent demands on the Spanish government to secure its fleet against capture and to move the prisoners to a place of greater safety (at the same time commenting to London that Spain's hesitation "is one among the various instances... of the deplorable want of energy and resolution on the part of the government.... [I]t is a circumstance, I fear, to be attributed to the defects of the Spanish character in general, rather than to be particularly applied to the characters of the individuals, who compose the Council of Regency.")[28] Wellesley's persuasive leverage in the negotiation remained his offer to send prisoners to England, and his ability to approve or deny the latest Spanish request for a British loan: but only if the remnants of the fleet would also depart from Cádiz.

In May (before the Spanish fleet had been moved) almost four thousand prisoners were despatched from Cádiz to England, most of them in British transports. In that circumstance of partial relief, the Council of Regency decided to accede to the Majorcan junta's urgent request to remove from Cabrera all the French officers held on the island, expecting that they too would somehow be included in the transfer to Britain. The Spanish foreign minister, however, neglected to report the council's decision to the British minister, who remained unaware of the decision until after the prisoners had left Cabrera en route to Cádiz in July.[29]

Despite the Majorcan junta's assurance to the prisoners that it intended to remove all of them from the prison island, its request to the Council of Regency apparently encompassed only officers and their servants; and that was what the Council of Regency approved. This was not a humane plan to give Napoleon's officers better care on English soil—though that might be its consequence. It was no more, on Spain's part, than a toss of the dice, a gamble that the Cabreran officers—once they were at sea on their way to Cádiz—would be removed to England rather than being left, against British wishes, in Cádiz Harbor under threat of rescue by the nearby French armies. The decision amounted to near fulfillment of the Majorcan plan to launch all the prisoners out to sea for capture by the Royal Navy. Since the Council of Regency had reluctantly promised to remove its ships from Cádiz as part of a diplomatic bargain, it was now pressing to get as much from that deal as it could.[30] A gamble for removal of the officers to England was a fair risk; an attempt to evacuate five times that number of prisoners, including common soldiers, was not. News of the Council of Regency's divisive edict to transfer the officers alone was not yet conveyed to the men on Cabrera.

The junta in Palma acted quickly when it received the decree from Cádiz, ordering the local naval commander to prepare two warships for escort duty and to hire a transport convoy for the prisoners. But there were difficulties on all sides: the ships were initially unavailable; the captain of the Royal Navy's brigantine

Espoir suspected that Palma was proceeding without authority from Cádiz (as in a sense it was, since there was no British knowledge of the initiative); and the fleet, once requisitioned, would accommodate less than half the officers. Envoys were sent to Minorca to contract for further transports and assure the cooperation of the Royal Navy. Gradually, over several weeks in June and July, the convoy and its escort ships gathered in Palma Harbor while the junta arranged for its provisioning.[31]

Because the ordinary prisoners knew nothing of the decision, they were unaware of the bureaucratic delays in carrying it out. On July 22, the *Espoir* made its charitable delivery of clothing collected from the British fleet for the prisoners—and sailed away without any hint of liberation. The captives were not told to prepare for departure until July 24—just two days before the relief fleet set sail from Palma for Cabrera; and even then, the decision to evacuate officers only was obscured. When the warships and ten transports reached Cabrera on July 26 the whole colony greeted them with shouts and displays of happy delirium, until the prisoners were forcefully restrained. Next day, as the restricted lists of evacuees were revealed, euphoria turned to tears and cries of despair. Common soldiers realized that they would once again be abandoned. Their officers would live comfortably in England on free parole "while we, poor devils... would be here until the departure of the last guard.... They are leaving us to our graves on Cabrera!" Just one officer, the renegade Lieutenant Vidal, chose to remain on the island.[32]

As the prisoners were segregated for embarkation, some soldiers did everything they could to escape with the officers.

What intrigues, what devices and subtleties were used to trick the Spanish commissioners or appease their own French officers! Passing as an aide, as a cook, as an aide-de-camp to a general; carrying on board the officers' equipment and then hiding in the most obscure corner; taking the name and the uniform of some dead lieutenant or sergeant.... All these things were considered and attempted. To escape from Cabrera was a matter of life or death; and the struggles that this provoked revealed violent egos and heroic virtues. Thus the accusations, the rages, the fistfights..., thus the generosity of giving up one's place to a brother or to a weaker comrade.... As these passions seethed, the convoy set sail on July 29.[33]

Louis Gille was among the favored prisoners allowed onto the transports. Captain Duval, Lieutenant de Maussac, Carbonnel, Thillaye, Gérodias, Boniface, the canteen-women, and hundreds of others were with him. As he prepared to depart, Gille passed on his place in the solid stone house at Palais Royal to his old friend and helpmate Golvin.

While the prison convoy was being prepared for departure, in Cádiz the Spanish government had some catching up to do. The Council of Regency's foreign minister, Don Eusebio de Bardaxi y Azaña, wrote to the British ambassador to tell him what was afoot and to plead belatedly for his help.

In consequence of the events that occurred in the island of Majorca, in the month of April last [sic], on account of the excessive number of French prisoners in that island, the Superior Junta of the said island, entreated the Council of Regency of these Kingdoms, to remove from them at least, the Generals, Officers, Serjeants, and Sailors, which were those prisoners who in addition to the uneasiness they gave,

occasioned an expense that could not be supported. The
Council promised to accede to their desires, and consequently
the said Junta has apprized us, that it is about to send to this
Bay eight hundred and seventy six prisoners of the above-
mentioned description, which may be expected every moment,
the Council of Regency on this account [reflected on] the
serious importance of these prisoners being allowed to remain
in this Bay at this season, and under the present circumstances,
commands me to submit to your consideration, and to entreat
you most earnestly, as I now do, that you should have them
sent to England, whereby you will render a most important
service to Spain, and will relieve His Majesty from a charge
most serious, under whatever point of view it is considered.[34]

Wellesley replied in tart language that the Spanish government
had done nothing to fulfill its repeated promises to remove its
fleet from Cádiz to a place of security. Instead the squadron
remained "exposed to every accident that may occur in the Bay
and … of no kind of service in its defense."

Under these circumstances I feel it to be my duty explicitly to
declare to Your Excellency that until there shall be at least an
appearance of an intention on the part of the government to
fulfill these conditions upon which alone I consented to send
to England half the number of prisoners confined at Cádiz, I
cannot comply with the application contained in Your
Excellency's letter. By a very little exertion the greater part of
the Spanish squadron stationed in this Bay might be fitted out,
a portion of it employed for the conveyance of the prisoners to
England, and the remainder sent to Minorca.
I must at the same time enter my protest against the
admission of the French prisoners into this Bay, and I cannot
help observing that if the Spanish govt. had no means of

disposing of them without my assistance, it would have been as well if they had consulted previously to their removal from Majorca.[35]

By this time the transport ships were at sea. A resolution of the diplomatic impasse was necessary. The rebuke prompted Bardaxi to inform the British ambassador in solicitous tones on July 31 that the Council of Regency, "impressed with the most anxious desires to satisfy you & to fulfill exactly the stipulation with His Britannic Majesty,... has made dispositions without losing a moment, for the preparing to sail from this Bay the ships *Príncipe, Sta Anna, San Justo, Neptuno, Paula, & Glorioso*" to places of security in either Minorca or Cuba. Since the Spanish navy could not provide crews for four of these ships, the Royal Navy agreed to do so for their journey to Minorca, and at last, on August 6, 1810, the remnants of the Spanish fleet set sail from Cádiz for safe harbor under British protection. In return, Henry Wellesley gave his permission to remove the drifting French officers to detention in England.[36] The Majorcan junta and the Council of Regency had won the toss for the prisoners, if they had lost the reassurance of Spanish warships in port at Cádiz.

When the prison convoy reached Gibraltar after a listless journey of eleven days, there was a flurry of tension between the Spanish and British captains: while the Spanish commander still expected to take the prisoners onwards to Cádiz, Captain Mitford of HMS *Espoir* insisted that they were to go ashore at once on British soil. Mitford knew where dominant power lay, and maneuvered his ship to block the convoy's departure. The Spaniards prudently conceded the point. The French General Privé noted gratefully in his journal: "11 August. This morning, the English took command of the Frenchmen who were on Spanish ships and transferred them to their own vessels, without advance warning to our Spanish guards."

In Gibraltar Bay close to the Rock, the senior French officers were ceremonially piped aboard HMS *Espoir* to dine on deck under a tent decorated with French and British flags, and then escorted ashore to view the local sights. For three days more they were entertained at a lavish series of banquets and receptions in Gibraltar town. General Privé wrote of one evening at the officers' mess of the Ninth Infantry Regiment: "The meal was splendid and, as long as it lasted, an excellent orchestra played charming musical pieces followed by French patriotic tunes. When we left the table we were taken on an agreeable walk, where the prettiest women of the town displayed their finery and their graces...." Privé was impressed. "The English officers vied with one another to make us forget—if that were possible—the horrible period we had spent with the Spaniards. The Spanish officers who witnessed the honors we received from their allies could not hide their astonishment; they did not realize that, among civilized nations, military men only recognize enemies on the battlefield." But he added a few words of balance: "Nevertheless, I must say that I met several among them for whom honor, justice, and humanity are not unknown; if I have not named them in this journal, it is only out of consideration for them. Their countrymen would not pardon them for being kind to us!" (Two of those who qualified for Privé's guarded praise were Don Antonio Desbrull, the Cabrera commissioner, and General Nazaire Reding, the Palma commandant, who had combined to save the officers' lives a few months before. Another officer expressed similar sentiments about Reding in his own memoir: "This noble military man did all he could to make our position tolerable, and this to the peril of his own life, for if the overexcited Spaniards had ever known the cordiality with which he treated us, they would probably have massacred him.")[37]

On August 21 the French were put onto English transports destined for Plymouth and Portsmouth. In England the officers were granted liberty on their own word of honor, while the sergeants were detained in Porchester Castle. There Louis Gille spent three relatively agreeable years—well dressed, well fed, consorting with his masonic friends, studying mathematics, making artificial flowers for sale, and performing in the prison theater under a director from the Théâtre Français. Exile and confinement were still grating; but the contrast with life on the desert island was profound.[38] Meanwhile the British foreign secretary warned Cádiz in November that "the Spanish govt. should desist from the practice which they have lately adopted, of sending from their prisons detachments of French prisoners to be confined here, and maintained at the expense of Great Britain."[39]

❖ ❖ ❖

AS THE SHIPS LEFT CABRERA, the remaining prisoners fell into melancholy. "In the hearts of all who witnessed it," wrote one of the departing officers, "the memory will remain of the farewells and the cries of those eighteen hundred unfortunates. Long after our departure, we could still see them through the telescope, perched on the rocks and waving their arms at us." The disappearance of the officers marked the moral low point of life on the prison island. The captives' previous disappointments had been imposed on them by unkind fate: but this abandonment was the choice of every officer who boarded the transports and left his men behind.

All the officers, in good health or bad (aside from the disgraced Lieutenant Vidal), went onto the transports freely. Former councillors, surgeons, and pharmacists departed with the rest. What justified an abandonment in 1810 that councillors and doctors had refused in 1809? Where was the honor that had previously kept a few commanders on Cabrera with their men?

On one side of the moral balance, the prospects on Cabrera were more bleak than ever. No end to the war was in sight. No one believed any longer that the desolate imprisonment was temporary. Everyone knew that thirst and starvation could strike again at any time. It was hardly an exaggeration to say that those who remained were being left to die. Even for the hardiest spirits among the officers, the instinct for survival was bound to assert itself.

On the other side of the balance, councillors and physicians could tell themselves that they had done all they could for their troops, that Palma had grown more sensitive to the islanders' plight, that the seriously ill were being cared for in Majorca, that more transfers off the island might follow, that fresh contingents of prisoners (including officers) would soon take their places on the island. But despite all the rationalizations, the departing transports carried with them a cloud of guilt and shame.

After so many disappointments, some of the prisoners clung only to the stoic faith that "in truth, we could count only on ourselves to escape the abyss."[40] They comforted one another, keeping close to their companions in the hours that followed. The common mood of the abandoned prisoners was deeply troubled.

> The resigned and the blasphemous, the intrepid and the apathetic, the calm and the agonized: all of them mixed with one another. Many broke into tears; not a few threw themselves onto the ground, seized by violent shaking. A kind of collective epileptic fit swept the whole colony; and after that frenzy of the first days there was a wild silence, a wave of desire for escape— or for bloody reprisal. And thus things remained for a year, and another, and another, until four had passed, with their scorching summers, their shortages of water, their winters and torrential rains, their hungers, their continuing death....[41]

Just before the disappearance of the officers, as high summer approached, the seamen of the Imperial Guard had begun preparing a gala celebration and show of defiance in honor of "the feast of Saint Napoleon." These career soldiers (for despite their title, they were not sailors) were always the most disciplined and defiant of the prisoners. In their quarters near the harbor entrance just below the castle, they saved portions of each day's rations for a full month, and determined—despite the latest calamity, and now nursing a deeper sense of bitterness—to hold the fête as planned on August 15. The building was cleaned and festooned with garlands; the store of food was laid out on a deco- rated table; and throughout the day the feast was served, toasts were drunk in fresh water and wine, stories were told, and there was increasingly frenzied singing and dancing. The celebration climaxed that night in a parodic and blasphemous act of com- munion, as the prisoners ate the minced remains of a roasted cat, drank water declared to be transubstantiated into champagne,

toasted the Emperor Napoleon and Cabrera in their wild inebria-
tion—and then "slept satisfied," worn out and innoculated briefly
against despair.[42]

Soon afterwards Henri Ducor and five friends secretly built a boat
and stocked it with supplies; but as they prepared to launch it, they
decided that it would not hold them all. Ducor reluctantly withdrew
from the party, and watched his fellow prisoners cast off, undiscov-
ered, into the darkness. He remained in captivity for another year.

Through 1810, 1811, and 1812, new shipments of French prisoners
arrived on the island from mainland Spain, in groups ranging
from a few dozen to more than one thousand. By February 1812
official calculations showed that a total of ninety-four hundred
prisoners had been deposited on Cabrera since the spring of 1809.
In fact the population of the island was considerably smaller,
since several thousand had died and hundreds more had been
transferred to England or gone over to the opposing armies.[43]

The sources disagree on whether island life was harder or easier
after the departure of the officers in the summer of 1810. The Majorcan author Miguel de los Santos Oliver wrote that new arrivals on
Cabrera were typically less able to survive starvation and disease
than hardened veterans of the exile. Their bodies were less adapted
to the strains of island life and their spirits suffered under Cabrera's
bleak civil anarchy. New prisoners could see the horrors of life and
death on the island with startling clarity—a perception only gradually numbed by self-protective indifference and apathy.

The community continued to reject firm supervision or discipline. Petty thievery was endemic. Drought and late shipments of
food periodically reduced the island to crisis. But in the later years

of captivity these hardships became somewhat more bearable because the colony possessed primitive housing, familiar habits of daily life, and regular commercial activity—which brought cash and goods to the island to supplement the minimal rations provided by official shipments from Palma. The junta's initial prohibition of trade with the captives remained on the books, though unenforced: each day there were independent Majorcan vendors touting their wares at Palais Royal. But the margins of comfort were dangerously narrow for those who lacked cash, goods, or talents to trade.[44]

One witness reports that the supply ships failed to arrive for a week at the end of August 1810. "Our days would have been slowly consumed in painful agony, if the English (who pitied us) had not thrown casks of biscuit and salt meat into the sea. These floated ashore and saved our lives.... But death still reaped its heartless toll in our thinning ranks. During four days of anguished waiting, the remains of more than four hundred among us ended up in the Valley of the Dead and—something previously unrelated—even some who dug the graves of their comrades breathed their last and fell into the ground beside them."[45]

The Majorcan writer Jaime Garau offered a decidedly optimistic account of events after July 1810. "The departure of the officers had a happy effect on the men who lived on Cabrera," he wrote, "for they could occupy the buildings and tents vacated by their commanders. Everything became easier, as the records of the junta in Palma demonstrate. No notable incident was reported for a long time." But Garau admits that the inadequacy of food supplies led to gradual changes in the island's administration: henceforth a larger Spanish frigate took the place of the gunships in the port, and in September 1811 both a military and a civil governor came ashore on the island to supervise the distribution of supplies. Rations were allocated more fairly; and orderly warehousing of Cabreran supplies meant that there could be advanced warnings of decreasing stocks. At least once, in October 1811, when another shipload of food failed to arrive, the prisoners were given cash as a substitute, in the hope that the market might provide what the winds had withheld.[46] By 1813, the Majorcan junta's funding of all its tasks—including the maintenance of prisoners—was eased when it decided to stimulate the economy by freely issuing its own currency and accepting sterling and French francs as legal tender.

The problem of clothing the prisoners was never resolved. The junta made no provision for clothing in its budgets. In January 1811 commissioner Desbrull and the junta encouraged the bishop of Majorca to support a fundraising appeal made by Father Estelrich to the people of Majorca. Estelrich's proclamation called for generous contributions on Christian grounds:

> ... It is true that they are waging an unjust, barbaric, and ferocious war against us, but this evil means that we must meet and exterminate them on the battlefields, while maintaining and clothing those who have been defeated and captured. The divine faith which we profess imposes this obligation on us, an obligation mutually observed by cultured and civilized nations even if they are not Catholic. Moved by the purest spirit of charity, I have been commanded by the government to offer spiritual comfort to the three thousand French prisoners placed on Cabrera, and am fully confident when I ask for your support, in spite of their crimes, as brothers in need of the most urgent charity.[47]

The appeal raised a total of 780 Majorcan pounds, including a contribution of 60 pounds from Don Antonio Desbrull himself. The money was far from sufficient to dress the prisoners adequately; but in Jaime Garau's forgiving judgment, "after this demonstration, there can be no doubt that the prisoners would not have been tormented by nakedness and a lack of warm clothes if the junta had possessed sufficient funds."

After the officers' departure, there were no further official efforts from Cádiz to arrange for transfers or exchanges of prisoners from Cabrera. The British offered no more initiatives. But in Palma, the local government made periodic attempts on its own to arrange for new transfers off the island. Twice, in 1811 and 1812, the central government vetoed Palma's proposals. Finally, in 1812—proceeding this time without any authority from Cádiz—the Majorcan junta arranged through intermediaries to send several hundred prisoners (either noncombatants or men judged to be incapable of bearing arms) from Cabrera to France. As their departure neared, the junta faced the familiar problem of providing suitable clothing for the nearly naked prisoners before they returned to their homeland, fearing that the appearance of soldiers in tatters might provoke retaliation against Spanish prisoners held in France. This time, the town council of Palma undertook a public subscription, raised close to five hundred pounds within a month, and at midyear about six hundred freshly clothed prisoners sailed for France, the belated beneficiaries of this act of Majorcan goodwill and self-interest.[48]

Palma's compassion was restrained by the junta's political realism: it knew that any mass transfers from Cabrera would weaken

Majorca's case against accepting large new shipments of captives from the mainland. The junta continued to protest that the Balearic Islands could not sustain those already on its hands. Despite Majorca's vocal complaints, a steady flow of ships carrying French prisoners was granted landing rights on the islands; nevertheless over the three years 1810 to 1812 the junta did successfully turn away twelve transports carrying a total of fourteen hundred prisoners.[49]

From time to time, in desperation at their plight, fresh groups of captives on Cabrera—in numbers that are impossible to calculate with accuracy—went over to the Spanish or British forces and made their departures into another form of captivity. As the tides of war periodically altered Napoleon's alliances, the local junta was also quick to grant freedom to prisoners from any newly independent territories of the French empire. Still, thousands remained, gathered in their makeshift houses and barracks at Palais Royal or dispersed in hermit communities across the island, the hapless victims of wartime bureaucracy and indifferent fate.

❖ ❖ ❖

FOR THOSE WHOSE SPIRITS HAD NOT FAILED, escape remained the everlasting dream. The authorities in Palma had less and less desire to prevent this kind of slow leakage from the prison island— as long as it did little damage to Majorcan lives and property. There were dozens of attempted escapes, small and large: one commentator suggests over a hundred, perhaps two-thirds of them frustrated. Conspiracies abounded, and the intrepid Henri Ducor was frequently involved. In June 1811, working secretly with a group of prisoners newly arrived from Catalonia, Ducor prepared a fresh plan to seize a Majorcan fishing boat. By this time the fishermen—knowing the dangers of hijacking in the bays of Cabrera—were reluctant to fish or anchor too close to shore. Ducor and his friends determined to seize one of the boats by throwing a grappling iron on deck and winching the vessel close enough in for boarding. Their planning was patient and meticulous. The conspirators stole a pair of grappling tongs from Father Estelrich, forged a chain of iron from an ancient cannonball, lengthened the chain with ropes, and gathered enough food and water to keep them for two weeks at sea.

On July 1 they moved their supplies and the grapnel to a cache on the west coast close to a familiar fishing ground, and began their watch. No boats were seen until July 16, when two barques came in close. Fourteen men took their places quietly for a night assault. The strongest of them, trooper Leroy of the 121st Grenadiers, was chosen to throw the grapnel; six men would hold the rope to pull the boat in after it had been hooked; four (including Ducor) would overcome the crew with a hail of rocks and then leap on board; and four more would hold the Spaniards once they had been taken ashore, to prevent any signals to the guardships in Cabrera Port. As the anxious Cabrerans waited, one of the fishing boats sailed away. But the other remained, and just before midnight the attack was launched. The grappling iron made contact, the boat was snared, the rocks hailed down, and the Spaniards— firing their weapons in panic—were noisily captured. All fourteen Frenchmen came on board, dumped the crew's fishing nets, and set sail to the northwest for Tarragona or Barcelona.

At sea in the darkness, the liberated prisoners used the fishermen's jackets as shields from the cold—and celebrated their conquest with cries of enthusiasm and embraces for the strongman Leroy. Ducor recalled their jubilant shouts, ending in ritual praise for the emperor: "Farewell, pestilential island, devil's rock! You'll never recapture us! Goodbye forever! Long live liberty! Long live France! Long live the Emperor! Our miseries are ended!"

About forty-five minutes out, a ship approached. The escapees were silent, and as it closed, they recognized the Royal Navy brig from Cabrera. The fishing boat passed near the warship, but thanks to their fishermen's clothing the Frenchmen were taken by the English watch for Majorcans. They slipped past in safety.

Next morning, before a weak wind, the Frenchmen sighted two guardships from the port, evidently giving chase. After two hours of desperate tacking, they moved out of reach. In the afternoon they were seen again and pursued by an English frigate, and once more managed to elude it. After another three days at sea, the mainland came into view, and one of the soldiers identified Tarragona in the distance. The escapees were uncertain whether the town was under French or Spanish occupation, but took the risk of raising a makeshift tricolor torn from pieces of clothing. (Tarragona had in fact been taken by the French after a destructive siege only one month before.) A ship left harbor to meet them, itself flying the French flag; when it came alongside, the captain and crew turned out to be Spanish pirates for the moment loyal to France. They welcomed the prisoners with a bottle of brandy, and led the fishing boat into port. There they were received by the French commandant and his staff, questioned, fed, and offered lodging wherever they wished in the empty town. Henri Ducor negotiated the return of the captured fishermen to the Spanish lines and eventually home to Majorca, while the fishing boat was sold as a prize for the profit of the fourteen escapees.

Ducor immediately wrote to the emperor's commanding officer in eastern Spain, Marshal Suchet of the Third Corps, to report on the distress of the prisoners on Cabrera, and was called to an interview with the marshal. Suchet offered his praise. Ducor's report was dispatched, in his own hands, to the chief of the general staff in Paris, with the advice that the escaped prisoner was a man with "great presence of spirit, much intelligence, and courage" who deserved further service. After an arduous march accompanying Spanish prisoners of war on their way to exile in France, Ducor reached Paris and delivered his messages. He located two friends who had made earlier escapes from Cabrera, and (without pause beyond a short interlude to greet his mother) was welcomed into the newly formed Sixth Company of the Seamen of the Imperial Guard—the elite unit that he admired above all after his three years' experience as a prisoner in Spain. From Paris, this young man who had joined the navy at the age of twelve to share in the glory of French triumphs, was dispatched in 1812—his zeal apparently intact—into the calamity of the Russian campaign. He survived imprisonment there as he had in Spain, and was freed in 1814.[50]

In August 1813 thirty-three prisoners under the direction of Lieutenant Mathieu Fillatreau and Sergeant Bernard Masson (both of them new arrivals on Cabrera in 1811) carried out another bold escape. When he reached the island as a prisoner, Masson was twenty-two years old, and an experienced three-year veteran of the Spanish campaign. He viewed the passivity of his fellow prisoners with dismay. "Most of our companions," he later wrote, "could see no end to their misfortunes and fell into a despair that I could not share. In my youth I had read the adventures of Robinson Crusoe and, like him, I was alert to any circumstance favorable to an escape.... There was no use waiting for help from our oppressors or from political events. Our only resources were within ourselves."[51]

To equip himself and acquire provisions for an escape, Masson knew that he would need cash. Along with an associate, Auguste Maillé, he became a woodcarver, and was soon selling small madonnas to the visiting Majorcan traders and accumulating tools, food, and silver coins in exchange. Ten months passed while Masson made plans like those of Henri Ducor to seize a fishing boat. But the plot was discovered, Masson was placed under close surveillance, and the scheme was abandoned. Twice similar conspiracies came to nothing. "I can hardly believe," the old soldier wrote in 1839, "how, after such carefully prepared failures, I had the spirit to throw myself repeatedly into these adventures.... Fortunately, a prisoner's desire for freedom and a good Frenchman's love of country are sentiments that overpower reason."

Masson grew more daring, recruiting a crew who would join him in seizing a longboat from the side of the Spanish guardship. For forty-six days they watched and labored, manufacturing ropes, masts, sails, oars, and a rudder, hoarding food and water, and secreting them in isolated caves. On the rainy night of August 19, 1813, the adventure was begun. Masson and a companion, Jean-Baptiste Rosier, entered the water and swam to the longboat, uncoiling a rope from shore as they swam. The rope was secured to the launch, the boat's cable to the frigate was cut, and on signal a gang pulled the longboat ashore. There the desperate men equipped it with rudder and oars, and rowed away in darkness to the cave where the remaining supplies had been cached.

After hours of spine-tingling (and mishap-filled) work, the boat was ready to flee south under makeshift sails, carrying sparse supplies of food and water—just sixty-two biscuits, a pitcher, and two barrels of water. Five days later the escapees reached the North African shore at Cherchell where their boat was broken up on the rocks. There they were taken into protection by a regional Algerian chief, the Khaid of Cherchell, who reported their arrival to the French consul-general in Algiers. In a dispatch to the minister of war in Paris, the consul commented that if the prisoners had landed a few miles further west, "they would have fallen into the hands of rebels, where they would have faced great danger of massacre." Because one of the consul's wartime duties involved the supervision of French privateers operating out of friendly ports on the Barbary coast, he was able to place the escapees aboard the corsair *Les Représailles* at Cherchell for repatriation; and on August 30, 1813, the fortunate soldiers set sail from North Africa headed for France or occupied Spain.[52]

Ten days later the brigantine made land at Peñíscola, north of Valencia, where the escapees joined a small French contingent under siege in the town. Masson and some of his fellows asked for authority to return to Cabrera to rescue more prisoners. The local commander refused; but the sergeant persisted in his request in the months that followed. Eventually,

> I presented myself to the governor to tell him my plan, of which he was already aware. This time, I was received as I wished to be, and strongly encouraged. In the port there were several Spanish ships captured by our corsairs. One of them was placed at my disposition with ten willing sailors and grenadier corporal Morel, who had escaped with me from Cabrera. It was important for me to be joined by someone who knew both the place and the prisoners, to help in finding comrades we wished to liberate, who would have to be approached with infinite care.... The ship was made ready with rigging, food supplies, fifty rifles, and a hundred cartridge pouches. The next day, March 1, at four in the morning, I was at sea.[53]

One league out from Peñíscola, the privateer sailed into a British convoy escorted by six men-of-war. Because the ship was flying Spanish colors, the British accepted the Frenchmen's word by loud-hailer that they were friendly and headed for Valencia. Masson sailed on towards Cabrera with the Royal Navy's good wishes. In darkness a few nights later, the ship came in briefly to Cabrera at Cala Ganduf, Masson and Morel went ashore on the small sandy beach, and the vessel put out towards Majorca to return before daybreak. The two rescuers walked in silence over the low pass to Cabrera Port where they moved from house to house, seeking a hundred of their friends without alerting the whole community to their mission and creating a dangerous commotion.

> Morel and I knew the cabins and the men that I had named; he went one way and I went another, and before long our hundred soldiers had been raised. It didn't seem safe to tell them the place where the ship would be found, so we limited ourselves to saying that the meeting place would be at the camp's spring. Unfortunately, the joy with which they received this

unexpected news meant that about half of them failed to
identify the correct rendezvous point. There were only two
springs on the island: one inland and the other near the shore.
Those who failed to listen carefully believed they were to meet
at the latter. You can judge my despair, when I reached the
meeting place, to find only some of those who should have
been there. I wanted to locate the missing men. But how to do
it? We had been on land for at least two hours, and would have
to leave before daybreak. To be prudent, we hardly had time to
save ourselves. Leading the group we had—now reduced by
this misfortune to thirty-eight men—I returned on foot to the
bay with an anguished heart.

Once we were at sea, the dawn came. I had no doubt that the
noise of our expedition must have been heard, and that the
guardship would be sent in pursuit. Believing that, rather than
sailing with the wind and quickly gaining distance, I ordered
that we sail upwind towards Majorca, where no one would
expect us to be. We did so until darkness came, with all our
previous precautions. Then we tried to sail towards Peñíscola,
but the wind made it impossible. Finding ourselves on the
coast [of Majorca] facing Minorca, we decided to go ashore
there. We spent the entire day of March 6 on land, several times
answering questions which no longer alarmed me—because in
both manners and language I had adopted the tone of a true
Spaniard.[54]

Next day the ship set sail for Peñíscola, to find itself confronting
the same British flotilla as it had on the outward journey. Masson
chose boldness, dropping anchor in their midst and playing his
practised role as a Spaniard. The escapade accomplished, the corsair sailed on in darkness towards Barcelona, where the adventur-
ous band were welcomed enthusiastically by the French com-

mander Baron Habert. Masson pleaded that he had promised to bring the prisoners back to Peñíscola to reinforce its four hundred besieged French soldiers; but Habert insisted that a further voyage was too dangerous—and that he wanted such exemplary men among his own forces. The ship returned without them to Peñíscola. Thus the thirty-eight Cabrerans, along with Masson and Morel, rejoined the French armies for the final weeks of the war, while those left behind on Cabrera drew a faint draught of faith that France had not forgotten them.[55]

❖ ❖ ❖

FROM THE EARLY MONTHS OF 1812, the war in the peninsula began to turn against Napoleon's armies, as Wellington led his combined allied forces out of their protective cover in Portugal and through a series of victories in western Spain. In Cádiz, the Cortes adopted the nation's first liberal constitution, which was reflected in more centralized direction of Spain's provincial governments, a loosening of wartime restrictions on public debate, and a deepening of domestic political conflict between liberals and reactionaries. In Palma, French military reverses on the mainland (and the obvious security provided to the Baleares by the Royal Navy and an enlarged local militia under command of the English General Whittingham) meant that anxiety about a French naval attack, and the related uncertainty posed by the enemy prisoners resident on Cabrera, had diminished or disappeared.

By 1813, in this more fluid political atmosphere, the subject of the prisoners' treatment could become a matter of open public discussion for the first time since their arrival four years earlier. A flurry of new newspapers and periodicals appeared in Palma during the short interlude of freedom from 1812 to 1814 ("from bad to worse," commented the satirical paper *El Nuevo Diario del Liberal Napoleón* in its single issue of June 1813). In August 1813 one of these papers, the *Diario de Palma*, published a long article signed with the initials R.A., arguing afresh on grounds both of humanity and self-interest that the prisoners of Cabrera should be brought to Majorca.

> Humanity cries out and the heart trembles to see three thousand or more men abandoned on an uninhabited desert island, exposed to storms, naked and hungry when weather blocks the supply ships. If they were cruel and armed enemies, we would not treat them with such atrocious torments: Religion prohibits it and nature rejects it. Such conduct is never seen in the dungeons of Algiers or Tunis, nor in the brutality of the Tartars. This is no more than sending men to their graves before their deaths: Yes, the island of Cabrera is the prisoners' tomb. Is such a thing possible in Spain, at the very center of Catholicism?[56]

The initial claim to compassion seems heartfelt. What follows is more curious. Maintaining these prisoners—the writer asserts—has caused grave economic hardship in Majorca; thus the Frenchmen have not been alone in their suffering. Yet they are a potential boon for the whole community, rich in skills and talent as farmers, technicians, artists, and intellectuals. They would make good citizens. Meanwhile, wartime over-regulation has paralyzed commerce on Majorca, while indolence, apathy, and ignorance have plunged the villages of the island into destitution.

Here, it appears, speaks the cosmopolitan free marketeer, the prophet of liberalism and progress, the enlightened heir of Adam

Smith, Jean-Jacques Rousseau, and Napoleon himself, almost a Frenchman of the Revolution. All this has the tone of bitter caricature. Dividing the prisoners among the communities of Majorca, the writer continues—recalling the generous "Aurorista" proposal of 1809 and wildly extending its logic—would turn them, within a generation, into loyal and productive Majorcans, dedicated to their new life and no longer Frenchmen, Italians, Germans, or Poles. They would have no reason to escape, or to seek exchange; their interest would lie in their new homes. The prisoners' labor would transform Majorca into a worldly utopia, "an opulent and useful province, a place of distinction and satisfaction for all of Spain; in every respect this would benefit all humanity, the state, and its interests." The junta, the writer asks, should proceed at once with this uplifting project—or at least invite the central government to undertake it.[57]

For those who took the letter at face value the scheme might seem farfetched or mad; but it was safely fanciful talk. No one was going to act upon it. More likely, it was a Swiftian challenge to liberal fatuity, the very opposite of what it appeared to be.

At least one correspondent approved. Another, writing a week later, granted the benefits of bringing the prisoners to Majorca to civilize the island, but doubted that the goal could be achieved without complications. If these soldiers worked all day, what would they do at night but mix their seed with that of the maidens of Majorca until, one day, they possessed all its lands? This would not, he thought, be opportune. These foreigners, after all, had inherited from their ancestors all the evil and slyness that they had shown in the war on the mainland. It remained in their blood.

The writer conceded that Majorcans might be donkeys; but they would have to show more cleverness than the captives in order to control them. He suggested that the prisoners of war should work for Majorca's improvement during the day, as the previous correspondent had proposed, but be securely locked up every night. The author was certain that his own proposal could be adapted to the original plan in a way that would bring real benefit to the public and the nation.[58]

Thus R.A.'s utopian scheme was trumped in fresh mockery. And that was the extent of debate about the captives' fate in the newspapers of Palma. The exchange must have echoed some kind of continuing public gossip and ribaldry about Cabrera; probably it reflected the widespread and vicious reactionary scorn being shown towards the new political leader of the Baleares, the liberal Don Antonio Desbrull, whose concern for the prisoners had been demonstrated during his term as commissioner for Cabrera in 1809–1810. (As a local symbol of the new liberal constitutional regime, he was the target of violent protest by traditionalists throughout 1813.) If there was talk of the prisoners' plight in the councils and cafes of Palma in 1813, there was no evidence of any popular desire to give them shelter on Majorca—just as there had been none in 1809, or during the riots of 1810. Even a tolerant local governor, supported by the central government, could not ignore the overwhelming sentiment of the Majorcan population. The prisoners were destined to remain on the desert island, conveniently out of sight, until the end of the war.

5
LIBERATION

THE FLOW OF NEW PRISONERS to the desert island gave the captives an indistinct sense of the fortunes of war on the Spanish mainland. From midsummer in 1812, the tides shifted unevenly. In August Wellington's Anglo-Portuguese armies entered Madrid. Joseph Bonaparte responded by ordering his forces to abandon Andalusia, concentrating French units in central and northern Spain. In November the British were driven from Madrid and Burgos, and Wellington, in headlong retreat, took his sick and wounded armies back to the safety of Portugal. The French marshals could have destroyed them as they fled if the offensive had continued; but the cautious King Joseph halted the pursuit and inadvertently condemned his own military prospects.

In Portugal Wellington added thousands of reinforcements from home and regrouped, while the French armies simultaneously lost several regiments of the Imperial Guard and many more experienced junior officers, called away from Spain to staunch Napoleon's immense losses on the Russian and German fronts. In northern Spain, irregulars tied down large numbers of French troops. By the late spring of 1813 Wellington was on the march again, advancing rapidly through the northern provinces, forcing Joseph to abandon the entire central plateau as he moved French forces north to protect the lines of retreat into France. On June 21 Wellington decimated the French armies at Vitoria, seized King Joseph's personal wagon train with all its rich plunder from the Spanish royal collections, and pursued the French as they retreated to the Pyrenees and across the frontier. Except for some straggling units isolated and under siege in Catalonia, the French war in Spain was over. On July 1, 1813, Napoleon removed Joseph from his puppet throne as abruptly as he had appointed him in 1808.

The state of anarchy in the peninsula following the collapse of the French regime could not be contained by the liberal Cortes of Cádiz. British armies and Spanish guerrillas alike, in their exuberance, sacked the cities and the countryside. To replace his unfortunate brother on the Spanish throne, Napoleon released the Spanish claimant, Ferdinand VII, from his French captivity; and as the legitimate leader proclaimed under Spain's liberal constitution of 1812, Ferdinand entered peace negotiations with his former captor from his French place of exile in Valençay. Ferdinand's negotiators ignored the views of his liberal government in Cádiz. In December 1813 the terms of peace were agreed upon, formally returning Spain to its condition before the beginning of hostilities in 1808. The treaty provided that prisoners on both sides, wherever they were held—and including those who had taken service in the enemy armies in order to escape incarceration—would be repatriated as rapidly as possible. Ferdinand's treaty of Valençay had little immediate effect. The king remained in exile on Talleyrand's estate. The war continued as the allies drove the French back into their homeland. Wellington's troops were now advancing against Napoleon in southern France, and Marshal Blücher's Prussian armies were moving towards France from the north. The prisoners on Cabrera remained ignorant of negotiations and the disposition of the armies. The emperor, as usual, had more pressing affairs on his mind.

In Palma the arrangements for provisioning Cabrera had been further improved and simplified in 1813, under the experienced and enlightened direction of Don Antonio Desbrull, for a brief period the political chief of the Baleares under the liberal constitution.[1] Cabrera's newly resident military governor, Lieutenant Baltasar Fernández (accompanied by his wife and servants), kept a nervous eye on the disorder around him, while Father Estelrich maintained his disapproving pastoral watch. The record no longer makes clear who spoke for the captives. Time had stopped. On the best of days, boredom was the common fate. The seasons came and returned: scorching summers, rainy autumns, chilling winters, once-hopeful moments under the warming spring sun. Rumors swept the camp in 1813 that the new military governor's wife had been caught in flagrant lovemaking with a prisoner, and banished to Palma by her angry husband. Thefts of food and minor acts of violence could not be controlled. The makeshift markets of Palais Royal carried on their daily trade. In Palma, a complainant protested to the city council in March 1814 that obscene wooden statues carved by the prisoners were on sale in Majorca, an evil that "threatened the innocence of the young, the self-control of adults, and scandalized our elderly."[2]

Through the early months of 1814 the French emperor's retreating armies fought rearguard actions in Italy, the Rhineland, the Low Countries, Catalonia, and southern France, until Paris itself fell to Prussian forces moving in from the north on March 30. At last Napoleon's ministers and marshals deserted him, and on April 4 he abdicated, banished to the island of Elba with a guard of four hundred men, but retaining the title of emperor. In defeat

Napoleon too would know island exile. As the emperor departed, the exiled king, Louis XVIII, crossed the Channel from England to take the throne of France; and ten days later his provisional government signed a general armistice agreement with the allies. In mid-April the Spanish king returned from France to Madrid; and with the support of traditionalists, church, and army, Ferdinand dissolved the Cortes and undertook a brutal purge of liberals and constitutionalists. In both France and Spain the counterrevolution had triumphed; the absolute monarchy was restored. Spain's exiled king—known throughout the war in Spain as "Ferdinand the Desired" because he represented the dream of liberation—revealed himself in power as a ferocious and reactionary absolutist, setting the pattern for a century-and-a-half of extremist conflict and failed parliamentary liberalism in the peninsula.

A series of bilateral, local armistices and military orders renewed the call for an immediate return of prisoners of war to their homelands. The captives of Cabrera knew nothing of their pending change of fortune until early May 1814, when a schooner flying a white flag entered the port. A crew member on the mainmast cried out repeatedly "Liberty! Liberty!" to the astonished inhabitants. Word passed rapidly through the camp. Still there was scepticism—until the vessel's French captain climbed to the castle to inform the governor, while his first mate announced to the prisoners that Napoleon had gone and Louis XVIII had become king. What they saw in the harbor was the flag of the Bourbons. The fervent admirers and loyal soldiers of the emperor absorbed the unlikely news: they would be liberated by the old monarchy. Whatever the source, they would be free men! Santos Oliver described the scene:

An incomparable happiness seized everyone. Some seemed to lose their minds: they broke into nervous and incessant laughter. Others embraced, crying, lacking words. The schooner's commander ordered a distribution of wine; sailors and soldiers, Frenchmen and Spaniards, poor fishermen from the fleet, all were overcome by the same flood of emotion. They walked about, they ran, they leapt into the air, they let out incoherent shouts. After dark the schooner was illuminated, rockets were fired, and music played on the quay. An enormous bonfire burned in the camp; everyone carried firewood, and no one slept.[3]

Next day the messengers sailed off, promising to dispatch a fleet of transports to take away the prisoners. The exiles organized search parties to scour the island, informing the hermits hidden in remote caves that liberation was at hand. Father Estelrich and Lieutenant Baltasar (facing the final collapse of their precarious island empire) decamped on a departing guardship. In Louis-Joseph Wagré's account, "the impertinent priest" asked for one final proof of the prisoners' friendship before he left Cabrera: a letter of commendation for his zealous assistance during the long internment. The captives' reply was sardonic: they must have regained their freedom because his walking stick had flowered and their tent posts had taken root. As for his request, "... we are ready to swear to all the humiliations you have imposed on us, and all the offences you have committed at our expense. If you will wait here, we promise that on our return we will sign your cer-tificate of good conduct."[4] This confection, published more than twenty years after the event, has more the ring of fable than of fact. The truth it conveys is emotional and literary. If no one actually said these words to Damián Estelrich, someone surely felt them. And they add a nice flourish to the prisoners' story, the insolent priest at last helpless and rebuked, his worldly empire forever abandoned.

Eight days later a frigate, a brig, and two cargo ships arrived from France to rescue the internees. A young ensign on the frigate *Zéphir*, writing to his sisters, described the island:

> It is impossible to picture a scene so strange and horrible as the one we saw on this island: Imagine a totally barren rock, not a tree, not a house, the climate scorching in summer; and in winter, often enough, a stinging north wind. Add to this complete isolation from everything living, except for a few visiting fishermen and some hovels and caves to shelter from the storms. This was the place chosen by the savage Spaniards to hold nine thousand French prisoners. Today, only three thousand survive; the others have perished from hunger, thirst (there is only a single spring, trickling drop by drop, on the whole island), the heat of the sun, and the cold.
>
> The labor of these unfortunates has created a small camp made of bramble and thorn to shelter them from the weather. Others have retreated into caves; a large number, for several years, have been totally naked, while some have only a shirt or a tattered pair of trousers. The Spaniards sent them, from Majorca, just enough to sustain their miserable existence: but sometimes the bad weather delayed the food ship for up to eight days. Then they either died or had the strength to live on a diet of roots.[5]

Since the convoy could not carry away the whole population of Cabrera in a single journey, there were disputes about the order of departure. Should the ill, or those longest on the island, be the first to go? The argument was prolonged for three days, until the seamen of the Imperial Guard pleaded for generosity: the weak should go first. So the sick were taken on board for Marseilles; and a week later the convoy returned for those who remained.

As they prepared to depart, the last prisoners engaged in a boisterous orgy of destruction, sacking and burning the supply shed and the governor's apartment, burning their own primitive homes, the taverns and shops, even the cistern theater, "... as though all these things were accomplices in our torments, and their destruction an act of revenge demanded by our ill-feeling."[6] The French naval commander protested in vain. As the fleet sailed out of the bay with the ruins of Palais Royal behind them, some of the freedmen sang their long-awaited "Farewell to Cabrera," composed in hope for this day:

> Farewell to cliffs and rocky slopes,
> To grottoes, deserts, ghastly caves;
> Leaving your melancholy wastes,
> Regaining the joys of hearth and home.
> Together now we raise our song
> For peace will bring us back to life
> Returning from the nether world,
> The survivors of Cabrera.[7]

The two convoys brought 3,700 liberated prisoners back to France; and by early 1815 a further 1,200 soldiers who had escaped Cabrera by transfer to the Spanish forces were repatriated. The imprecise calculations of arrivals and departures on the prison island from 1809 to 1814 made by the Majorcan authorities suggest that—of a total of about 11,800 transported prisoners—from 3,500 to 5,000, or up to forty percent, had perished on the rock. Their graves were unmarked, their bodies unidentified. Initial French estimates of about 10,000 dead seem substantially exaggerated, unless those who died on the hulks in Cádiz are included.[8]

The maritime prefect of Toulon, reporting to the French minister of marine after an official Spanish complaint about the destruction of property on Cabrera by the departing prisoners, gave this explanation of the incident:

> It is true... that the cabins were torched, but this was not an evil act: it was more the result of the pleasure felt by the prisoners at the return of peace, the consequences it brought for them, the raptures of freedom, the return to their homeland, to their families and their loved ones. What is more, these buildings were—so to speak—the property of the French prisoners who, thrown ashore and discarded on a desert island, built them with their own toil to shield themselves from the rigors of the seasons.

"I have already told you," the prefect continued, "of the frightful condition in which the prisoners were found, deprived of all clothing, dying of hunger, even reduced at times to cannibalism to prolong their sad lives for a few moments longer." The change of fortune for those who survived "should be enough—if I can put it this way—to excuse their joy and exuberance at the moment of their deliverance."[9] The Spanish request for compensation was rejected.

Fortune's wheel had turned full circle. Louis XVIII's minister of war who supervised the return to France of these captives taken at the battle of Bailén was Count Pierre Dupont de l'Etang, their own defeated and disgraced commander of 1808. Dupont had lived through the war in humiliation until Napoleon's abdication, when the restored king rewarded him with fresh (and higher) favor. Dupont was untainted by the recent military collapse and no favorite of the departed emperor, and Bailén was long forgotten.

When the rescue ships reached the port of Marseilles, the prisoners faced new trials. No military bands, no ceremonies of welcome greeted the returning exiles. Instead of disembarking on the mainland, they were put ashore on a quarantine island, "solidly surrounded by walls and guarded like a prison." The mood of the Cabrerans turned foul.

> After surviving the tests of the most frightful misfortune for the sake of fidelity to our flag, humanity and the wide sympathy we had inspired should have been enough to set us free. We shouldn't have to suffer any more; our chains were broken, and freedom called us to enjoy its benefits![10]

Yet they seemed doomed to a further forty days of captivity. When the prisoners were moved to quarantine barracks only slightly less harsh on the mainland, they guessed that they were being punished for allegiance to the exiled Emperor Napoleon. The suspicion was confirmed by a visit from the camp commander. He listened to their tales of suffering and responded that their fate was the responsibility of that great usurper and murderer now in detention on the island of Elba. Voices murmured in protest.

> "Do you mean," General Lobau cried, "that in spite of all the evil he has done to you, you still love him?"
>
> "Yes, we will always love him," the most rash among them yelled.
>
> "Well, in that case," the general replied, "I despair for you.

The king's orders are that you will be divided into companies,
and the regiment you form will be transported to Corsica
tomorrow on two frigates waiting in the port."

Now the protests exploded: "France! France! No, we will not go to
Corsica! Sooner death than a second exile!" Lobau and his companion officers were threatened with violence.

By this time friends and family members of the Cabrerans were
waiting in Marseilles for their release. When they heard reports of
the commotion and the reason for it, they were joined outside the
barracks by other sympathizers. The prisoner Sébastian Boulerot
recalled the scene:

> Suddenly we heard a noise like the ocean breaking against the
> rocks. Vague at first, it grew until we had no doubt that it was a
> giant mob coming toward the prison. It was the women of
> Marseilles who—at the news of the cruelty intended for us—
> rose up generously together as one!

On both sides of the entrance, inside and out, prisoners and rescuers battered with shoulders, fists, and clubs until the doors gave
way. When the crowds surged together and the mob saw the Cabrerans for the first time, all voices suddenly went silent.

> Our shabby and half-naked condition made an indescribable
> impression on the crowd that blocked the passage and
> surrounded us. They thronged around us with expressions of
> pity, without daring to question us because the signs of our
> suffering spoke for themselves and said more than we could. It
> was a matter of who would first offer us a hand, an arm, or a
> word of consolation.... We were all mixed together without
> distinction: misery and humanity could hardly be separated.

Tears poured from every eye as though the prodigal son had returned. The skin infections affecting some of us were no obstacle to the handshakes and embraces that left us breathless. They saw us all as brothers and suffering companions. Everyone looked for acquaintances, but our changed and disfigured features made [recognition] impossible....[11]

The prisoners streamed out of the broken gates among the swirling masses, cheered on by more crowds in the streets and on the balconies. Twice terrorized by the mob in Cádiz and Palma, they received its rewards in Marseilles. Coins rained down on their heads; they were pulled into cafes for food and drink; shirts, trousers, cloaks, and shoes were thrust into their hands to replace their rags. The carnival of generosity continued through the day. Fearing the enthusiasm of this rabble, General Lobau issued urgent orders that the Cabrerans should return to barracks at Fort Saint-Nicholas for the night. His commands were ignored. Most of the liberated prisoners preferred to cling to their freedom by walking out of the city in shuffling clusters, heading homewards with the solid earth of *la patrie* beneath their feet. Within days the government in Paris acknowledged their initiative and sent out maps, travel warrants, and medical aid to all the Cabrerans they could find on the roads leading away from Marseilles.[12] As the prisoners reached their destinations, the families of the thousands who died at Bailén, or on the hulks of Cádiz, or on the prison island, would learn of their deaths only by their continuing absence.

6
MEMORY AND FORGETTING

M OST OF THE SURVIVORS OF CABRERA were still young in 1814. They returned home to recover and rebuild their lives as officers, policemen, bureaucrats, farmers, engineers, architects, wine merchants, fishermen, laborers, butchers, tailors, doctors, drummers, shoemakers, masters and servants of all the trades and professions. Henri Ducor, the observant and ingenious sailor who traded his uniform with a soldier to get onto the Majorcan transports, had escaped from Cabrera and was rewarded with service in the Imperial Guard. He was demobilized to Le Havre in 1815, where he became a steamship company agent and reserve officer. His memoirs of the adventure were published in 1833.

Louis Gille, the literate and observant Parisian conscript, returned to France from England, was appointed secretary of the military college of Saint-Cyr, and later became an eminent Paris magistrate. He was named a knight of the Legion of Honor under the Emperor Napoleon III. For years he intended to publish the story of his wartime experiences but never did so. When he looked at his diaries in 1860, Gille laughed at the exaggerated "declamatory style of the Empire and the Restoration," and put them aside. His son Phillipe regarded the rococo language as a charming evocation of another era, and a true reflection of a man "full of integrity and simplicity, brave without being vain, a patriot above all." He edited the manuscript memoirs for publication after his father's death in 1863.

When the Napoleonic wars ended, the apprentice baker Louis-Joseph Wagré, "Corporal of the Fountain" and captive entrepreneur, returned to the trade of his father and became a master baker. Some of his "more literate friends" shaped his reminiscences into a book, which was first published in Paris in 1828. Later versions—adding further episodes to his Cabreran adventures, which were probably those of another prisoner or prisoners—appeared in the 1830s and were reprinted for the rest of the century.

Robert Guillemard, Cabrera's self-proclaimed theatrical impresario, retired from his military career in his late thirties in 1823. He dreamed of the glorious past, recalling that "the dazzling illusions, with which more than once in my life I had a right to flatter myself, have altogether disappeared amidst the solitude of a wretched village." In 1826, still bedazzled by Napoleon's genius, he published his romantic wartime memoirs. "Methinks I hear the words of that king of kings, who was only the first soldier of his army, and who shared in our toils as we shared in his renown. I was then proud of my lot and would say to myself: *I too was one of the Grande Armée!*"[1]

Charles Frossard—another career officer—handed his manuscript memoirs on to his family. His son Charles-Auguste Frossard, born just before the Cabrera internment, became a general, aide-de-camp to the Emperor Napoleon III, and commander of the Second Army Corps in the War of 1870. Frossard's Cabrera memoirs were first published in the French journal *Historama* more than a century after his death.

The intrepid Bernard Masson, twice an escapee from Cabrera and the rescuer of seventy-one other prisoners, was recommended for promotion to sublieutenant and to receive the cross of the Legion of Honor in March 1814. But France was about to capitulate, and Paris failed to confirm the appointment. Instead Masson became an adjutant in the Forty-second Regiment of the Line, and after the armistice reverted to sergeant in a newly constituted regiment. Back in France, he behaved heroically in a fire and was finally rewarded with membership in the Legion of Honor. Masson soon tired of the army of Restoration France, which he believed to be dominated by green and cocksure young officers he could not respect. He transferred to the Corsican police force. "Here I am," he wrote in 1839, "still in this job, happy to find in it new occasions to prove my unalterable devotion to my country." Masson's twenty-five-page account of his double escape from Cabrera offers an engaging glimpse of an irrepressible spirit. Twenty-five years on, the episode remained a high point in his life.[2]

Little can be known of the effects of imprisonment and deprivation on the surviving captives. The English historian Sir Charles Oman judged that the survivors "were for the most part mere wrecks of men, invalids for life." France (like other European countries of the period) offered no rehabilitation and kept no records about its former prisoners of war beyond their names. Medical studies in the twentieth century suggest that a high proportion of the Cabrerans probably experienced long-term stress reactions manifested in anxiety, depression, sleep disturbance, or similar complaints. Many of the prisoners undoubtedly suffered other physical ailments, the results of undernourishment, starvation, and exposure. The speed and extent of their recovery would have been positively related to their youth, their level of education, and the degree of social support available to them both during and after captivity. The hermits and recluses who survived isolation in the island's caves—those least able to cope with Cabrera's anarchic social life—probably suffered most in the aftermath. If the language of "post-traumatic stress disorder" was unknown to them, the symptoms would not have been.[3]

In 1836, two groups of former captives from Cabrera signed petitions to the National Assembly on behalf of about four hundred survivors, pleading for sympathy and support. They were common conscripts from the reserve legions, not career soldiers of the elite guard. Many of them, the petitioners said, were ill and could no longer work. They spoke of three thousand survivors and sixteen thousand dead among the captives taken at Bailén, and compared their fate to that of their brothers-in-arms on the Russian front, whose suffering and death in a brief two-month campaign had violated no treaty. The Cabrerans had endured five years in purgatory. The list of signatories to one of the petitions was headed by Louis-Joseph Wagré, the "Corporal of the Fountain," now forty-six years of age and faltering.

The call for aid remained unfulfilled. When the National Assembly debated the appeal in the following year, the rapporteur noted that the Frenchmen had suffered "contempt for the law of nations, violation of the laws of war, all the torments of their dreadful sojourn on the hulks of Cádiz Bay, and finally the hideous captivity on the island of Cabrera. . . . Their cruel situation evokes in us every sympathy that the Chamber always displays towards our soldiers." The men of Cabrera deserved public pity, and the Assembly wished that it could respond to their rightful demands; but it could not do so because that would provoke "innumerable claims of the same kind, for which the law also offers no justification."[4]

By the thirties and forties, old conflicts and old sufferings were mostly forgotten by the public as France endured its continuing domestic upheavals. The memories of Cabrera had faded into grotesque legend or tall story. In 1847, fewer than a hundred survivors of the captivity met for a service of memorial in Paris. The nation took no steps to commemorate the prisoners of Cabrera until the same month, when the Prince of Joinville, son of King Louis-Philippe, brought his naval squadron to Majorca, visited the island of Cabrera, and determined to raise a monument to his lost countrymen. The memorial stone was designed and quarried in Majorca, and solemnly installed on the prison island two months after the Prince's visit. It referred sparely to "the memory of the Frenchmen who died on Cabrera," without mention of the terrible circumstances of their exile.

Later in the nineteenth century, the island's owners planted irrigated vineyards in the central valley beyond Palais Royal in the hope of creating a wine industry; but the business soon failed. By 1907, the Majorcan editor Pedro Estelrich reported that Cabrera was populated by no more than fifteen peasant farmers, a small colony of fisherman, and a few soldiers, all of them living close to the harbor on the site of the old prison colony. Estelrich was perplexed by the contrast between the prisoners' claims that the island was "a bald rock, useless for farming" and other reports that it offered excellent prospects for agriculture; to satisfy his curiosity he visited the island in July 1906. There he found lands similar to those in the mountains of Majorca, with identical flora and fauna.

"The hillsides," he wrote, "are fertile enough, and once terraced with dry stone walls they could sustain fruit trees and planting just as well as similar productive lands in Majorca." He found superb fig and almond trees in full production, comparable to those across the strait on Majorca. But despite these favorable signs, Cabrera in 1906 offered as bleak a face to Estelrich as it had to the prisoners a century before. The hills lacked all growth because the shrubs and trees were constantly devastated by goats. "The name of the island," he concluded, "indicates that the trees have been ravaged from antiquity by the most destructive of domestic animals." To recover the land, he judged, the goats would have to be permanently expelled. Beyond that, there was the problem of adequate water supplies: Estelrich estimated that the single freshwater spring that had supplied the prisoners would not support more than a thousand residents in a dry year. He called for reforestation of the island, which would draw fresh rainfall. But despite all the drawbacks, the visitor was moved by what he saw. Cabrera harbor "is so beautiful, so tranquil, so clear and protected from the winds, that it seems more like a lake than a corner of the sea. No port in the Baleares compares to it, and a day will come when its beauty and freshness will be recognized to create a summer residence and a sea-bathing place that will be an enchantment, surpassing all others in this so beautiful Mediterranean.... Its air is so pure that it restores health to all who breath it...."[5]

Soon after this visit, Cabrera became a Spanish military camp, populated by a small establishment in the port that was swollen by temporary summer invasions of army recruits in training. Fishermen continued to harvest Cabrera's waters, and in the twentieth century yachtsmen made it a familiar overnight haven. Late in the Franco era, a developer drew up plans for the kind of summer resort dreamed of by Pedro Estelrich; but the plans lay dormant as speculators invested their capital in Majorca's beachfronts. In 1991, after years of campaigning by environmentalists on Majorca, Cabrera was designated as a nature reserve and the National Park of the Balearic Islands. Today the island shimmers in the dazzling Mediterranean light while the winds still blow on the castle ramparts. A sprinkling of tourists in excursion boats marvel at the turquoise waters in the caves of Cala Ganduf. Blue-black lizards bask and scuttle on the walls above the port. The goats are long gone, and the pine forests have renewed themselves and advanced closer to the harbor on both north and west. The dusty trails tramped out from the port by the prisoners of 1809 still survive, while on the stony plaza of Palais Royal no relics of the Frenchmen's town can be found. No hills or valleys, no bays or promontories, bear their names. But high up on the ramparts, alone with the winds, the names of two soldiers of France remain, chiselled deeply into the castle wall. "Fleury. Grapain," they have written, "prisonniers en 1810."

❖ ❖ ❖

THE CABRERAN ADVENTURE WAS DEADLY FOLLY. The prison camp was the product of a chain of circumstance leading inexorably—if unpredictably—from the overweening ambition of Napoleon Bonaparte. On the scale of human suffering, Cabrera was just one of the emperor's small disasters among all the horrors of the Peninsular War. Within that larger panorama, the fate of the prisoners of Bailén was born of a few key events: Dupont's spectac-ular mismanagement of his armies in the field; the calculated British and Spanish decision to violate the terms of surrender by keeping the Frenchmen in Spain; the removal of the captives from the hulks in Cádiz Harbor for what might conceivably have been more tolerable detention in the Balearic Islands; the Majorcan and Minorcan refusal to accept the prisoners on the main islands; the British veto on an early exchange; and so on down to all the details of inadequate provisioning, shelter, and care on the prison rock. Even when goodwill and occasional generosity in Palma softened the harsh realities of life on Cabrera, the result was a cruel captiv-ity. Grand strategy took no account of a few thousand distressed and isolated prisoners in the care of an impoverished local govern-ment. Reason of state was an unfeeling god.

Spanish treatment of the prisoners of Bailén was not markedly different from that offered by Spain's allies or the French enemy, though it was more haphazard because the rebel governments remained weak and impoverished. When confronted with so large a mass of captives, the authorities could only improvise. Civilian bystanders on the roads and in the towns—when they had the opportunity—demonstrated their prejudice, fear, and vengeful spirit in acts of wanton cruelty towards the prisoners, as ferocious mobs have always done when balance and civil authority break down. The military and civil authorities rarely challenged the hos-tile sentiments of the crowd, preferring cautious efforts to calm them by appeasement. But when they were able to deliberate in relative calm, the authorities could act with measured (or trou-bled) responsibility—and sometimes with spontaneous kindness.

Despite what the prisoners may have believed in their moments of despair, the governments of wartime Spain did not set out intentionally to kill prisoners of war away from the battlefield. But they lived in a lawless world without benefit of rules to guide them; and local officials, who found the prisoners thrust on them by default and against their will, never had the resources to supply or care for them adequately.

Another century, and more bloody wars, would pass before the conscience of mankind could be imperfectly reflected in formal international declarations and treaties aimed at the protection and care of prisoners of war. These documents initially codified existing practices, and gradually elaborated on them. The Brussels declaration of 1874 on the treatment of prisoners remained unratified, and the Hague Conventions of 1899 and 1907 achieved uneven acceptance during the First World War. The Geneva Convention of 1929 was more generally recognized (although with vast and horrific exceptions) during the Second World War. The Geneva Convention of 1949, which was widely ratified, for the first time treats the status and care of prisoners of war comprehensively; but it has failed to protect combatants and civilians taken prisoner, or kidnapped and held hostage, in the many domestic conflicts of collapsing states that erupted late in the twentieth century. The gradual extension of international law since the Napoleonic Wars has been accompanied during the age of nationalism, imperialism, and postimperialism by a simultaneous weakening of moral restraint and the recognition of limits on the battlefield. It would be rash to insist that mankind has benefited wholly in that exchange.

Through modern eyes, probably the most anomalous distinction apparent in the treatment of prisoners of war in Napoleon's time was the one between officers and common soldiers. After the surrender at Bailén, French officers enjoyed privileges unknown to their troops: they were allowed to keep their personal possessions (including cash and some of their booty), were paid larger allowances, billeted in private houses on the march to Cádiz, imprisoned in more commodious quarters, fed better meals, transported to Majorca in a less crowded ship, and at first permitted to remain in Majorca when their men were dumped on Cabrera. Although the surrender agreement of Bailén was, in general, dishonored by the Spaniards and the British, many of the senior French officers were repatriated along with their commander within a few months. While the mob forced the Majorcan authorities to ship most of the remaining officers from Palma to Cabrera in March 1810, the allies nevertheless proceeded with arrangements to move them onwards to Gibraltar and England, where they arrived later that summer to enjoy the comforts of open detention for the rest of the war.

These privileges were reflections of Christian, chivalric, and aristocratic principles, developed as armies became professional institutions during the late Middle Ages, applied from one officer class to another, and enforced by sanction and disgrace if they were dishonored. Even in the midst of a brutal war, they reflected a civility lost to the slaughters of the late twentieth century. There was no similar respect shown towards common soldiers, who were usually unsophisticated peasants and laborers, indentured or press-ganged into unwilling service as cannon fodder.

Napoleon's revolutionary armies were a novelty in warfare. Aside from the elite professional units and the mercenary regiments, they were recruited by general conscription in annual call-ups applying across the nation, in towns and countryside, and throughout the empire's conquered territories. The Napoleonic regiments were, for the first time, citizen armies drawn from all elements of the population. The strangely intense loyalty of the French prisoners on Cabrera reflected the revolutionary spirit of the times, which acknowledged that all the sons of France and its empire shared something in equality with their emperor and their officers. They lived in a time of momentous transition, retaining the instincts of historic deference towards their betters while also sensing that the nation had changed forever. They could not quite accept—as previous generations of soldiers had done—that officers deserved privileged treatment without earning it. They had heard the revolutionary proclamation of the rights of man. When the officers were removed to England from Cabrera, the ordinary ranks showed emotions deeper than resignation at their inevitable fate: there was anger and a sense of injustice too. The considerations of humanity and the laws of war that emerged during the nineteenth century—and applied to all combatants—were a product of this revolutionary period. Logic insisted that those who fought as citizens would have to be treated as citizens, and decency demanded certain minimal standards of treatment for all prisoners of war. In 1836, when the survivors petitioned the National Assembly for support, they made this claim explicit. They had been wronged and deserved redress.

The soldier memoirists made the same point by recounting their sufferings on the battlefields, on the hulks, and on the prison island. They were doing more than telling a good story. The lesson of the witnesses of Cabrera was that—once literate—no common soldier with the pluck and good fortune to survive need remain an unknown soldier. "To serve one's country well," the master baker Louis-Joseph Wagré insisted, "it is not necessary to be able to expound Virgil or Cicero." To serve well, and to be able to proclaim it, was a kind of redemption. Bearing witness did not diminish the waywardness of mankind, the cruelties of politics, or the barbarities of war; but it was an assertion of dignity deserving its honorable place beside the calculations of emperors and generals.

Seen in long perspective, the evidence of the Cabreran imprisonment suggests that all sides acted in this affair with about equal measures of inhumanity and compassion as desperation or opportunity permitted, and none with any great and liberating acts of humanity. On all sides there were instances of grace, decency, courage, stoicism, anguish, folly, cowardice, betrayal, cruelty, and greed: the contradictory staples of human behavior.

A NOTE ON SOURCES

THERE WERE NO REPORTERS AT THE BATTLE OF BAILÉN, or on the hulks in Cádiz Bay, or on the prison island of Cabrera. The armies of Dupont and Castaños, the Royal Navy's Mediterranean squadron, and the juntas of Seville, Cádiz, and Majorca did not employ press officers to put their actions—and their official spin—on the record. But major events in the Peninsular War were reported in the press of Britain, France, and Spain on the basis of firsthand accounts, military documents, and parliamentary reports. Official materials relating to the prison island can be found in the decisions of the Spanish Junta Central, the Council of Regency, and the Majorcan Junta Superior, in the Spanish national archives, the French war archives, and the British Admiralty and Foreign Office papers. The records and communications of the armies and navies became available afterwards to historians; and the Peninsular War became one of the most closely studied subjects of military history. But the fate of prisoners on both sides of the conflict has been only glancingly treated in this vast bibliography. In Spain (with a few notable twentieth-century exceptions) this lapse may be, in the words of the Catalan writer Lluís Roura I Aulinas, "owing to a chauvinist tradition about the War of Independence, which ignores all the black Spanish episodes like that of the prisoners of Cabrera."

Accounts of life among the prisoners were written after their liberation by a handful of the captives, and published during the nineteenth and twentieth centuries. Several of these reappeared in later editions, sometimes revised. Not surprisingly, as memoirs they tend to enlarge the significance of their authors' roles; and they vary in reliability and precision. Apparently only one of them, bearing the name of Robert Guillemard, was published in an English translation in London in 1826. All are long out of print. I have relied chiefly on five of the memoirs for direct descriptions of events, and especially on those of Henri Ducor, Louis Gille, and Louis-Joseph Wagré—though some of their anecdotes must be treated with scepticism. (For example, there is just one reliable firsthand account of cannibalism; but some commentators wrote of other incidents in later years. The memoirs do not establish whether these stories arose from a single event or more than one.) While the soldiers' tales can be vague about dates and almost always exaggerate the numbers of prisoners and deaths on Cabrera, they sustain one another in the general outlines and many of the details of the story.

Through the eyes of these veterans, Spanish policy was vicious and unfeeling, its agents mostly monstrous and uncivilized. The memoirs contributed to the "black legend" of Spain in northern Europe; according to the Majorcan Jaime Garau (writing in 1907), their exaggerations were "one of the infinite ways in which the French try to influence their readers and excite indignation against us."[1] By contrast, the prisoners regarded their British naval guardians more warmly, because the Royal Navy from time to time performed small acts of mercy towards the Cabrerans. The captives had no means of knowing that the policy that halted their repatriation, delivered them to Majorca, and ruled out any prisoner exchange had been dictated from London.

There are five especially useful secondary accounts of the Cabreran captivity: Miguel de los Santos Oliver, *Mallorca durante la primera revolución (1808–1814)*, Vol. II, (1901, reprinted 1982); Pedro Estelrich, *La Isla de Cabrera* (1907); Miguel Bennásar Alomar, *Cabrera: La Junta Gubernativa de Mallorca y los prisioneros del ejército napoleónico* (1988); Théophile Geisendorf-des-Gouttes, *Les Archipels Enchanteurs et Farouches: Baléares et Canaries, Vol. 1, Cabrera, L'Ile Tragique* (1936); and Lluís Roura I Aulinas, *L'Antic Règim A Mallorca: Abast de la Commoció dels anys 1808–1814* (1985). Santos Oliver's *Mallorca* contains an expressive historical narrative of the Cabreran episode from a balanced Spanish perspective, making use of Majorcan sources and some of the memoirs; Estelrich gathers together a classic nineteenth-century physical description of the prison island, a prisoner's memoir, and a justification of Majorca's treatment of the captives based partly on previously unexploited personal papers; Bennásar Alomar examines the Majorcan official records of the affair, and gathers useful statistical summaries and documents in his appendices; Roura I Aulinas examines the social and demographic condition of Majorca before and during the Peninsular War; and Geisendorf-des-Gouttes thoroughly surveys the official and memoir records available by the 1930s. (His long account was originally published as a doctoral thesis for the University of Neuchâtel in 1936.)

Geisendorf is particularly helpful for his judgments about the authorship and credibility of earlier sources. He notes, for example, that the memoirist Louis-Joseph Wagré (whose account of the Cabreran captivity he describes as "one of the most striking for its simplicity, its tone of honesty, and an amiable candor") recounts his imprisonment after Bailén and his escape from Cabrera into further French military service in one book (1828), while claiming in a later version (1835) to have been recaptured and returned to Cabrera for the duration. Geisendorf speculates from internal evidence that Wagré, hoping to gain from public interest in the Cabrera story in the 1830s, appropriated the recollections of another, unnamed soldier and absorbed them into his own tale in his new editions. (Wagré's 1828 version of the story credits another captive with his brief account of the prisoners' treatment after repatriation in Marseilles, and makes no claim to have been present at the liberation.) He appears also to have relied upon Ducor's 1833 text in the later versions of his adventures.

Geisendorf, like others before him, expresses "certain reservations" about the identity of the author Robert Guillemard, the self-described theatrical impresario of Cabrera (who claimed in his memoir, incidentally, to have been the deadly marksman at the battle of Trafalgar who shot Lord Nelson). Guillemard's name is not mentioned by other memoirists, and his chronology of events on the island is vague and inconsistent with other accounts. An anonymous writer, Geisendorf suggests, might have called himself Guillemard, the marksman of Trafalgar, to promote his own lively memoir. Geisendorf offers the names of two prisoners, Lardier and Barbaroux, as possible authors, while another memoirist, the Swiss officer Amédée de Muralt, identifies the theater director as "a captain of artillery named Foucault."

The justificatory essay in Pedro Estelrich's book, written in 1907 by the Majorcan writer Jaime L. Garau, makes use of a remarkable collection of papers from the Desbrull family, which is now preserved in the Archivo Municipal of Palma. These documents include the surviving, handwritten manuscript records from the French prisoners on Cabrera, and a large collection of correspondence to and from the Cabrera commissioner Don Antonio Desbrull. Garau's purpose, he wrote, was not to deny "that the drama took place as it was told," but to show that it lacked "the intensity and exaggerated scale" that Ducor, Wagré, Turquet, and Gille gave to it. "What is unacceptable," Garau wrote, "is that they made such repeated sacrifices of truth for the sake of telling the story that they turned it into legend, and offered it to us as fact."[2] Garau tries to balance the legend against the official record of the Junta Superior, and in doing so sometimes tips the scale too far in favor of the Majorcan authorities. In a recent article, the Catalan historian Lluís Roura I Aulinas offers similar demythologising comments: "... we must find the balance between the record and the tendency to romanticize it: there were fewer prisoners, less that was exceptional and outrageous, lower costs for Majorca or the central state, and less heroism" than the memoirists claimed. On the other hand, he concedes that the grand themes of traditional history too—Nation, Honor, Army, Empire, Independence, Religion—turned to dust on Cabrera.[3] Reduced and measured, the legend of Cabrera re-emerges, phoenixlike, an antiheroic epic of petty inhumanity.

Gabriel Froger, who published his *Souvenirs de l'Empire: Les Cabrériens, épisodes de la guerre d'Espagne* in 1849, called himself the "chief copyist" of an uneducated artisan called Sébastian. Geisendorf identifies the source convincingly as Sébastian Boulerot, a Parisian leatherworker.

The Abbé Turquet of the diocese of Amiens, who published his *Cinq ans de captivité à Cabrera ou Soirées d'un prisonnier d'Espagne* in 1853, identifies himself as the son of a captive, telling his father's story. But Geisendorf points out sections of the book that have been "borrowed" without acknowledgement from Ducor and Wagré. (Turquet's account is republished in Estelrich's *La Isla de Cabrera* as a foil for Jaime Garau's defense of the Majorcan junta.) Similarly, the Parisian art critic Philippe Gille published the memoir of one of the last survivors of the imprisonment, his father Louis-F. Gille, after the ex-captive's death in 1863. Gille kept journals throughout his military service and imprisonment, reflected on his experiences and added to his historical knowledge in the aftermath, and left a detailed, judicious, and scrupulously fair account of the events that followed the defeat at Bailén. Further stories of the terrible episode continued to appear in France until early in the twentieth century.

In Britain, the superb manuscript records of the Foreign Office and the Royal Navy, available in the Public Record Office at Kew, reveal the leading role of Great Britain in the wartime alliance with Spain, and offer essential evidence of her influential part in creating and perpetuating the misfortunes of the Cabreran prisoners.

Two recent books have used the prisoners' memoirs as the basis for fictionalized tales of the captives' lives on Cabrera: Pierre Pellissier and Jérôme Phelipeau, *Les grognards de Cabrera (1809–1814)* (1979, also published in Spanish as *Los franceses de Cabrera*, 1980) and Jesús Fernández Santos, *Cabrera* (1981). As this book went to press, another novel about the Cabreran imprisonment, *El Emperador o el Ojo Del Ciclón*, by the Majorcan writer Baltasar Porcel, was published in Barcelona. My brief reference to water sprites as guardians of the springs on Majorca comes from Lucia Graves' inspired memoir, *A Woman Unknown: Voices from a Spanish Life*.

Historical accounts of war are (consciously or unconsciously) prone to reflect national feelings about enemies and allies. Such national stereotypes were common in so passionate a conflict as the Peninsular War, and polemical debate on the nature of the Cabreran episode that incorporated simplification and exaggeration continued for a hundred years. Spain needed the incomparable Francisco Goya to deliver the message of man's impartial inhumanity to man—whether French to Spanish, or Spanish to French—in his terrifying series of etchings, the *Disasters of War*. Among the memoirists of Cabrera, Louis Gille in particular made notable efforts to counter popular prejudices and to report the actions of both sides in the struggle with balance and honesty. As memories and passions faded, more distant observers could usually do the same. But stereotypes born of the Peninsular War (or even earlier events) remained embedded in British, French, and Spanish views of one another for almost two hundred years after the conclusion of the war, belatedly fading only with the integration of democratic Spain into the European Union at the dawn of another century. The new national images, one may hope, will be less distorted than the ancient ones.

BIBLIOGRAPHY

Admiralty Board. *In Letters to Admiralty Board: Mediterranean, Admirals' Correspondence, 1810*. London: Public Record Office: Admiralty 1/416, 417.

Amédée de Muralt, R. K. "Les conséquences de la capitulation de Baylen (1808–1810)," *Revue Rétrospective: Recueil de pièces intéressantes et de citations curieuses, Nouvelle Série*. Premier semestre (Janvier–Juillet 1890). Paris, 1890.

Archives Historiques de la Guerre, Paris. *Carton: Prisonniers de la Guerre Français, 1808–1816*.

Archivo Municipal de Palma de Mallorca. *Fons Desbrull*. XXXVI, Legajo 1,1; 2,1; 2,2; 3,1; 3,2, Comissió de Cabrera; XVIII, Cáfeta 52.

Archivo Histórico Nacional, Madrid. *Orders and correspondence relating to the French prisoners*. Sección III, Estado, Legajo 46 D. Baleares.

Bennásar Alomar, Miguel. *Cabrera: La Junta Gubernativa de Mallorca y los prisioneros del ejército napoleónico*. Palma de Mallorca: Ajuntament de Palma, 1988.

Best, Geoffrey. *Honour Among Nations: Transformations of an Idea*. Toronto: University of Toronto Press, 1982.

Bovér, D. Joaquín María. *Cabrera: Sucesos de su Historia que Tienen Relación con la Francia*. Palma de Mallorca: Imprenta de D. Felipe Guasp, 1847.

Briggs, Asa. *England in the Age of Improvement, 1783–1867*. London: The Folio Society, 1999.

Broers, Michael. *Europe Under Napoleon: 1799–1815*. London: Arnold, 1996.

Canning, George C. *Drafts from the Secretary of State to Mr. Frere, October 4–December 24 1808*. London: PRO: Foreign Office 72/60.

Collingwood, Vice Admiral Lord. *Journal of Vice Admiral Lord Collingwood, Commander in Chief in the Mediterranean (1808–1809)*. London: PRO: ADM 50/60.

Cotton, Admiral Sir Charles, Bt. *Letter Books of Commander, Mediterranean, 1808–1811*. London: PRO: ADM 7/41.

Cuming, Capt. Wm. *Captain's Log on Board His Majesty's Ship Bombay, From 3 June 1808 to 25 May 1809.* London: PRO: ADM 51/1929.

Cuming, Capt. Wm. *A log of the Proceedings on board His Majesty's Ship Bombay, commencing the 2d of November 1808 and ending the 21st July 1809 kept by W. Giekie/Masters Mate.* London: PRO: ADM 52/3887.

Dempsey, Guy C., Jr. *Napoleon's Soldiers: The Grande Armée of 1807 as Depicted in the Paintings of the Otto Manuscript.* London: Arms and Armour, 1994.

Ducor, Henri. *Aventures d'un marin de la Garde Impériale, prisonnier de guerre sur les pontons espagnols, dans l'île de Cabrera, et en Russie,* 1. Paris: Ambroise Dupont, 1833.

Durban, Capt. Wm. *Captain's Log on board His Majesty's Ship Ambuscade, 1 April 1808–18 August 1809.* London: PRO: ADM 51/1969.

Estelrich, Pedro. *La isla de Cabrera.* Palma de Mallorca: Rotger, 1907.

Fernández Santos, Jesús. *Cabrera.* Barcelona: Plaza & Janes, 1981.

Frere, John Hookham. *Letters and Papers from Mr. Frere to the Secretary of State for Foreign Affairs, October 21 1808 to December 28 1808.* London: PRO: FO 72/61.

Froger, Gabriel. *Souvenirs de l'Empire: Les Cabrériens, épisodes de la guerre d'Espagne.* Paris: 1849.

Frossard, Charles. "Prisonnier des Espagnols: mémoires du capitaine Charles Frossard," *Historama, Nos. 305, 306.* Paris: n.d.

Galdós, Benito Pérez. *Bailén: Episodios Nacionales, 4.* Madrid: Alianza Editorial, 1985.

Garau, Jaime L. *Noticias Históricas del Cautiverio de los Prisioneros Franceses en Cabrera* (in Estelrich, P., *La Isla de Cabrera*).

Gates, David. *The Spanish Ulcer: A History of the Peninsular War.* London: George Allen & Unwin, 1986.

Geisendorf-des-Gouttes, Théophile. *Les Archipels Enchanteurs et Farouches: Baléares et Canaries: Cabrera, L'Ile Tragique.* Genève/Paris: Les éditions labor, 1936.

Gille, Phillipe. *Les prisonniers de Cabrera: Mémoires d'un conscrit de 1808*. 3me édition, Paris: Victor-Havard, Editeur, 1892.

Glover, Michael. *The Peninsular War, 1807–1814: A Concise Military History*. Newton Abbot, London: David & Charles, 1974.

Graves, Lucia. *A Woman Unknown: Voices from a Spanish Life*. London: Virago Press, 2000.

Guedella, Philip. *The Duke*. Ware, Hertfordshire: Wordsworth Editions, 1997.

Guillemard, Robert. *Adventures of a French Sergeant, During his Campaigns in Italy, Spain, Germany, Russia, etc. From 1805 to 1823*. London: Henry Colburn, 1826.

Hibbert, Christopher. *Wellington: A Personal History*. London: HarperCollins, 1998.

Isaacs, A. Lionel. *The Jews of Majorca*. London: Methuen, 1936.

Longford, Elizabeth. *Wellington: The Years of the Sword*. London: Weidenfeld and Nicolson, 1969.

Lovett, Gabriel H. *Napoleon and the Birth of Modern Spain: I. The Challenge to the Old Order*. New York: New York University Press, 1965.

Madariaga, Salvador de. *Spain: A Modern History*. London: Jonathan Cape, 1961.

Marcus, G. J. *Heart of Oak: A Survey of British Sea Power in the Georgian Era*. London: Oxford University Press, 1975.

Masson, Bernard. *L'évasion et enlèvement de prisonniers français de l'île de Cabrera*. Marseilles: Nicolas, 1839; Paris: Ivan M. Labry, 1951.

Mitford, Captain Robert Esq. *Captain's Log on board Her Majesty's Ship Espoir, 1810–1811*. London: PRO: ADM 51/2406.

Napier, William (Abridged and with an introduction by Charles Stuart). *History of the War in the Peninsula*. Chicago and London: The University of Chicago Press, 1979.

Napoléon 1er, *Correspondance de Napoléon 1er, publiée pour ordre de l'Empereur Napoléon III*. Paris: Henri Plon, J. Dumaine, 1866.

Naval Chronicle, The. London: J. Gold, 1799–1818.

Oman, Sir Charles. *A History of the Peninsular War: Volume I: 1807–1809; Volume II: January–September 1809; Volume III: September 1809–December 1810.* London: Greenhill Books, 1995.

Partridge, Richard and Oliver, Michael. *Battle Studies in the Peninsula: May 1808–January 1809.* London: Constable, 1998.

Pellissier, Pierre and Phelipeau, Jérôme (Traducción de Carlos Garrido). *Los Franceses de Cabrera, 1809–1814.* Palma de Mallorca: Aucadena, 1981.

Philbrick, Nathaniel. *In the Heart of the Sea: The Tragedy of the Whaleship Essex.* New York: Viking, 2000.

Pujol, Louis. "Le repatriement des prisonniers de Cabrera (1814)," *Revue Rétrospective: Recueil de pièces intéressantes et de citations curieuses, Nouvelle Série.* Premier Semestre (Janvier–Juillet 1890). Paris: 1890.

Rathbone, Julian. *Wellington's War: His Peninsular Despatches.* London: Michael Joseph, 1994.

Roura I Aulinas, Lluís. *L'Antic Règim A Mallorca: Abast de la Commoció dels anys 1808–1814.* Barcelona: Conselleria d'Educació i Cultura del Govern Balear, 1985.

Roura I Aulinas, Lluís. "Els Presoners de l'illa de Cabrera (1809–1814)," *L'Avenc,* 78 (gener 1985), 22–28.

Salvador, Archiduque Luís. *Las Baleares: I. La Isla de Cabrera.* Palma de Mallorca: 1885, 1954 (also reprinted in Estelrich, P., *La Isla de Cabrera,* 1–29).

Santos Oliver, Miguel de los. *Mallorca durante la primera revolución (1808–1814), Tomos I, II.* Palma de Mallorca: 1901; Segunda Edición, Luis Ripoll, 1982.

Solís, Ramón. *La Guerra de la Independencia española.* Barcelona-Madrid: Editorial Noguer, 1973.

Tranie, J. and Carmigniani, J.-C. *Napoleon's War in Spain: The French Peninsular Campaigns, 1807–1814.* London: Arms and Armour Press, 1993.

Turquet, Abbé C. *Cinq ans de captivité à Cabrera, ou Soirées d'un prisonnier d'Espagne.* Lille: L. Lefort, 1853 (also reprinted in Estelrich, P., *La Isla de Cabrera,* 33–174).

Wagré, Louis-Joseph. *Les Prisonniers de Cabrera: Souvenirs d'un Caporal de Grenadiers (1808–1809)*. Paris: Emile Paul, 1902.

Wagré, Louis-Joseph. *Mémoires des captifs de l'île de Cabrera et adieux à cette île où 16,000 Francais ont succombé sous le poids de la misère la plus affreuse*. Paris: by the author, 1835, 1843–4.

Wagré, Louis-Joseph. *Mémoires d'un Caporal de Grenadiers ou le Prisonnier de l'île de Cabrera* [published anonymously and signed Le Caporal de la Fontaine]. Paris: by the author, 1828.

Wellesley, Henry. *Letters from Mr. Wellesley at Cádiz to the Secretary of State for Foreign Affairs, March–October 1810*. London: PRO: FO 72/94, 95, 96, 97.

Wellesley, Richard, Marquis. *Letters to Mr. Henry Wellesley at Cádiz from the Secretary of State for Foreign Affairs, March–November 1810*. London: PRO: FO 72/93.

Williams, Lieut.-Colonel. *The Life and Times of the late Duke of Wellington*. London and New York: John Tallis, n.d.

NOTES

NOTES TO PROLOGUE

1. Bovér, 22–23.

2. Primo Levi, *The Drowned and the Saved*, 83–84.

NOTES TO CHAPTER 1: ANDALUSIA

1. Madariaga, 59.

2. Guedella, 151; Longford, 138. Until the Spanish rising, Wellesley's army had been training for embarkation to Spanish America, where it would have fought against Spain for Latin American independence—a cause promoted in Britain by the Venezuelan adventurer Francisco de Miranda. Wellesley was cool to this expedition, and was happy to turn his attentions directly against the French enemy. If no advantage appeared in Spain within a month, he suggested that the expedition could carry on from Gibraltar to South America.

3. Glover, 53–55.

4. Gates, 50–51; Solís, 137–138; Lovett, I, 188–192. The historical novelist Benito Pérez Galdós describes the events at Córdoba in his *Episodios Nacionales 4: Bailén*, 63–64.

5. Lovett, 192–193; Glover, 53.

6. Gille, 11–28.

7. Ibid, 76.

8. Ibid, 77.

9. Ibid, 88–90, 97–98.

10. Vedel's march south and the battle of Jaén are recounted by Gille, 73–106.

11. Gates, 55–56.

12. Glover, 54.

13. Gille, 116–120; Oman (I) 621–623. As one of the quartermasters, Louis Gille transcribed the capitulation in his book of orders. The provision in the agreement calling for payment of prisoners at the rates of the Spanish army was normal European practice; but prisoners' food and lodgings were charged against their pay. The privileged treatment of officers was also common practice.

Responsibility for assuring that prisoners were adequately clothed remained a matter of uncertainty. In the earlier period of war between France and Britain in 1799–1800, the British claimed that the French were responsible for clothing their prisoners held in Britain, while the French insisted that, under a Napoleonic decree of May 1800, "prisoners of war are entrusted to the care and humanity of the nations in the power of which they are placed by the chance of war." French commissioners reported that French prisoners of war in England were being held in conditions of "dreadful meagerness," many of them "literally naked." In France, by contrast, they wrote that English prisoners "not only receive a wholesome and plentiful subsistence, but are clothed at the expense of the Republic. . . ." The disagreement was resolved in 1801 when the British government undertook "that warm clothing, proper for the season, be provided with the utmost expedition, for all French prisoners now detained in this country as the only means of alleviating their distress, and putting a stop to the sickness and mortality already too prevalent among them." The British insisted that this decision created no precedent; but the French practice seems to have been generally accepted by Great Britain during the Peninsular War and henceforth. Neither Britain nor Spain sought payment from France for French prisoners held under their care during the Peninsular War. The Spanish authorities, however, supplied no clothing to the French prisoners from public funds. (See "The Treatment of French Prisoners of War: Official Correspondence 1799–1800," in www.cronab.demon.co.uk/fpow.htm)

14. Gille, 120.

15. Amédée de Muralt, 337.

16. Gille, 123.

17. Quoted in Ducor, 68–70.

18. Lovett, 222, 226.

19. Castlereagh to Vice Admiral Lord Collingwood, August 19, 1808, Public Record Office [hereafter PRO]: FO 72/60.

20. Ibid.

21. Oman (I), 201–202, 624–625; Lovett, 224–225.

22. Gille, 125. Gille says that the massacre was witnessed by a domestic servant, who was the sole survivor.

23. Guedella, 160–168; Longford, 152–160.

24. George Gordon, Lord Byron, *Childe Harold*, quoted in Longford, 158.

25. The official mood in London was reflected in the opinion of one member of the court of inquiry, Lord Moira, who wrote in an appendix to its report in December 1808 that the British aim of destroying France's military resources had been disregarded in the Convention. Instead, Junot's army had been "extricated . . . from a situation of infinite distress" and restored, with all its equipment, to a position where it directly threatened British interests. (Oman (I), 628–630) The poet Robert Southey wrote of Cintra: "Were we then to annul this treaty with our enemies, or to betray our friends?—for to this alternative our triumvirate of generals had reduced us! No law of nations could justify them in making such stipulations; no law of nations, therefore, could justify us in performing them. . . . In whatever way we acted, some loss of honor was inevitable; but it was less disgraceful to break the terms than to fulfill them; better that the French should reproach us, than that they should compliment us upon a fidelity which enabled them to injure our allies." (Quoted in Williams, 51.)

26. Gille, 126–134; Wagré, *Les Prisonniers*, 23–39.

27. Once a central government came into existence, Britain established formal diplomatic relations with it and negotiated a treaty of alliance that took effect from January 1809.

28. Quoted in Glover, 55.

29. Wagré, *Les Prisonniers*, 40.

30. Gille, 143–148.

31. Gille, 150–161; Wagré, *Les Prisonniers*, 43–54.

32. Gille, 161.

33. Ducor, 1–13, 52–53.

34. Ibid, 56–59; Gille, 169–174.

35. Ducor, 59–61.

36. Gille, 163.

37. Ibid, 164–165, 177.

38. Wagré, *Les Prisonniers*, 1–13, 55–61.

39. Gille, 165, 167.

40. Amédée de Muralt, 343.

41. Quoted in Ducor, 90–91.

42. This account of the prisoners' life on the hulks is based on a doctor's story given to Henri Ducor and inserted as three chapters of his book. The details are from pages 91–97.

43. Ducor, 100–106.

44. Ibid, 153–154.

45. Ibid, 169.

46. Quoted in Ducor, 174.

47. Frere to George Canning, December 28, 1808, No. 42, PRO: FO 72/61.

48. Bennásar Alomar, 39–41.

49. See Wagré, *Les Prisonniers*, 61–62; Ducor, 177–183; Gille, 178–182; *Captain's Log*, HMS *Bombay*, April 3, 1809, PRO: ADM 51/1929.

NOTES TO CHAPTER 2: A DISGRACEFUL AND REPULSIVE IDEA

1. The census of 1787 showed a total population of 137,222 in Majorca, 30,264 of them in the city of Palma. (Roura, 408–409.)

2. Both Majorcan pounds and Spanish reales were legal tender in the Baleares. One pound equalled twenty sous, or approximately thirteen Spanish reales. (Roura I Aulinas, 454, 513.)

3. Ducor, 179.

4. Gille, 181.

5. Wagré, *Mémoires des Captifs*, 61–62; Geisendorf, 381.

6. Gille, 188–191; Geisendorf, 9.

7. Quoted in Briggs, 147.

8. *Journal of Vice Admiral Lord Collingwood, Commander in Chief in the Mediterranean, August 1808 to 30 April 1809*, PRO: ADM 50/60.

9. Ibid.

10. Ibid.

11. Bennásar Alomar, 15–20.

12. Ibid, 40.

13. "Actas de la Junta Superior, sesión del 27 de marzo de 1809," quoted in Santos Oliver, II, 251–252; Bennásar Alomar, 43–44; Garau, 184–190.

14. Junta Central to Junta Superior of Majorca, March 22, 1809, Archivo Histórico Nacional, Legajo 46 D., Baleares, 96; Santos Oliver, 254–255.

15. Ibid, 255–256.

16. "Actas de la Junta Extraordinaria de la Noche del 21 de Abril de 1809," in Bennásar Alomar, Appendix V, 139; see also Santos Oliver, 258–259.

17. Santos Oliver, 259–261; Bennásar Alomar, Appendix V, 141–145; Gille, 192–195.

18. Santos Oliver, 262–263; Bennásar Alomar, 51–52.

19. Bennásar Alomar, 53–55, 146–147. The information provided by the health commission contained some inconsistencies. The commission reported that there had been no evidence of contagion during the voyage from Cádiz to Palma, and that "the absence of any deaths or illnesses on the days at sea is convincing evidence of their good health." But an accompanying chart reporting illnesses and deaths on eleven of the transports indicates that there had been 39 deaths among 3,780 prisoners taken aboard in Cádiz. It may be that these deaths occurred after the arrival of the fleet in Palma, and especially during the week of May 5 to 11, when supplies had run low and only some of the prisoners had disembarked on Cabrera. Benássar

Alomar also attributes the high death toll on the island in the first months of deten-tion to the conditions on the transports in these last days on board the ships.

20. Captains' Logs, HMS *Bombay, Ambuscade,* May 4–11, 1809; *Journal of Vice Admi-ral Lord Collingwood,* May 6–8, 1809, PRO: ADM 50/60, 51/1929, 51/1969, 52/3887.

21. Santos Oliver, 264–265; Bennásar Alomar, 58–60.

22. The newly appointed commissioner for Cabrera, Don Jerónimo Batle, reported to the junta that 2,979 prisoners were disembarked on Cabrera on May 7 and a fur-ther 1,548 on May 10 after a stormy crossing. He recorded the total number of pris-oners, including those held in Palma and Mahón, as 5,255. (Garau, 203–204.)

23. Santos Oliver, 266; Bennásar Alomar, Appendix VI, 153; Gille, 195–198; Ducor, 184–189; Wagré, *Les Prisonniers,* 64–66.

NOTES TO CHAPTER 3: CABRERA

1. Ducor, 187–188; Gille, 195–197.

2. Geisendorf, 72, 74–75, 350–351. The enlisted men's rations compared unfavorably with those provided for in an agreement on prisoners of war made between Great Britain and the United States of America in 1813, calling for "a subsistence of sound and wholesome provisions, consisting of, one pound of beef, or twelve ounces of pork; one pound of wheaten bread, and a quarter of a pint of pease, or six ounces of rice, or a pound of potatoes, per day to each man; and of salt and vinegar in the pro-portion of two quarts of salt and four quarts of vinegar to every hundred days sub-sistence." (See "Cartel for the Exchange of Prisoners of War between Great Britain and the United States of America May 12, 1813," 6, in *The Avalon Project at the Yale Law School,* http://www.yale.edu/lawweb/avalon/diplomacy/cart1812.htm.)

3. Gille, 198; Ducor, 194–195; Frossard (I), 67.

4. Garau, 209–211.

5. Wagré, *Mémoires des Captifs,* 15.

6. Masson, 9.

7. Ducor, 188–190, 209–213; Santos Oliver, 289–291. None of the memoirs reports on the subsequent fate of the two children.

8. Gille, 225–226.

9. Ibid, 198.

10. Ibid, 198–199.

11. Ibid, 201.

12. Bennásar Alomar, 152.

13. Ibid, 157–158; Garau, 205–208.

14. Geisendorf, 222–223, 227.

15. The stonings were reported at second hand by one of the memoirists; another speaks of "bloody executions." There is no evidence of their occurrence in the official Majorcan records. (Guillemard, 100–101; Geisendorf, 88–91.)

16. Santos Oliver, 298; Ducor, 197–198.

17. Santos Oliver, 284–286; Bennásar Alomar, 60–64, 170–171, 175.

18. Garau, 244–245; Geisendorf, 98–102; Ducor, 202–203; Guillemard, 105.

19. Estelrich to Desbrull, November 17, 1809, quoted in Geisendorf, 108.

20. Gille, 228; Geisendorf, 108–109; Amédée de Muralt, 355.

21. Santos Oliver, 286; see also Gille, 202–204; Ducor, 217–219.

22. Maussac to Don Antonio Desbrull, October 27, 1809, quoted in Garau, 246.

23. Quoted in Garau, 246.

24. Bennásar Alomar, 70–71.

25. Wagré, *Les Prisonniers*, 97–98; Geisendorf, 116–119, 125–128.

26. Gille, 204–207; Ducor, 220–221; Geisendorf, 119–122; Santos Oliver, 292–294.

27. Santos Oliver, 293–294; Gille 207; Frossard (I), 68.

28. Quoted in Santos Oliver, 300.

29. Maussac to Pons, September 18, 1809, quoted in Garau, 228.

30. Santos Oliver, 300–302.

31. Legajo 2,1; 2,2; 3,1; 3,2;7, Fons Desbrull; Garau, passim; Bennásar Alomar, 71–74.

32. Don Antonio Desbrull, "Al tratan de obras..." September 28, 1809, Legajo 1,2, f.7, Comissió de Cabrera, Fons Desbrull; Bennásar Alomar, 72, 162–163; Santos Oliver, 302–303.

33. Garau, 242–243.

34. Gille, 208; Bennásar Alomar, 178–179.

35. Estelrich to Don Antonio Desbrull, October 17, 1809, Legajo 1,3, No. 9, XXXVI, Comissió de Cabrera, Fons Desbrull.

36. Geisendorf, 144–149; Garau, 247–251.

37. Ducor, 224–229; Santos Oliver, 298–299; Gille, 216–217; Geisendorf, 151, 356–357; Garau, 253. Other estimates of the dead ranged from eighteen to three hundred.

38. Garau, 249–251; Geisendorf, 148–149; Wagré, *Les Prisonniers*, 93.

39. Ducor recalls twelve to fifteen deaths per day; Bennásar Alomar cites slightly lower figures from the Majorcan records. The junta's medical reports show the island's population at 4,047 on October 21, 1809, and at 3,969 on November 24, 1809, for a loss of 78 prisoners during the month. (Ducor, 229–230; Bennásar Alomar, 166; "Relaciones sanitarios de los prisioneros franceses de Cabrera—Años 1809 y 1810," Legajo 1, 1, XXXVI, Comissió de Cabrera, Fons Desbrull.)

40. Ducor, 230–231.

41. Dr. Juan Cerdó to Don Antonio Desbrull, December 5, 1809, Legajo 2–1, 2, Comissió de Cabrera, Fons Desbrull.

42. Quoted in Garau, 256.

43. Ducor, 231–233.

44. Geisendorf, 81, 83; Gille, 210–216; Wagré, *Les Prisonniers*, 102, 119; Santos Oliver, 299; Guillemard, 89.

45. Guillemard, 95–96; Frossard (II), 65–66.

46. Gille, 209–211, 217.

47. Guillemard, 108.

48. Guillemard, 108–109; Gille, 217–218. Gille dates the opening of the cistern theater to November 8, 1809, when Guillemard had not yet arrived on Cabrera. Gille was probably mistaken in his dating, since this would have placed the opening just after the destructive November storm; or Guillemard may later have taken over an unfinished amphitheater and altered the motto. Guillemard's account of the details is more complete. The first motto is attributed to the Abbé Jean de Santeuil, who coined it in 1665 to accompany a portrait (or bust) of Domenico Biancolelli, famous for his role as Harlequin and one of Louis XIV's favorite performers. The epigram was later adopted by the Comédie Italienne and its successor, the Opéra Comique, with which Cabrera's Parisian players would have been familiar.

49. Guillemard, 109–110.

50. Guillemard, 110–111; Gille, 246–247.

51. Guillemard, vii, 1–2, 116–118.

52. Ducor, 246–247; Santos Oliver, 308. In October 1809 the junta sent an agent to Cabrera to review the number of healthy prisoners on the island; he reported a total of 4,020, compared to 4,074 reported by the prisoners themselves, or a minor discordance of only 54. Maussac's sworn census statement for December 1, 1809, showed a total of 3,839 prisoners on Cabrera just after the removal of 120 patients to a hospital in Palma. The figure was about 700 lower than the numbers originally left on the island in May, or about 1,700 lower than the total of all transfers to Cabrera since that time. (Unsigned document, October 8, 1809, No. 23; Maussac, Revue du mois de Décembre 1809, Legajo 1,3, XXXVI, Comissió de Cabrera, Fons Desbrull.)

53. Gille, 6–7, 207–208, 218–219; Ducor, 246–247; Guillemard, 95–96, 107; Geisendorf, 143.

54. Ducor, 186–187; Gille, 219–223.

55. Ibid, 223–228.

56. Ibid, 231–235; Carbonnel d'Hierville to Monsieur Del Rio, lieutenant de Vaisseau à Cabrera, n.d., Legajo 2, 2, No. 236, Comissió de Cabrera, Fons Desbrull.

57. Gille, 240; Wagré, *Mémoires des Captifs*, 52–54, *Les Prisonniers*, 166; Masson, 10; Geisendorf, 200, 296–298. Some sources date the incident to 1812 (when Gille was

no longer on the island), and vary the details. In a twentieth-century display of nationalist *amour-propre*, the Swiss writer Geisendorf-des-Gouttes suggests that the threadbare Swiss uniforms reported by Gille must have been unidentifiable, and could just as easily have been Polish. Froger, writing in 1849, also identifies the errant soldier as a Pole. Masson adds: "Happily this monster was not French."

58. A vivid account of cannibalism among the crew of the Essex appears in Nathaniel Philbrick's *In the Heart of the Sea: The Tragedy of the Whaleship Essex* (see especially pages 151–206).

59. Garau, 260.

60. Ducor wrote that more than 150 died in the first days of the famine. An accounting of the costs of maintaining both the prisoners and the Spanish military garrisons on Majorca and Ibiza in May 1811 prepared for Don Antonio Desbrull showed that a minimum of 277,000 reales per month was needed to maintain the prisoners. Taxes and rents on Majorca recovered only 324,000 reales per month for all purposes. (Gille, 242–244; Ducor, 239–242; Santos Oliver, 310–315; Geisendorf, 210–218; "Notice of numbers of troops on this Island, including Iviza, and the monthly subsistence they need," May 8, 1811, Cáfeta 52, File 2, Fons Desbrull.)

61. Privé to Desbrull, April 22, 1810, Appendix 15, Garau, 343–345; 281–282.

62. Guillemard, 89.

63. Admiral Sir Charles Cotton to John Wilson Croker, July 16, 1810, PRO: ADM 7/41. Cotton's trust in the Admiralty's approval probably reflects his hope that the costs would be recovered from London. A postscript to his letter notes that a full account is enclosed, "together with the ships from which the Slops in question have been furnished, and the prices of each article." The correspondence is just one indication of how closely the Royal Navy and the Admiralty Board were monitoring the incarceration on Cabrera. When the account, amounting to £622/7, was duly passed on to the Foreign Office, the foreign secretary noted that it would be "posted to the debit of Spain in the account between the two countries." (Marquis of Wellesley to Henry Wellesley, September 24, 1810, No. 29, PRO: FO 72/93.)

64. Gille, 245–246; Wagré, *Mémoires des Captifs*, 171.

65. *Captain's Log*, HMS *Espoir*, July 15–November 12,1810, PRO: ADM 51/2406; Gille, 232, 244–247; Wagré, *Mémoires des Captifs*, 48–49.

66. Marquis of Wellesley to Henry Wellesley, September 4, 1810, No. 30, PRO: FO 72/93.

NOTES TO CHAPTER 4: A REMOTE AND FLEETING HOPE

1. Santos Oliver, 280.

2. Ibid, 280–283.

3. Ibid, 306, 322–323.

4. Frossard (I), 70.

5. Ibid, 70–71.

6. Santos Oliver, 325; Garau, 220–22.

7. For accounts of this incident, see Santos Oliver, 323–326; Geisendorf, 397–412; Garau, 220–223.

8. Frossard (I), 73.

9. Geisendorf, 229–233; Legajo 3,2, Nos. 254, 260, Comissió de Cabrera, Fons Desbrull.

10. Capitaine Richard to Desbrull, April 7, 1810; Edward S. Reistetz to Desbrull, April 21, 1810, Legajo 3,2, Nos. 280, 317, Comissió de Cabrera, Fons Desbrull.

11. Ducor, 253–255; Santos Oliver, 328–329.

12. Frossard (II), 66–68; Desbrull Dossier, quoted in Garau, Appendices 6,7,8, 331–334.

13. Geisendorf, 232; Santos Oliver, 329–330; Ducor, 255–257.

14. Le Général Morand à Son Excellence le Duc de Feltre, June 2, 1810, in Geisendorf, 594–595.

15. Napoleon: Décision, 12 juillet 1810, No. 16638; Napoleon au vice-amiral Comte Decrès, ministre de la marine, 25 novembre 1811, No. 18287; Napoleon au captaine de frégate *Feretier*, 25 décembre 1811, No. 18369; Napoleon au vice-amiral Comte

Decrès, 23 mars 1813, No. 19751, in *Correspondance de Napoléon 1er*, vol. 20, 462–463; vol. 23, 35–36, 108–109; vol 25, 118. One further letter from the emperor to the minister in June 1811 asked that an argument should be made for repatriation of the Bailén prisoners who were by then being held in England. No action followed.

16. Quoted in Geisendorf, 599–600.

17. Ibid, 600–601.

18. Ibid, 601.

19. Frossard (II), 62–64.

20. Gille, 228–9.

21. Geisendorf, 160–161; Gille, 229.

22. Quoted in Geisendorf, 162.

23. Father Estelrich's letters are quoted at length in Geisendorf, 161–166. See also Garau, 245–257, 312. The letters were part of the Desbrull Dossier, now in the possession of the Archivo Municipal of Palma—although not all those quoted by Garau and Geisendorf seem to have survived.

24. Actas de la Junta Superior, May 29, 1810, quoted in Santos Oliver, 327.

25. Admiral John C. Purvis to J.W. Croker, Admiralty, April 6, 1810, PRO: ADM 1/416, No. 134.

26. In a letter to Antonio Desbrull reporting directly on this conversation between Colonel Lanti and the dying Admiral Collingwood, Admiral Hood discreetly failed to mention the exact nature of the Majorcan proposal, advised Desbrull that Lord Collingwood alone had prevented the dispatch of even more prisoners to the Baleares, offered his opinion that maintaining the prisoners on Cabrera caused only slight hardship compared to that being borne by all Spaniards on the mainland, and welcomed advice on how the Royal Navy could add to the islands' security from the French. This was a more discouraging rebuff than Collingwood had delivered in person to Colonel Lanti. (Hood to Desbrull, March 31, 1810 [in Desbrull's Spanish translation], Cáfeta 52, 2, XVIII, Fons Desbrull.)

27. Henry Wellesley to the Marquis of Wellesley, March 9 and 10, 1810, Nos. 3 and 4, and enclosures, PRO: FO 72/94.

28. Henry Wellesley to the Marquis of Wellesley, May 30, 1810, No. 35, PRO: FO 72/95.

29. This lapse was perhaps only inadvertent, one of the many confusions arising from the fog of war. Or it could have been a deliberate application of pressure on the part of the Council of Regency.

30. The details of this arrangement are laid out in a series of dispatches between the British foreign secretary and the British ambassador in Cádiz in early 1810. See, for example: Marquis of Wellesley to Henry Wellesley, March 12, 1810, No. 9; Henry Wellesley to the Marquis of Wellesley, March 9, 1810, No. 3; March 10, 1810, No. 4; March 20, 1810, No. 7; April 5, 1810, No. 15; May 30, 1810, No. 35; July 31, 1810, No. 70, PRO: FO 72/93, 72/94,72/95,72/96.

31. Ducor, 326–331.

32. *Captain's Log*, HMS *Espoir*, July 22, 1810, PRO: ADM 51/2406; Ducor, 258–259; Santos Oliver, 331. Free parole meant that the officers were granted liberty, on their word of honor not to escape to France, enabling them to live without guard in lodgings arranged for themselves.

33. Santos Oliver, 331–332.

34. Bardaxi to Henry Wellesley, July 24, 1810 [British Ambassador's translation copy], enclosure with Wellesley to Marquis of Wellesley, July 31, 1810, No. 70, PRO: FO 72/96.

35. Henry Wellesley to Bardaxi, July 26, 1810, copy enclosed with Wellesley to Marquis of Wellesley, July 31, 1810, No. 70, PRO: FO 72/96.

36. Bardaxi to Henry Wellesley, 31 July 1810 [British ambassador's translation copy], ibid; Henry Wellesley to Marquis of Wellesley, August 6, 1810, No. 73, PRO: FO 72/96.

37. Privé, quoted in Geisendorf, 289–290; Amédée de Muralt, 349.

38. Gille, 250–295; Frossard, (II) 68–69; Santos Oliver, 330–332.

39. Marquis of Wellesley to Henry Wellesley, November 1, 1810, No. 31, PRO: FO 72/93.

40. Geisendorf, 291; Gille, 259.

41. Santos Oliver, 332.

42. Ducor, 260–263.

43. Bennásar Alomar, 175–177.

44. Santos Oliver, 333–334.

45. Méry, quoted in Geisendorf, 294.

46. Garau, 282–302, 314–315; Geisendorf, 294–295.

47. Quoted in Garau, 279.

48. Bennásar Alomar, 80; Garau, 281.

49. Bennásar Alomar, 80, 168.

50. Ducor, 2, 267–295.

51. Masson, 11.

52. Dubois de Trainville, Consul général, Chargé d'affaires de France et d'Italie, Alger, à Son Excellence Monseigneur le Duc de Feltre, Ministre de la Guerre, September 6, 1813, Archives Historiques de la Guerre (hereafter AHG): *Liasse: Prisonniers français évadés de Cabrera et débarqués en Alger 1813, Carton: P.G.F. 1808–1816, Pièce 6993;* Geisendorf, 602–603; Bennásar Alomar, 179; Masson, 12–19.

53. Masson, 20.

54. Ibid, 22.

55. Ibid, 22–24; Geisendorf, 318–319.

56. Quoted in Bennásar Alomar, Appendix XIII, 191–193.

57. Ibid.

58. Ibid, 193–195.

NOTES TO CHAPTER 5: LIBERATION

1. Bennásar Alomar, 89–90.

2. Wagré, *Mémoires des Captifs*, II, 25–27; Bennásar Alomar, 186.

3. Santos Oliver, 335.

4. Wagré, *Mémoires des Captifs*, 89–90.

5. Louis Pujol à ses soeurs, à bord du *Zéphir*, May 29, 1814, "Le repatriement des prisonniers de Cabrera (1814)", *Revue Rétrospective*, Janvier–Juillet 1890, 357–358.

6. Wagré, *Mémoires des Captifs*, 87.

7. Quoted in Santos Oliver, 337.

8. The most careful discussion of numbers occurs in Roura, 150–158. See also Bennásar Alomar, 175–180; Geisendorf, 606, 613; Garau, 285–286.

9. Le préfet maritime de Toulon à S. Ex. M. le Baron Malouet, Ministre de la Marine et des Colonies, August 27, 1814, AHN: *Carton: Prisonniers de Guerre Français, 1808–1816.*

10. Wagré, *Mémoires des Captifs*, 108.

11. Ibid, 120–122.

12. Ibid, 107–132; Geisendorf, 321–343.

NOTES TO CHAPTER 6: MEMORY AND FORGETTING

1. Guillemard, 2.

2. Masson, 23–24. The document was reprinted in 1951 by Masson's great-nephew Ivan M. Labry, and can be found in the Bibliothèque Nationale of France. It is also quoted at length in Geisendorf, 305–320.

3. Oman, (III), 323; for recent medical studies of prisoners, see, for example, R.J. Ursano, J.R. Rundell, "The prisoner of war," *Military Medicine*, April 1990, 155 (4): 176–80; B.E. Engdahl, W.F. Page, T.W. Miller, "Age, education, maltreatment, and social support as predictors of chronic depression in former prisoners of war," *Social Psychiatry and Psychiatric Epidemiology*, March 26, 1991 (2):63–67; W.F. Page, B.E. Engdahl, R.E. Eberly, "Prevalence and correlates of depressive symptoms among former prisoners of war," *Journal of Nervous and Mental Disorders*, November 1991 (11): 670–7; P.E. Galanti, "Different wars, same hardships," *Virginia Medical Quarterly*, Winter 1994, 121 (1): 35, 39–41.

4. M. de Vatry, rapporteur, Chambre des Députés, March 11, 1837, *Le Moniteur Universel*, 308.

5. Estelrich, v–i.

NOTES TO A NOTE ON SOURCES

1. Garau, 260.

2. Garau, 182.

3. Roura I Aulinas, "Els presoners . . ." *L'Avenc*, 78.

ACKNOWLEDGEMENTS

I FIRST READ OF THE CABRERAN IMPRISONMENT during an extended interlude on Majorca in the 1980s, and returned to the story after finding only the most fleeting references to it in English-language histories of the Peninsular War. Curiosity about the experiences of war, and about the life of islands, led me on. I was aided and encouraged in pursuit of the tale by my wife Dawn's scholarly career in Spanish literature and drama; and I am, as ever, thankful both to Dawn and to our son Stephen, who have been perceptive readers of the manuscript.

I am greatly indebted to my Canadian publisher and editor, Jan Walter, for her insights and guidance throughout; to my American editor, Kathryn Belden; to my friend Phyllis Grosskurth for her advice and encouragement; and especially to Bella Pomer, a gracious and indefatigable agent.

For generous assistance in the Paris archives I am indebted to Harry Seydoux; for a bit of detective work on Latin epigrams familiar to Parisian theater-goers of the early nineteenth century, I am grateful to the classicist Ian McDonald; and for wise comments on various matters military and historical, my thanks to Jack Hyatt, Ian Steele, and Art Cockerill.

For access to materials, I am grateful to the obliging librarians and archivists of the Biblioteca Municipal de la Ciutat de Mallorca, the Biblioteca Bartomeu March, the Archivo Municipal de Palma, the Archivo Histórico Nacional de España, the Public Record Office, the British Library, the Archives Historiques de la Guerre, the Bibliothèque Nationale of France, the University of

Sherbrooke Library, the Trent University Library, the Toronto Public Library, the Library of the University of Neuchâtel, and the Napoleon Series webpage. They preserve history for all of us, whether we know it or not.

My thanks to HarperCollins Publishers Ltd. for permission to use a short quotation from David Gates, *The Spanish Ulcer.*

Pursuing material for this book has given me more good reasons to return to Spain and to the enchanted island of Majorca than I need. I am grateful for the good fortune to have known them over thirty years.

Banyalbufar, Majorca, and Port Hope, Ontario

INDEX

214 | THE PRISONERS OF CABRERA

Cabrera *(continued)*
departure of prisoners
from, 166–167
donkey on, 63–64, 99
descriptions of, xv, 60,
61, 63, 175–177
escapes from, 76–77,
90, 92–93, 115–117,
148–156
food supplies on,
62–63, 70, 89, 94–95,
97, 98–102, 144–145, 146,
200n2
French knowledge of,
117–121
French monument on,
xvi, 175
governors of, 146
hospital on, 77, 81–86
housing on, 64–65,
77–79, 87–89, 96
Majorcan traders on,
95
Masonic lodge on, 95
medical staff on, 67,
81–82
Napoleon's interest in,
119, 205n15
plants and animals on,
96–97
prisoners' council on,
66–68, 70, 126–129
punishments on, 68,
77, 99
relief expeditions to,
80, 95
society on, 68–69
subsidies to Majorca
for prisoners on, 44,
50, 52, 55, 56, 9–70, 78,
129, 131

supply ships to, 62, 68,
97–99, 101–102
theater on, 89–93,
203n48
transfer of prisoners
from, 107, 129–141, 147,
148, 206n26
water supply on, 65,
72, 74–77, 176
Cabrera commission,
65–66, 70, 73–74,
77–80, 101–102. *See
also* Batle, Desbrull,
Pons
Cádiz, viii, x, 3, 8, 9, 22,
30–42, 43, 47, 49, 51, 52,
53, 54, 56, 60, 105, 106,
107, 114, 120, 124,
130–139, 161, 170, 174,
178
camp followers, 20, 44,
60, 121–129, 137
Campaner, Nicolás, x,
108, 110
Campillos, 27
Canary Islands, 41, 42
Cañete La Real, 27
cannibalism. *See*
Cabrera, cannibalism
on
canteen–women, 36, 44,
60, 121–129, 137. *See
also* camp followers
Carbonnel-d'Hierville,
lieutenant, ix, 67, 98,
137
Carolina, La, 8, 17, 18
Castaños, Francisco
Javier de, xi, 9, 10
at battle of Bailén, xi,
14, 17, 18, 19, 20, 23

Castlereagh, viscount, x,
22–24, 28
Catalonia, viii, 43, 52, 55,
57, 58, 106, 161
Charles IV, xi, 2, 4, 5
abdicates, 4
deposed, 5
Cherchell, 153
Chobar, 92–93
Cicero, 182
Cintra, Convention of,
26–27, 197n25
Collingwood, Cuthbert,
x, 22–24, 26, 46–49,
54–55, 58, 59, 60, 69,
130–132
Compiègne, 5
Conejera, Isla de, 97
Continental System, 3
Córdoba, 8, 9, 17
Cork, 7
Cornelia, xi, 42, 43, 44,
48, 53, 57, 59, 60
Corsica, 1, 117, 119, 169, 173
Cortes, 106, 161
Coruña, La, 6, 32
Cotton, Sir Charles, x,
103
Council of Regency, x,
105–106, 129–139, 183
Crusoe, Robinson, 152
Cruzel, ix
Cuba, 139
Cuming, William, x, 42,
47, 48
Cyclops, 96

Degain de Montagnac,
lieutenant, ix, 67
Dameto, Juan, 56
Darlier, 92–93